The Breakaway

Michelle D. Argyle

ꓵ chi
we
ꓵook i̶

gello

The Breakaway / Second Paperback Edition

Summary: "Naomi Jensen tries to escape her kidnappers by pretending to fall in love with one of them."

This book is a work of fiction. Any resemblance to actual persons, living or dead, events, or locales, is entirely coincidental.

ISBN: 978-0989970006

Edited by Diane Dalton

Cover Design by Melissa Williams Cover Design

Author Photo by Meg Hall Photography at
http://meghallphotography.blogspot.com/

Visit author Michelle D. Argyle at http://michelledargyle.com/

To Mom,
for being there, now and forever

I
February

THE KIDNAPPER LOOKING DOWN AT NAOMI HELD A book of poetry to his chest. She didn't know what he was doing with the poetry, but it was the first thing that fueled her hope of staying alive.

"I'm Jesse," he said, and bent down to touch her arm. His hands were small, but she guessed he was stronger than he looked. "How do you feel? Dizzy? Sick?"

She tensed. Why did he care how she felt?

"Not dizzy," she said slowly. Her tongue was dry, and her voice was strange through a faint ringing in her head, like the sound of a muffled bell. "I don't know. I thought I was home. I thought—"

A few things came back; screeching tires, darkness, the smell of leather. Now she felt a flattened, unfamiliar pillow beneath her head. It smelled of dirty hair. She hated that smell, and held her breath. Up until this moment, her life had been simple. Or at least she had thought so. Now it all felt upside-down.

"I won't hurt you if you do what I say," Jesse said, pressing her forearm with his thumb. With his other hand he clutched the book closer, if that was possible. Naomi winced at his touch. She wanted his hand off her, but she didn't dare resist him. The calm side of her brain took over. It told her to stay still, do what she was told, and an opportunity for escape would come later. There was always a chance for things later.

She clutched the bedspread as she looked around. Sunlight peeked through a thin gap in the curtains across the room. There was a patch of blue sky, parked cars. She was in a motel. Her heart picked up pace and it made the ringing in her head louder. What would they do to her here? She didn't want to think about that. She couldn't. She shoved the thought away and focused on the moment.

Jesse curled two more fingers around her arm. "What did you see in the parking lot last night?"

"Parking lot?" She looked into his eyes, hoping she would find an answer. All she found was a beautiful green. It was a striking combination with his short, reddish brown hair. That was unexpected, like the poetry. What kind of a kidnapper read poetry? It was the only thing she could cling to—a delicate flower in the middle of a burned field of weeds.

"You mean the parking lot outside the window?" she asked. She had no clue what he meant by asking her what she had seen. What day was it? Friday? She had gone to school, done her homework, spent most of the night with her boyfriend, Brad. His sheets had smelled like his cologne, so strong she thought he might have spilled the bottle. When she complained, he kissed her. Then he kissed her some more. One thing led to another. She hadn't finished her homework, she realized. They had walked to the park at two in the morning, Brad hauling her camera equipment.

"Think," Jesse urged. "I need to know what you remember. Try, please."

Why didn't he just leave her alone? She didn't want to talk or think. She touched the base of her skull. A tender wound. Red flakes on her fingers. Her head must have hit something hard. She blinked and scrambled to sit up, groaning as pain shot through her arms and legs. Aching bruises everywhere. None of them hurt as badly as the one on her face. She knew what had caused that one.

Jesse backed away when she let out a cry and fell back to the pillows. "What happened to me?" she whimpered. "What did you do to me?" She craned her neck to find the motel door. It was across from the bed, begging her to run.

"Tell me what you remember." He was starting to look angry.

She didn't remember anything! She should be in a hospital, or at least her own bedroom. She should be in Brad's arms. His bed was familiar, his embrace comforting and protective, until last night. No, it was earlier. She lifted a hand to her left cheek. She still couldn't believe he had done it.

"Start talking," Jesse ordered. He was obviously losing patience. Naomi looked up, frantically searching her mind for one scrap of memory. Would he hurt her if she didn't come up with something right this second?

She kept her mind focused on the poetry. A strange side. A soft side.

"The park," she said, remembering a grove of black eucalyptus trees, misty through a veil of fog. Brad leaning against a tree with his hands pushed into his pockets. "I was taking pictures."

She remembered squinting through the lens of her camera, deciding what exposure she should set to capture the fog rolling through the grove. "I wanted to go home, so I cut through the parking lot."

"And?"

Garbage dumpsters loomed through the fog. Out of nowhere, a set of blurry, yellow lights slammed into her.

"A car."

"What kind of car?" His voice was more urgent.

"I don't know. I just remember the lights. I–I was hit, wasn't I?"

"You're certain that's all you saw? No license plate? No make or model of the car? Nothing else?"

"Nothing." She glanced at the book. Seamus Heaney, a poet she had studied last month in her advanced English class. That was weird. Nothing about this seemed right. She wanted to curl up and hide, but instead she looked at Jesse's face. The stubble across his jaw was a deeper red than his hair. He was dirty and messy, not much older than her, maybe in his twenties. Rough. Dangerous. Not like somebody who read poetry.

"You like to read?" he asked.

She clamped her lips together, darting her attention to the door. He was distracted. This was her chance.

Scrambling off the bed, she ignored her pain and ran to the door. Her body was fluid and strong, her mind instantly focused. She reached for the handle, but Jesse was too fast. He knocked her to the floor so hard she yelled out. The scratchy rug reeked of cigarette smoke.

"Damn it! I said I didn't want to hurt you!" He gripped her shoulders and pulled her to her feet, his hands surprisingly gentle compared to how rough she expected a kidnapper to be. She focused on the door, feeling her knees give out as she strained to pull away.

"Let. Me. Go!" Her voice came out louder than she thought. Her throat swelled like it was filled with cotton.

Wrapping her in an embrace, Jesse kept her upright. His chest smelled of stale cologne and sweat. It was similar to Brad's smell after he finished working out at the gym, and she almost gagged with the realization that she might never see him again. Or maybe it was something else. That smell could make her do anything she was told.

"Let you go? No, no, we can't do that." He steered her to the bed, but she didn't fight. She couldn't. She was limp and heavy like a wet towel that would never dry. "Stay here on the bed." He helped her lie down on the flower-patterned blanket and picked up his poetry book that he had dropped. "Eric will kill you if you try to run again."

Kill her? He hadn't said it sarcastically, and she believed him. A smudge of dried blood stained the pillow. She held her breath as she rested her cheek on it. Jesse sat on the opposite bed to watch her. She fought the desperate urge to curl into a ball and cry, but it was too late. Tears were already forming. A cold burst of air from across the room made her jump. The door closed. Oh, crap. That was probably Eric.

"Is she awake?"

Jesse nodded as a man walked between the beds. His jeans were dirty and wrinkled around the knees.

"She doesn't remember anything, Eric. It looks like this was all for nothing."

"What?" Eric leaned down to look her in the face. He had dark brown eyes. His mouth was drawn into a taut line. "Sit up."

She obeyed and squeezed her knees to her chest. He was older than Jesse. She guessed maybe forty. The oddest thing of all was how nice he looked, almost handsome. He was clean-cut except for the black scruff on his jaw. His thick, carefully shaped sideburns were knifelike.

"What did you see in the parking lot?" he asked.

It was hard to make her voice come out. She was sure he wanted a specific answer. He wanted her to say something about the car and the headlights.

"I don't remember very much," she said and looked up just as his fist met her cheek. She hadn't expected that.

"You don't have to hit her!" she heard Jesse yell as her head collided with the headboard. She kept the scream bundled inside her throat. If she let it out he would hit her again, she was sure of it.

"You said you wouldn't hurt her." Jesse glared at Eric.

"Shut up."

Naomi pressed two fingers to her numb cheek. Her face felt broken. She couldn't tell if she was crying. She had to stay calm and give them what they wanted. That was the only way out of this mess. If there was a way out without getting herself killed.

"Like hell, you don't remember." Eric curled his upper lip into a snarl. "Even if you don't, it doesn't matter now. You've seen us." He pulled her off the bed, past Jesse, and into the bathroom.

"What are you doing?" Jesse asked.

Eric glanced down at the poetry still gripped in Jesse's hand. "Ditch the damn book and help me out. Go get the scissors." He wrapped a cold hand around Naomi's neck and leaned her over the sink with a fierce shove. Her tears dropped into the porcelain sink. She was crying. Great. So much for staying brave. Of course, she had never thought of herself as particularly brave. This was not a situation in which she would shine.

Her lip was bleeding, turning her tears pink as they slipped down the drain. She wondered why these men didn't just kill her. Not that she wanted them to, but keeping her alive meant they were going to do something with her, and that was what she didn't want to think about in any amount of detail.

"Here." Jesse stepped into the bathroom and handed Eric a pair of office scissors, the kind with the bright orange handle. Her dad had a pair of those in his office. She remembered cutting her own hair with them when she was six. Her nanny had spanked her so hard she couldn't sit down for the rest of the day.

Eric snatched the scissors from Jesse and pushed her head down farther. He parted her hair in the middle. It was so long it coiled into the basin of the sink like two golden snakes. She stared at it, somewhat relieved. At least he wasn't planning on stabbing her. She hoped. She repeated the same phrase in her head over and over—*stay calm, stay calm, stay calm.* Her body relaxed.

"Don't," Eric said when her knees wobbled and her body went limp. He shoved her against the counter before she fell over.

"I'm sorry," she mumbled into the sink. The little resolve she had left was unraveling quickly, and she couldn't tie it back together fast enough. All she wanted to do was curl up into a ball and cry.

He finished the first section in four strokes and moved to the other side. He yanked. He tugged. He had obviously never cut hair before. When he gripped her shoulders and forced her to straighten, she stared at herself.

Her hair was gone. He had cut it a few inches above her shoulders. She gripped the counter so hard she thought her fingers might break. What was this? Why? Why any of this?

"Take off your sweater."

After wiping the last of the blood from her lips, she pulled off her hoodie. It was the one Brad had bought her at the mall a year ago. She handed it over, hoping he wouldn't ask her to take off anything else. She would freak out if he did. If Brad ever met this man, he would break his neck.

"Take your earrings out."

She lifted a hand to her ear. "Why?"

"Because I said so, that's why." He leaned forward as he spit the words at her.

The earrings were a Christmas gift from her parents. Or what they wanted to call a gift, taking her to the jewelry store two days before the holiday to pick them out. Two diamond studs, a full carat each. Had she been kidnapped for ransom? Her parents had a lot of money, but that didn't seem to be what these men wanted.

Eric slipped the earrings into his pocket. "It would be a hell of a lot easier to kill you, but I don't want to do that if I don't have to." He shrugged. "It's your choice. If you try to escape, I'll kill you. If you want to live, stay with us and do exactly what we say."

She took a step back.

"You're not a fighter," he said, rubbing the knuckles of the hand he had hit her with. "That's good."

The rest of her strength unraveled as she realized the truth of what he said. Of course she wasn't a fighter. If she was, she would have kicked him in the balls by now, or slammed her elbow into his stomach, or bitten his arm. Anything but do whatever he said. She lowered her eyes.

He filled a plastic cup with water and set two pills on the counter. "Take those."

They were blue and round, bitter and tart on her tongue as she swallowed them. She convinced herself they were only to make her sleep because she didn't have any will left to resist. She took another step back and glanced at the toilet. She needed to pee.

"You need to go?"

She nodded, and when he didn't move she realized he was going to stay there the whole time. He cleared his throat and turned around.

Could she do this? She had to.

Unzipping her pants, she pulled them down and sat on the toilet, her face growing hotter by the second. Her urine hitting the water was the loudest, most embarrassing sound she had ever heard. She squeezed her eyes shut. She felt naked. The only person who had ever seen her naked outside of childhood was Brad, and now this idiot man could turn around and watch her pee and there was nothing she could do about it. Where was Brad? What had happened? Why was going to the bathroom taking so long? At least the man wasn't watching. His name was Eric. Was it wrong to think of him by his name? How long would she have to do that?

Finally, she finished. "I'm done," she said after zipping up her jeans. She flushed the toilet.

He led her back to the bed. "Lie down and stay quiet." He watched her crawl under the blankets and curl into a ball.

On the other bed, Jesse looked up from his book. Naomi closed her eyes and turned away from him before she could decide if his compassionate expression was well-intentioned or not. At least they hadn't tied her up, but what would they do to her once she was asleep? She hugged herself and breathed slowly for what seemed like hours. Blank slate. She had to push her mind somewhere safe, somewhere empty. Then the men started to talk.

"How much did you get?" Jesse asked.

"Three-fifty. Better than we thought. Your friend says there's a push for gold overseas. We'll head home tonight once the pills knock her out."

Their words were starting to slur and fade in her head. Great. Why now when she could maybe pick up something useful from their conversation? She probably wouldn't remember any of this. Stupid pills. She should have pretended to swallow them, but a part of her wanted to fade away and never wake up.

"Did they get everything ready? You're sure you want to go through with this?"

"Of course I'm sure. I left the choice up to Evie, and this is what she wants. It'll work out. It's my own damn fault. I didn't see her in all that fog until it was too late, and who the hell knows if she's telling the truth?" He cleared his throat and it sounded like a train wreck inside her head through whatever drugs he had given her. "We'll need to clean up in here before we leave. Fingerprints, hair, everything. We can't leave anything behind. She's all over the news now. Is she out yet?"

A hand touched her arm. Her body jerked, but she couldn't open her eyes.

"Getting there."

The hand lingered on her elbow, warm and pressing. It slid up her skin, a gentle, trembling stroke. Then it was gone.

II

KAREN JENSEN LOVED HER OFFICE. SHE LOVED THE thick, leather-bound law volumes lined neatly on the bookshelves. She loved the smell of coffee from down the hall. She especially loved the windows behind her desk overlooking the city and the ocean beyond that. It was often dark when she left for work early in the morning and always dark when she went home late at night. Traffic moved down below, but she was so far removed from it that it couldn't possibly bother her. Anna, her secretary, always let her know ahead of time if there was an accident or construction and which route would get her home fastest. Anna was a lifesaver.

This morning as Karen entered her office and flipped on the light, she sensed something was wrong. Anna had already arrived. That was odd; she usually didn't show up until nine. Karen glanced at her watch. It was only eight. She peeked into the adjoining office where Anna was hunched over her desk, one hand supporting her chin as she drowsed in front of her computer monitor.

"Anna, what are you doing?"

The girl jumped and spun around in her chair. "Karen!"

Anna was twenty-eight, thin, alert, and quirky—a breath of fresh air every time Karen looked at her. The girl could talk faster than a spinning top, but Karen liked that. She liked her wildly curly, chestnut-brown hair and dramatic hazel eyes that flickered about like two moths trying to find their way out of a room.

Today, however, Anna looked anything but quirky. Dark circles sagged underneath her eyes. Her hair was limp.

"Karen," she repeated, and rolled her chair back from her desk. Her face drained of color as if she was seeing a ghost. "What are you doing here? I thought you wouldn't come back for weeks, or until Naomi is found. I thought—"

"Forget what you thought." Karen waved her hand. "There's nothing I can do about Naomi right now. The detectives are on the case. The press is having a field day, and I've got clients with cases that aren't going to wait just because I have a personal crisis going on in the background. I already missed yesterday."

"Personal crisis?"

"Yes, isn't that what this is?"

Anna blinked. "Yes, and you should be home."

"Doing what? Crying? Fretting? What is *that* going to solve? Anna, be realistic for two seconds."

Karen straightened her shoulders and tried to force her thoughts away from yesterday morning when Brad had shown up just before breakfast. Naomi was missing. She had been missing for two days, but Brad was too afraid to tell anyone he couldn't find her. He had stood on the front porch with his hands shoved into his pockets, his blond hair falling in his eyes as he confessed that he had hit Naomi in the face the night before she disappeared, and maybe that's why she was gone. Karen knew her husband, Jason, would likely scream at the boy for ten minutes if he heard such a confession, so she kept that quiet when he arrived home to a house full of police officers asking questions. But it all came out later, anyway.

"I *am* being realistic." Anna's voice interrupted her thoughts.

So much for not thinking about yesterday. Karen gave Anna a cold look and headed for her desk. She didn't have time for this. She sat in her chair and looked up at Anna, who seemed to be fighting the urge to put on the crusty glare usually reserved for her ex-boyfriend when he called her at work.

"Anna," she said in a calm voice, smoothing the wrinkles out of her blouse and adjusting her pearl necklace. "The police are trying to find Naomi. Nothing more can be done right now. We spent yesterday searching our area with the police, and I've hired my own private detective to work with them as well. I've seen enough in the courtroom to know how pointless it is for me to get involved with the investigation right now. I'd only be a nuisance. This early on she could show up any second. She's almost eighteen, and she only wants to exert her independence. I'm sure that's all this is."

Anna folded her arms. "The first few days of a missing person case are the most important, and what do you mean it's pointless for you to get involved? You're her mother."

"Yes, I'm her very busy mother with five clients scheduled today." She glanced at her watch. "And I'm due in the courtroom in three hours. Very important people depend on me, Anna." She gave Anna a look that clearly said *let it go,* then jabbed the power button on the computer. "I sure hope you kept on top of things yesterday."

"Oh sure, I kept on top of things." Anna unfolded her arms and spun on her heel, disappearing into her own office. "I went through your emails," she called out as she sat down at her desk where Karen could only see her back. "I sorted through your voicemails; there were a lot of messages from people concerned about Naomi, and one from your sister, Elizabeth. Doesn't she have your cell number?"

"Nobody has my cell number except for you and Jason. You know all my other calls are forwarded from here."

"Not even Naomi?" Anna spun around in her chair, and it was then that Karen noticed her wrinkled clothes and the misplaced pillows on the leather sofa across the room.

"No, not even Naomi."

"What if she needs you? How can she get a hold of you if she doesn't have your number?"

"Naomi never needs me. Did you sleep here last night?"

Anna blinked.

"Anna?"

"Yes, I did."

"Why would you sleep here?"

Her face turned scarlet as she stood from her chair. "Why wouldn't I sleep here? I only had people and reporters coming in here every five seconds yesterday asking about you. I only tried to call your phone five billion times. I only sat here worried sick ever since they announced on the news that there was a robbery the night she disappeared *three blocks* from your house. What if someone took her, Karen? That's what they're saying. You and your husband are two of the most prominent people in this city, and you're hiding her under the rug."

Karen closed her eyes and forced her mind back to a calm place. She was starting to come undone, and she couldn't let that happen. A woman in her position had to stay strong. Her career depended on it. She wasn't showing remorse or guilt or anything over Naomi, and that obviously bothered Anna. The problem was that Anna couldn't possibly understand how her relationship with Naomi worked. She opened her eyes and stood.

"I'm going to go get some coffee."

"But I always get your coffee."

"Not today."

Karen marched out of the office as she rubbed a finger between her eyes. Was this how everyone was going to react? Shocked at her behavior? The reporters were already camping out near the house. It was only a matter of time before they realized she had snuck away to come to work. They would be here by afternoon pestering her with questions. Jason would have it even worse. He was the CEO of one of the largest companies in the western United States.

She snatched a mug from a cupboard and filled it with coffee. She needed it badly today. Jason had kept her up all night worrying about Naomi. He wondered if he should go back to work, if he should try to help search for her more than he already had, if it was his fault she was gone. Which was ridiculous. She was almost eighteen. When Karen was that age, she had left her family, excited to start her own life away from what was barely a home. She could still smell the burnt macaroni and cheese her sister had tried to make in the kitchen of their trashy trailer and the greasy hamburgers her father grilled outside every weekend until the snow fell. Her mother had worked at a factory, and whenever she came home she plopped herself onto the lumpy couch and chain smoked until Karen had to go outside so she could breathe. The only refuge was school. On her ceiling she had taped a poster of Harvard. One day she would go there and graduate and live in a big, clean house by the ocean.

"And that's exactly what I did," she mumbled into her coffee. She marched back to her office and sat down. Anna was still at her desk.

"I know what you're thinking," Karen said, causing Anna to turn around to look at her.

"What am I thinking?"

"That I'm a terrible person for reacting this way."

"That's not what I—"

Karen held up a hand "Everybody will think that, but they're wrong. They don't understand the pressures Jason and I deal with—what we have to maintain in the public eye. I've given Naomi everything I never had. If she's anything like me, she's not in any danger. She just needed some space. Her boyfriend hit her, and she probably thinks running away for a little while will teach him a lesson. She'll come back in a few days."

Anna turned back to her computer. "Seems like she had plenty of space before "

That wasn't worth answering. Karen couldn't believe she was wasting her time arguing with Anna. There was too much to do today. She stared at her email inbox and blinked as the screen turned fuzzy. Lack of sleep, that was all. She swiveled her chair to face the windows behind her as the caffeine from her coffee seeped into her system. The ocean was calm beyond the city, just like her. She would stay calm. Even if Naomi was truly in danger, showing the public her fear and insecurities would not help anyone. Nobody could understand her relationship with Naomi. It was like a flower trying to bloom. If someone disturbed it, it would die, just like her broken relationship with her own mother had died. She wouldn't let that happen, especially from reporters trying to pry into her life.

Taking a sip of her coffee, she turned back to her computer.

III

THE AIR SMELLED LIKE BACON. NAOMI KEPT HER EYES closed as sunlight warmed her face. She was comfortable beneath a heavy quilt. Turning, she snuggled her cheek into a fluffy pillow.

Wait a minute.

The motel room. The book of poetry.

She sat up, her heart hammering. The room was mostly empty and definitely not a motel room. There was a four-poster bed, a nightstand, a dresser. The door was dead bolted from the other side. There was a bathroom and a walk-in closet with clothes on hangers.

She wasn't dreaming. She couldn't be dreaming with this much pain. She touched the ends of her short hair as tears sprang to her eyes. She blinked them away. She had to think and keep a level head. First of all, where was she? Was she safe, or seconds away from danger?

She lifted the quilt from her body and stared at her bare feet. They had taken her shoes off, and she couldn't see them anywhere. She touched her lip. No blood. The split had closed. The wound at the base of her skull throbbed, but it was clean and healing over. They had taken care of her, and that frightened her more than anything else. She swallowed. Her throat was parched.

Trembling, she got out of bed and entered the bathroom where she leaned over the sink and drank straight from the tap. The water sloshing in her stomach, she straightened to look at herself in the mirror. She wasn't about to flip on the light to see more of the terrified girl staring back at her. She looked terrible. Her hair was uneven and serrated, not even fit for a punk star.

She peeked inside two shopping bags on the counter. Toothbrush and toothpaste, floss, a brush and comb, soap and shampoo. Even underwear. Her size.

She raced out of the bathroom to the window by the bed and pulled back the curtain. There was hard packed snow on the ground. The bedroom was on the second floor of a house facing a quiet street. Ancient maple and pine trees dotted the neighborhood of fancy houses and landscaped yards. Her fingers brushed across the window sill and she nearly jumped at what she saw. Someone had installed a lock on the outside. Why bother? Even if she managed to get out, the fall would break a leg or an arm.

So they wanted to keep her here like a caged animal.

Yeah, right.

Running to the door, she yanked on the handle. Locked. She threw herself at it, pounded, kicked, but didn't yell. She was already dizzy. White stars exploded before her eyes. She blinked and shook her head. More stars. Blackness. Her knees were suddenly Jell-O. She was going to crumple in a heap on the floor if she didn't make it back to the bed in time. All she needed was to lie down. Two seconds.

Finally, she made her way back to the bed and crawled under the warm blankets. Her stomach tightened. Hunger. That explained the stars, the exhaustion, and the ache in her stomach. She hadn't eaten in days. Maybe she would give up for now.

A clock near the bathroom showed that it was five. She focused on the second hand ticking its way around, around, around. She closed her eyes and saw two yellow lights speeding toward her. No time to run. No time to do anything but widen her eyes in the foggy darkness. An explosion ripped through her lungs as her feet flew out from under her. Gritty tar and gravel, slamming doors and panicked voices, breaths on her face. She was lifted up into nothing.

A hand brushed across Naomi's forehead and she opened her eyes. It wasn't Jesse or Eric, but a woman.

"Hello," the woman said with a sweet smile. "I'm Evelyn."

Naomi backed away and sat up. The sunlight shining through the windows was heavier than before. Evelyn blinked as the rich glow shifted across her face. She looked a lot like Eric—same clear olive complexion, angled cheekbones, and dark hair. Hers was in loose ringlets falling to her shoulders. Her lips were pretty, a deep red. She was sitting on the edge of the bed and leaned forward.

"Are you all right? Can I get you anything? I brought you some food. Eric said you haven't eaten for days."

She gritted her teeth. "He never gave me any food." Her voice was weak and frail. It felt strange to speak. She should probably keep her mouth shut in some sort of defense, but Evelyn wasn't threatening in any way and the words flowed to the tip of her tongue. "He gave me pills."

Evelyn sighed. "He thought rest was more important for you. We didn't want you dying or anything."

Naomi didn't know if she should laugh or be horrified. Why would these people care if she died? They wanted her to keep her mouth shut about whatever they thought she had seen. Dying would take care of that. Why waste the energy keeping her locked up like this?

Evelyn pointed to a sandwich and glass of milk on the nightstand. "Go ahead and eat, but take it slow or it might come right back up. Do you want me to leave?"

She snatched the plate with shaky hands. Bacon, lettuce, and tomato, something Brad had made her once. She sank her teeth into it, and a small groan escaped her throat.

"I'm glad you like it."

Naomi hardly heard her. The sandwich was so good.

Evelyn stood. "I want to cut your hair. It looks terrible. I'm sorry he ...." She chewed on her lip, blinking as she looked at the floor. "Eric is my brother. He didn't have any choice but to take you." She glanced at the door. "I'll be back in the morning."

She left the room in a hurry, the locks turning in place as Naomi looked down at her sandwich. It was the best food she had ever tasted.

❧

An intense, pounding headache and spells of stomach cramps plagued her most of the night. After deciding it was because of the food, she wished she had heeded Evelyn's advice and eaten more slowly.

Now she tossed and turned beneath the blankets, repeatedly waking in a cold sweat until she looked at the clock for the hundredth time, saw that it was six in the morning, and realized her headache was finally gone.

She heard muffled voices. Doors opened and closed, and the faint hum of a hairdryer drifted through the far right wall. One of her kidnapper's bedrooms was next to hers, but what were they doing awake at six o'clock in the morning?

She could pound on the door again.

No, she felt too sick. She couldn't remember the last time she had felt so crappy. Her nannies always took such good care of her when she was sick as a kid. They never let it get too bad.

The air was missing something. She was used to the sounds of crashing waves and screeching gulls. She longed for those sounds now, the smell of salt in the air when she woke up every morning to the brisk commotion of her parents getting ready for work. They woke up at six every morning, but they had jobs. Did her kidnappers work like normal people? It was so weird to think of them that way, but as the clock ticked through the darkness, she heard them passing her door, talking and clearing their throats as if nothing was wrong. Downstairs, dishes clattered, cupboard doors closed. Faint voices, laughter, the smell of coffee. All the voices sounded male except for Evelyn's smooth tones.

The minutes ticked by, each one building up the nervous tension inside her until she finally slipped out of the bed and rushed into the bathroom.

"Good thing there's a lock," she grumbled and switched on the light. She pressed both of her palms to her forehead and looked at herself in the mirror. She needed to think, to feel safe for two minutes. She closed her eyes and leaned against the wall.

Think. Think.

They thought she had seen something. She hadn't, but they weren't going to let her go now. It was obvious they were going to keep her here until ... until what? She groaned and dug her fingernails into her scalp. Whatever happened, she had to play by their rules until she could figure something out. Eric would kill her if she made one wrong move. She believed that with every fiber of her being. She had to obey.

For now.

She left the bathroom to search through the clothes in the closet. Jeans, long-sleeved shirts, sweaters, even a pair of cotton pants and a camisole to sleep in. They were all brand-new, the correct sizes, and clean. The smell of her own dirty body was getting on her nerves. She could at least take a shower before Evelyn came to cut her hair. She snatched a change of clothes.

Something urgent nagged at the back of her mind as she locked herself in the bathroom. Were the clothes kindness? The food Evelyn had brought her? The promise to cut her hair? It felt like kindness.

She peeked around the shower curtain every ten seconds to make sure the door was still locked. It felt good to stand under the water. The steam drifted around her like fog, and she thought of the banquet she and Brad went to the night she was taken. That night had ended in fog.

It was one of the few banquets she had attended for her father's company. He was the CEO. The press liked to take pictures, and her parents liked to be in the pictures. It would look strange if they didn't have their daughter with them when everybody else brought their older children to show them off like trophies.

She shook her head in awe as she and Brad entered the banquet hall decorated in blue and white roses. She didn't know blue roses existed, but apparently they did.

"Good thing you wore a blue tie," she mumbled as Brad's fingers closed around her hand. She thought of his knuckles slamming against her cheek the night before and almost pulled away as he squeezed her fingers and smiled. He looked at the spot on her cheek—right where she had caked make-up over the bruise.

He had been nothing but gentle and loving the entire day, but she was still annoyed with herself for forgiving him so quickly. It had only taken him ten minutes of tender apologizing for her to speak to him again. She finally yanked her hand away once they found her parents' empty table.

"So you think the food will be good?" he asked as he pulled out a chair and sat down next to her.

"It usually is."

The room was packed with over-dressed men and women. It was loud with what she liked to call corporate talk—things her father was always saying that made no sense to her. She didn't care, either. The only reason she was there, she reminded herself, was because they had basically ordered her to come. People found their seats, and after a few minutes the room fell silent.

"You look amazing, by the way," Brad whispered into her ear. His hand inched to her hip and slid across her lap. He nibbled at her ear when she leaned into him because she knew that's what he wanted.

Lowering her eyes, she stared at the straw-yellow satin that rippled against her legs when she walked. Brad slid his other hand across her bare shoulder blades, and she fought back a wave of tears. If she cried, the tears would wash away her makeup and reveal her bruise.

"Where are your parents?"

She lifted her eyes, folded her arms, and nodded toward the front. "Where they always are at these things—up there. We'll be lucky if they ever make it down here."

She was crying now, in the shower, still surrounded by steam. She didn't want to cry, but she was kidnapped. What else could she do? She was supposed to cry, fight, scream, panic. That's what all the books and movies showed. But now, as she faced the reality of where she was, those reactions seemed stupid inside her head. She didn't feel like crying. She felt numb, and that made the tears go away.

She turned off the water and leaned her shoulders against the dark stone tiles. The room was steamy and hot, but the tile was still cool and sent goose bumps down her body. She sucked in her breath and savored the rush of awareness.

Someone opened the bedroom door just as she stepped out of the tub. She snatched a towel from the rack and wrapped it around herself.

"Naomi?" Evelyn voiced through the door. "Are you all right?"

Her stomach fluttered. None of them had said her name before. It was strange. Too personal. It made her cold all over as water slid down her legs and formed little pools around her toes.

"I'm ...." Her voice was hoarse and quiet. She cleared her throat. "I took a shower."

Silence, a few movements. "That's fine. Open the door when you're finished so I can cut your hair. Hurry if you can, okay?"

She didn't answer. She had no idea what to say to her kidnappers any time they spoke to her. If anything, she felt stupid and embarrassed. She should have taken a different way home. She should have screamed and fought back in the motel room so Eric would have killed her. That way they wouldn't have to worry about her and go to all this trouble. She wasn't worth so much worrying. It was ridiculous. If only they would let her go. She didn't care about what they had done that night.

Slipping into her new clothes, she towel-dried her hair as much as she could before unlocking the door.

Evelyn had a barstool and small bag in her arms. She gave Naomi a brief smile and set the barstool in front of the mirror, then opened the bag and spread out a handful of haircutting supplies. Naomi sat down and watched her wipe off the foggy mirror.

"Is this all right with you—cutting your hair?" Evelyn asked, adjusting her white silk blouse on her perfect frame.

Naomi tried to keep her expression neutral. For some reason anger was surging through her. "I guess so."

"Okay, then." She ran the comb through Naomi's hair and stopped near the wound at the back of her head. Stroke after stroke, she gently worked through the snarls, then took a pair of scissors from the counter and started cutting.

Her hands were quick as she worked. She tilted Naomi's head, measured the hair on both sides with her fingers, and checked her work in the mirror with swift, thoughtful glances. After two minutes, Naomi was sure she was a professional hairstylist. For some stupid reason, that made her relax.

"It'll be short," Evelyn said after a few minutes. "I'm sorry."

Naomi let no emotion show on her face. She focused on Evelyn's hair, long and twisted in spirals down past her shoulders, like tumbling black water. She was so graceful and elegant, like a supermodel.

Except for the scar.

Naomi widened her eyes. She hadn't seen it before—a long, thin groove on the left side of Evelyn's face. It was barely visible beneath her perfectly applied makeup, but Naomi could see she took great pains to cover it up. It started at the top of her ear, ran down across her cheek, and stopped near the edge of her mouth.

Evelyn cleared her throat. "You look a lot like your mother."

Her mother? No, she didn't. She looked at her own reflection and frowned. How did Evelyn know what her mother looked like?

"I've seen her on the news reports." Evelyn shook her head and coughed. "I'm sorry. I shouldn't say things like that to you. I'm always saying things I shouldn't."

"It's all right."

"No, it's not." She took a clip from the counter, and Naomi caught a glimpse of a wedding ring on her finger—a large diamond and two deep red rubies. "You must think we're horrible, terrible people."

Yeah, just a bit.

Evelyn lifted the clip and twisted some of Naomi's hair to fasten it out of the way. She started cutting again. "I can't believe how calm you are—except for your kicking and banging on the door yesterday afternoon. We expected that."

So they had heard her and were okay with it. Maybe.

Evelyn narrowed her eyes. "I don't recommend any more of that kind of behavior. Eric doesn't like it. He said you haven't tried to get away, and it should stay that way." She softened her expression. "But if it were me, well, you're—"

"I didn't see anything," she interrupted, unable to hold back any longer. She gripped the edges of the barstool. "I don't know why you're keeping me here. Wouldn't it be easier to let me go? I won't say anything. I don't care about whatever it is you're trying to hide."

"No!"

The scissors snipped shut.

"Don't ask things like that. We can't let you go now that you're here. You've seen too much. Eric told me you had to come here or he'd have to kill you. That's how things are." She glanced at the watch on her wrist. "I'm almost done. Just a few more minutes or I'll be late for work. It's Wednesday. There's always a time crunch on Wednesdays."

So they had jobs for sure. Would she be left alone in the house? Were they so confident in keeping her locked inside the room? Not that she saw any possible way out short of tearing down a wall, and it wasn't like she had strength for that.

When Evelyn finished cutting, she combed through the hair framed around Naomi's jaw line. It looked better than Eric's haircut, at least.

Evelyn smiled. "I like it, but Eric might have me dye it. We'll see." She glanced at her watch again, then at the floor where hair was scattered across the tile. "I have to go, but I'll clean this up when I get home. I left you some fruit and a glass of milk on the dresser."

Naomi brushed the damp clumps of hair from her shoulders and chest, then stood and followed Evelyn out of the bathroom.

"Do you like milk?" she asked, turning to Naomi before opening the door. "You drank it before, but would you rather have something else? Orange juice? Coffee? We like coffee in the morning."

"Milk is fine."

A sigh that sounded relieved. "Thank you for being so calm. Eric told me you would do what I asked, but I wasn't sure what he meant until now." She opened the door and twitched her mouth into a nervous smile before leaving the room.

When the locks clicked into place, Naomi hurried to the window where she could keep an eye on the driveway. Ten minutes passed before a sleek, black sedan with tinted windows pulled out of the garage, followed by a small, fire-red sports car driven by Evelyn.

Naomi tried to read the license plates, but was too high up to see anything helpful. Utah or Colorado? Idaho or Wyoming? It didn't matter.

She ran her gaze along the horizon, following the mountains in the distance. She had never seen such sharp mountains before, at least not outside her own window. She was used to the smooth, flat lines of the ocean stretching on forever.

That night she dreamed of dragons and fairies. She sat at the edge of a cliff as storm clouds rolled across a deep valley filled with fire. Dragons circled the destruction, their wings transparent in the bright glow below them. When they shrieked, she covered her ears and fell off the edge of the cliff, her own screams matching the dragon-cries. Fairies flew in to rescue her, but their strength was insufficient. They wept when she landed on the rocks and broke in two like a china doll.

Later, a handsome, leather-clad man rode up on a horse, his battered, blood-stained sword glinting in the fire's glow. He was too late to rescue her, and before she could warn him, a dragon flew above him and breathed a jet of flame, burning him to ashes. She wept as the failed hero crumbled before her eyes.

With a start, she sat up in bed, breathing hard. It was midnight. Clouds covered the moon. The only light came from the lamps on the street. Slowly, she lay back down and tried to get her mind off the image of her face cracked in half. The quiet bedroom was better than a burning valley ridden with dragons. Besides, her kidnappers were not hurting her, so why was her subconscious panicking?

She groaned and rolled over to discover her pillow was wet with tears. She hit the pillow with her fist. She had to get a grip on her emotions before they took over.

Then again, she remembered that dealing with things inside your head could help you deal with everything outside. Wasn't that Psych 101? That had to be what her mind was doing.

Taking a deep breath, she closed her eyes and relaxed her body, trying to imagine herself melting away. The dragons came back, but this time they had settled on the rocks to quietly watch the burning valley.

It was then that she heard the locks on her door twisting open. She froze, as tense as if a dragon was breathing down her neck.

"I have to see her again." Evelyn's hushed whisper floated across the room.

"Don't wake her up, then." Another whisper, a male's voice, not Jesse's or Eric's. How many of them lived in the house?

"I won't. She's been quiet for hours, the poor thing. She's out cold, like always."

"She's still adjusting. She shuts down. It will be months before she accepts any of this." They stopped right by the bed. She could hear their breathing, feel their presence. She had no idea what they wanted, but she wasn't about to let them know she was awake.

"She's absolutely perfect," Evelyn said with a catch in her voice. "Every time I look at her I think she's more than I could have asked for."

"That's not why Eric took her, Evie."

"I know, I know, but look at her."

Silence. What were they doing? Just staring? Her back was to them. She didn't dare move. She tried to make her breathing slow and heavy as if she was asleep. They were buying it.

"You have to decide, Evie. We're not risking any of this shit for nothing."

"I already told you I could never live with myself if we hurt her. Never."

"It's settled, then, but you know the risks if she tries anything."

"I know." Her voice was weighted. A tinge of doubt flecked her words.

"You've got to wake up early," the man said, and they moved away slowly, as if they were still staring. She had the sick feeling this wasn't the first time they had come into her room to look at her while she slept.

IV

NAOMI TRIED NOT TO THINK ABOUT THE LAST TIME SHE had eaten or the last time she had talked to Evelyn or any of her kidnappers. Evelyn had said she would come back, but never did, unless she counted the creepy night-watching thing. The night had passed, then morning, and now it was evening again. She thought about pounding on the door again, but remembered Evelyn's warning.

She suffered as quietly as she could, curled on the bed, holding her stomach and groaning. The rancid aroma of old banana peel hung in the air, along with the rotting apple core and pit of an overripe plum. She had buried it all in the bathroom trash can beneath wads of toilet paper and the plastic bags she had emptied the previous day. She even shut the door, collapsed onto the bed, and turned to face the other wall, but she could still smell it.

It was unbearable. Did they want to starve her to death? If not, then they were going to drive her crazy by leaving her alone with nothing to do except exist in her crazy mind filled with other worlds scarier than this one.

She had caught sight of Eric only an hour earlier. He parked the black sedan in the driveway and stepped out with a quick glance at her window. He most likely saw her standing half-hidden behind the folds of the sheer curtain, her eyes red from crying.

He didn't exhibit any signs of acknowledgment as he ran his gaze across the window, then turned to grab a leather briefcase from the back seat, slammed the door shut, and headed to the front door.

Naomi was surprised to see him, especially dressed in a suit and tie beneath a black, knee-length trench coat, appearing as though his most immediate concern was to relax after a long day of work. He knocked his shoes against the sidewalk to clear off slush and then disappeared beneath the roof over the front porch.

He seemed like a normal, middle-aged man coming home from work, but she knew better. She could still feel his fist against her face like a violent explosion. The bruise still hurt, pressed against the quilt of the bed, tight and stiff and probably uglier than Brad's ever was. It was probably deep violet, maybe even black, swollen and shiny. She wouldn't know. She hadn't looked at herself since the morning Evelyn cut her hair. She hadn't showered, changed her clothes, or done much of anything but lie on the bed and feel sorry for herself. It was pathetic and exhausting.

As the clock ticked its way toward seven-thirty, the click of a lock made her jump off the bed. Evelyn opened the door and gave her a weak, apologetic smile. She wore a white apron splattered with what looked like spaghetti sauce.

Food. For a minute she thought she might claw her way past Evelyn to get to it. The smell was suddenly strong, drifting up from the kitchen in stages— tomatoes and garlic, oregano and sweet basil.

"I need you to come downstairs with me," Evelyn said quietly.

Naomi followed her out of the bedroom, her heart pounding. She had to eat. She had never been so hungry in her life. She didn't care if she had to see Eric or anybody else. It didn't matter. Nothing mattered but her stomach. That was more pathetic than anything.

They reached the end of the hall where Naomi saw a picture of Evelyn and a dark-haired man. She guessed he was Evelyn's husband, probably the man who had come into the bedroom with her the night before.

Downstairs, Evelyn led her into the living room where she told her to sit down on a leather sofa across from a TV. Books. They were everywhere, stacked neatly on the end tables, set in straight rows on shelves down the hallways, even in the kitchen. Most of the windows were covered with blinds and curtains. No phones anywhere.

Evelyn leaned down to her ear. "Stay quiet and don't move." She walked into the kitchen where Eric stood talking with the man from the picture. They were all holding bowls of spaghetti, eating during their conversation. The smell drove her crazy as she folded her hands in her lap, pushed her heels together, and sank farther into the leather cushions.

She couldn't believe they were going to let her eat. Her hands shook at the thought, but more than that, she didn't understand why they had left her on the couch. Didn't they think she would try to run? Because she could. There was a set of sliding glass patio doors in the dining room. It looked like they led to the backyard, but how fast could she run? She was weak with hunger, and if she managed to get out of the house, where would she go? She would only have one chance to make a run for it, and if she happened to knock on a neighbor's door and they weren't home or if there was nowhere to hide, what would she do then? They would catch her, and Eric would kill her just like he said. No, she had to wait. She had to make a plan. One mistake, she remembered from the hushed conversation in her room, and there would be consequences worse than she could imagine. Even Evelyn feared them.

A door slammed shut and Jesse walked in from the garage. He hung up his heavy, green coat, slipped off his shoes, and headed straight for the kitchen.

"Smells fantastic. I'm starving." He glanced at the empty dining table then at the bowl in Eric's hand. "Why are you all in here?"

Eric scowled, mumbling something as Jesse turned to look at her. From the way he had treated her in the motel room, she expected him to smile, but he narrowed his eyes and looked away.

Evelyn came into the living room and sat on a sofa. She grabbed a book from an end table and flipped it open, pretending to read as her husband sat down next to her, still eating his spaghetti. He had already splattered sauce on the sleeve of his white dress shirt, and gave Evelyn an apologetic smile when she glared at him over her book. Naomi thought he was nice looking—normal, like her dad. The sad thing was that she had no idea if her dad ever splattered sauce on his sleeves.

"Naomi," Evelyn said, "this is my husband, Steve."

Naomi swallowed and nodded as Steve smiled softly in her direction. He seemed nice so far. Making an introduction was a strange thing to do, but these people didn't seem like they were about to let her go anytime soon. She might as well get to know them. She hoped there weren't any others.

Eric came into the room next and pulled off his suit jacket. He tossed it next to Naomi and sat on the edge of the coffee table in front of her.

He was too close. She noticed his hair was shorter than before. His face looked sharper now since he had shaved, and as he placed his elbows on his knees and leaned closer, she smelled his aftershave mingled with garlic. Why did he have to be good-looking? His olive skin and dark lashes, the way his hair curled against his forehead—it all created the most satisfying balance. In the weirdest way, it made him that much creepier.

"Evelyn told me how cooperative you've been," he said coolly with a glance at her hair. "I'm not surprised. We brought you down here to see what you'd do, and well, here you are—sitting quietly." He smiled, but it was twisted all wrong. "You seem like a smart girl. You're not going to try to escape."

She pressed her lips tight as he chuckled. He started unbuttoning one of his sleeves. "Tell me about your parents," he said without looking up. "Tell me why your mom went back to work one day after she found out you were missing."

A weight slammed into her chest. One day? She had expected maybe a week or two, but *one day?* Had her dad gone back too? No doubt he had.

"Well?" He looked up from his sleeve.

"I don't know. I guess she—"

She had to stop. An ache tightened her throat and she couldn't talk anymore. She knew it was only a matter of moments before she lost it in front this man she hated more than anybody she had ever met. The last thing she wanted to do was cry in front of him. Again. He made her feel naked. He made her feel like puking.

"Look at me." He lightly placed a hand on her arm. "There are rumors your parents don't even miss you. What kind of relationship do you have with them?"

"They have important jobs," she stuttered. She hated the tears filling her eyes. She hated how hot Eric's hand felt on her arm. "They work all the time. A lot of people depend on them. They've never had time to spend with me, so I guess that's why they don't care about me. They've never cared about me."

That's all it took. Her tears broke free and streamed down her face. It was the first time she had ever admitted out loud that her parents didn't love her. It was the truth. A fact. Not even up for negotiation. She remembered her nannies making random comments about how odd it was that her parents didn't celebrate holidays with her, even her birthday—not because they didn't want to, necessarily. They bought her things, but that was it. "They're just too busy to do anything else," her nannies said in an attempt to explain it away. It was then that Naomi started noticing other children and how their parents dropped them off at school and kissed their foreheads, handed them sack lunches, scolded them for doing something wrong. Nobody cared about her like that.

Eric was quiet and Naomi looked up at him, her tears still running down her face. He removed his hand from her arm and started rolling up his sleeve.

"That's good enough," he said. "Now I need to know about your boyfriend, Brad."

He knew Brad's name? Her tears stopped. Now she really wanted to puke.

"What's your relationship with him?"

Her eyes widened. "That's none of your business!"

Before she knew what was happening, he slapped her right across the bruise on her cheek. She almost bit through her lip.

"Eric! You said—"

"Quiet, Evie." He took Naomi's arm again and leaned so close to her face that all she could see was the bridge of his nose. She hated his nose. She hated his dark eyes and the garlic on his breath. "Tell me how you feel about Brad."

She looked away, straining against his arm.

"If you don't answer me I'll lock you back in the room with no food for three more days."

That did it.

"I don't love him, if that's what you're asking," she whispered, blinking, finally aware of the sting from his slap. It didn't hurt. Nothing hurt now.

He nodded and stood up from the coffee table. "Good." He turned to Evelyn. "Take her back upstairs."

Evelyn stood up from the couch. She was still holding the book, her knuckles white. "You said we could give her something to eat."

"She can wait until tomorrow."

"Tomorrow? Eric, she hasn't eaten for two days!" Her lips quivered as Steve stood and wrapped an arm around her shoulders.

"Sweetie, calm down. You agreed to let Eric make the decisions, remember? We've discussed this."

"Yes, but you both said we're doing this because I—"

"That's enough." Eric glared at her.

She lowered her eyes and nodded.

"I'll take her upstairs," Jesse said. He was at the dining table eating his dinner. He swallowed the last of his wine, threw a half-eaten piece of garlic bread on top of his spaghetti, and motioned for Naomi to follow him. She was glad he was taking her. Something about him felt safe. They headed up the stairs and she realized he hadn't taken hold of her arm. He stopped in front of her door.

"Will you be all right?" he asked.

She lowered her eyes to the noodles in his bowl and held back a flood of tears. She was such an idiot. Why couldn't she be strong for five minutes? Her stomach clenched so tightly she wrapped her arms around herself to try to stop the pain. She blushed and looked away.

"I guess so," she mumbled, and turned to go into her room when Jesse wrapped a hand around her arm.

"I won't let them hurt you," he whispered, then gently nudged her into her room and followed her inside.

She stumbled backward. "Wh-what do you want?"

He turned and shut the door. "Here." He flipped on the light and held out his bowl of spaghetti. She snatched it from his hands, too hungry to care about anything else as she bit into the bread and turned away. She didn't care that he had already eaten half of it, that his mouth had been on it. She could feel his eyes on her back.

"How old are you?" he asked.

"You don't know?" She stared at her bed as she chewed so fast her temples started to hurt. She knew she should eat slower, but she couldn't help herself. "You guys seem to know everything else about me."

A pause.

"Okay, I know you're seventeen."

"Then why did you ask?" She spun around, food still in her mouth. It tasted so good. She wished he would leave so she could enjoy it.

"No reason." He stepped forward, and she saw a spark in his eyes as he leaned forward and drifted his gaze down her body.

She almost choked.

So far she had managed to convince herself that none of the men would touch her except to hit her or force her to move, but now a whole new fear opened up inside her. She swallowed. Hard.

"I'd like to be alone," she said and stepped back. He took another step to match hers. His green eyes were anchors attached to her body. She remembered the poetry book he had been reading in the motel room and her mind fought to cling to it, to anything that might mean he wouldn't hurt her. People who read poetry didn't hurt others, did they? Maybe that was the dumbest thing she had ever let herself believe.

"I'll stay until you finish." He nodded at the bowl and smiled. An idea, small and possibly insane, formed in the back of her mind.

"I'll hurry." She shoveled the food into her mouth as fast as she could. She wasn't hungry anymore, but the faster she finished, the faster he would leave—if that was his intention. She guessed it wasn't.

V

DESPITE HER SUSPICION, JESSE LEFT HER IN PEACE. SHE gathered the courage to finally take another shower and change into the pajama pants and camisole from the closet. The camisole was pale pink and thin. Too cold. She searched through the closet and found a velour sweatshirt hanging near two pairs of jeans.

It was pale pink too. Evelyn obviously liked pink, or at least thought Naomi did. It had been washed and smelled the same as the clean sheets and pillowcases on the bed, rain-scented fabric softener and Tide, the same as Brad's clean laundry. That wasn't comforting.

She crawled into bed and grew tense beneath the covers. Had she lied to Eric? Was she in love with Brad? She had certainly thought so for the longest time, but there were always periods of doubt. Eric had forced her to answer his question so quickly that maybe she hadn't thought through everything in enough detail.

Or maybe she didn't have a clue what love felt like. She used to think it was lying in Brad's arms as he whispered things like, *It will be this way forever, you and me. I will always protect you, hold you, love you.*

Now, thinking of her admission to Eric, she was almost positive the passions Brad stirred inside her heart were not impressions of love at all. Maybe she was wrong about that too. The only sure thing was the dangerous idea forming inside her head; Jesse was possibly the answer to her escape. He seemed to want her, and whether or not that was part of her kidnappers' plans, she could play into his hands and get out of here. If they trusted her, they might let their guard down. Maybe.

She rolled onto her side and tried to ignore both her uncertainty and the fact that her hair was wet. She hated going to sleep with her hair wet and tossed and turned for the longest time, irritated that her pillow was now damp and cold against her face. Maybe she should ask Evelyn for a hairdryer.

A soft knock on the door made her jump. The locks turned, and she sat up when Jesse slipped into the room. In the moonlight from the window, she thought she saw him smile as he approached. She hugged the blankets to her body, trembling.

"I thought you might like a book," he said softly, and placed a hardback on the nightstand. He was close enough now for her to smell his cologne—a peppery smell, like eucalyptus. She held her breath and looked up at him, confused. His smell burned in her throat.

"A book?"

"Yes, you seemed interested in my poetry book in the motel. I thought you might get bored during the day, so I brought you something to read. Do you like classics?"

What was going on? She shook her head, still confused. "I like fantasy, but I just found out my mom likes classics and I—" She stopped and looked away, finally letting out her breath. Too much information.

"Hmm," he said, and stepped closer to the bed. She could see his face now. It looked innocent enough.

"What do you want?"

He leaned down with that same spark in his eye. "I thought it was obvious." He came so close to her that she could feel his breath on her face. His attention fastened to her lips, hanging there until she shrank from him. She was surprised at every part of her reaction. If she was going to play into his hands, this wasn't the way to do it.

"I'm not going to hurt you," he whispered as he inched closer again, leaning halfway across the bed. His red hair seemed brighter now. His smell was nice, but it was too close. It almost made her choke.

"P-please," she cried as his hand reached out to touch her face. "Please don't ...."

He tilted his head as if he didn't understand her apprehension and curled his fingers around her face. There was a soft ache in his eyes. She tried not to whimper with the fear boiling beneath her skin.

"I think you're very beautiful," he said, moving even closer. "I keep thinking about you lying in the parking lot that night. You were beautiful then too, and I didn't want Eric to hurt you. You're so innocent, so frightened."

He stared into her eyes, his hand strong but gentle around her face. Then he let go.

"I only came in here to bring you the book. I hope you give it a chance." Clearing his throat, he backed off of the bed. She looked away. "Good night," he said softly, and left the room.

Her breaths came ragged. Fear throbbed in her chest. Being intimidated wasn't a foreign thing to her, but she didn't want to think about that right now. Nothing had happened, anyway. He hadn't hurt her. She was fine.

She smoothed the blankets around her and took a deep breath. No more Jesse. No more dragons. Maybe a classic would be good for her. Shaking, she picked up the book from the nightstand. It was old, and the smell of its pages reminded her of her parents' library. The book was *The Great Gatsby*. It had been an assignment for her English class, and she remembered first cracking it open in the library at home. As she had settled herself into her usual spot in the armchair, she glanced over the open pages at the Mercedes Lackey novel lying on the table. It would have to wait.

She had barely begun chapter three when her mother entered the room. That was odd. She was in jeans. Naomi rarely saw her in something so casual, but she still wore a work blouse and jewelry. She was all lopsided.

"I thought you would be in here," she sighed, and sank into an armchair across from her. "You know about your father's merger, don't you?"

Naomi closed the book around her thumb and lowered it to her lap. "I've heard you guys talking about it. I guess it's a big deal?"

She nodded. "Yes, a big deal. It's an overseas merger. There's a company in Germany …."

Naomi tuned her out, certain she was going to say something about moving to Europe, but soon realized it was nothing so drastic.

"They'll grow three times the size they are now," her mother was saying when she tuned back in. "It's a significant step for the company." She paused and wrinkled her nose. "Does that make sense?"

Naomi wondered why anything about her father's company had to be explained. "I guess so," she answered. Then with more trepidation, "Will he travel more than he already does?"

Karen frowned and glanced at the book in Naomi's lap. "I suppose he will for the first little while, yes." Her eyes narrowed. "Does that bother you?"

She didn't know what to say. Of course it bothered her. But how was she supposed to explain that to a mother who rarely sat down to talk to her? A mother who, most of the time, said things like, "I had no idea you were gone all last week on a school trip. Did you have a good time?" Or, "Naomi, I'm busy right now. Maybe later."

Later never came. Sometimes Naomi wondered why it mattered. Why did she care if her mother spent time with her? Most teenagers her age wanted nothing to do with their parents.

"Naomi, does that bother you?"

She looked up. "No, I guess not."

Another glance at the book in her lap. "What are you reading?"

Naomi looked down, her mind shuffling over the first paragraphs of chapter three—something about motorboats slicing their way across the water and oranges and lemons piled into pulpless pyramids. She liked the language and imagery. It was bright and colorful in her mind, even now as she looked up at her mother.

"It's for school," she stammered. *The Great Gatsby.* I just started it."

"Oh, that's one of my favorites." She smiled brighter than Naomi had seen in a long time. "Do you like it so far? Have you met Gatsby yet?"

A tremor shot from her heart to her toes. She had no idea her mother liked to read anything but thick, dry reference books with complicated law titles stamped into the leather spines. She assumed all the fiction in the library was for sheer decoration.

"Um, no, I haven't."

"Don't judge him too unfairly in the beginning. I promise he gets better."

Naomi was speechless. It wasn't that her mother had never surprised her before with random stints of conversation. She sometimes seemed genuinely interested in her life—for about two minutes, anyway, until her cell phone rang or the housekeeper needed something or a quick glance at her wristwatch reminded her that two minutes talking to her daughter was two minutes too long. That was how their relationship worked—little bits here and there like scattered breadcrumbs leading to a real family that spent time together. The only problem was Naomi seemed to keep getting lost in the woods. She had accepted it long ago, but now as she saw her mother looking at *The Great Gatsby* with a long, thirsty gaze, she wondered if she might be wrong. Maybe there was hope after all and she could catch a glimpse of who her mother really was, and that might lead to something long hidden about herself, as well—something she had always felt was locked away.

Karen shook her head as if waking herself up from a dream and stood up from her chair. Naomi sighed. Nope. There wasn't anything hiding beneath her mother's shell. She was who she was. She was probably going to leave. Seven minutes had already passed.

"Let me find something for you," Karen said, and walked across the room to a bookshelf. "I first read this when I was your age. I think it might be my favorite novel." She walked back and placed a slender book in Naomi's lap. "You don't have to read it. Just let me know what you think if you do."

She glanced at her watch, and Naomi saw the change in her face from the mother she barely knew to the efficient attorney she hated.

"I came in here to make sure you know about your father's banquet in two weeks," Karen said. "It's to celebrate the commencement of the merger. There will be photographers and dinner, and we want you there. Bring Brad, if you like."

Now they were back on normal turf.

She nodded without a second thought. "Okay."

Whatever.

She had heard it all before, been to the banquets, posed for the pictures. The only good thing about any of it was the excuse to buy a new dress. She opened her book again and started the chapter over, but stopped to glance at the novel her mother had placed in her lap.

It was a thin hardback, old and well-worn. One crumpled edge, a smudge of dirt near the spine. A part of her wanted to pick it up and start reading immediately, but another part pulled away and stayed away.

The buttery scent of scrambled eggs woke her up. It was seven o'clock. Blue morning light glittered through the curtains. She sat up and rubbed her eyes, looked at the eggs and toast on the nightstand, and lifted the plate to her lap.

The eggs were hot, fluffy, and lightly salted. They were so much better than Mindy's eggs. Mindy was her parents' current housekeeper, and the eggs she made were too dry.

She was halfway finished before she noticed Evelyn cleaning the bathroom. Already dressed for the day, she was kneeling on the floor with her back to Naomi. Her willowy frame bent over as she swept up the hair she had promised to get rid of two days ago. Then she stood and wiped down every surface in the bathroom. After emptying the trash, she opened drawers and cupboards so she could put away everything Naomi had taken out of the Wal-Mart bags a few days earlier.

Mortified, Naomi watched. She was used to somebody cleaning up after her—her nannies until she was thirteen, then Mindy—but they were paid to do it, and she had never sat and watched them clean up her messes. Should she have been tidier? Should she offer to help? Apologize?

Evelyn stepped out of the bathroom and smiled. "How are the eggs?"

She swallowed. "They're really good. Thank you."

Why was she being so damn polite? And why was she ashamed for feeling dependent when they were forcing her to be?

"I'm glad." Evelyn approached the bed. "Eric made them for you."

The fork nearly slipped from her fingers. "That was … nice of him."

"I thought so. He feels bad about slapping you last night." She stepped closer to the bed. "That's not how we're going to treat you from now on, okay? We want you to be comfortable. You'll learn to like it here, I promise. Just don't try to get away."

There was a pleading tone to her voice. Naomi wanted to promise her she wouldn't try to get away, but that would be stupid, so she kept her mouth shut. She wondered what went through Evelyn's mind when she looked at her. Was she merely a prize Eric had brought home one day? Someone Evelyn could "play with" and take care of? For some reason, that didn't disturb her nearly as much as it should.

"I won't be able to bring you lunch on weekdays," Evelyn said, "so today I'll pick up some snacks at the store you can keep up here to eat during the day. I get home at four and start dinner around five or six. Eric might let you eat with us downstairs, but I'm not sure yet." She glanced at the toast left on Naomi's plate. "Is there anything you don't like to eat?"

She fidgeted with the fork in her hand, considering the fact that the house would be empty for most of the day, and that her own mother had never asked her such a simple question as what she liked to eat. She looked up. "I can't stand fish."

"I'll keep that in mind." She turned and headed for the door. "I'll bring up a hamper for your dirty clothes. Laundry's done once a week."

When she was gone, Naomi looked down at the remaining eggs on her plate. She was no longer hungry. The mere thought of Eric preparing something for her to eat made her stomach twist. She set the plate on the nightstand and curled back under the covers. She needed Brad's arms around her. He would tell her she was doing the right thing by not fighting back. She missed him no matter what the rational side of her mind kept telling her about not loving him. He only wanted to protect her and love her. What was so bad about that?

The late January air was frigid the night she first realized he might hit her. It was only a few weeks before she was kidnapped. The cold air was expected since the entire winter had been cooler than normal. She had been forced to pull out old, heavy sweatshirts and coats she hadn't worn in two years.

Brad was lying on his stomach on top of her bed and reached his hands to the floor where she sat Indian-style. She was trying to finish the last chapter of *The Great Gatsby.*

"Wear your white hoodie," he said when she told him she couldn't possibly go since all her winter clothes were downstairs in the laundry room.

"What white hoodie?" She kept her eyes focused on her book, annoyed that he wasn't letting her finish, and even more annoyed that he wanted her to go for a three-mile walk down the beach to party with a bunch of people from school she didn't even like.

"The one I bought you, remember? You wore it yesterday; I can see it in your hamper."

She twisted around. He was right, and she scrunched her nose. "It smells like fish. It got wet when I reached into the tide pool, remember?"

"It does not." He jumped off the bed and went to the hamper. "Well, maybe a little," he mumbled after pressing one of the sleeves to his nose. "But who cares? You won't be able to smell it outside."

He was right. Again.

As they headed down the beach hand in hand, the only thing she could smell was the drifting, hot scent of a bonfire. When they finally reached the party, she was freezing. She had only worn flip-flops and could hardly feel her sand-covered toes as Brad led her to a log close to the fire.

He left her sitting between two groups clustered in their own conversations, and as she patiently waited for him to get her some food, she pressed her knees and elbows together and stared into the flames. She was admiring the color when somebody sat next to her.

"You're Brad's girl, right?" a deep voice asked.

She jumped and turned to face the guy. He was skinny, but not nerdy, with longish, dark brown hair swept across his forehead. She thought he looked handsomely philosophical, with thin, wire-rimmed glasses perfectly balanced on his polished, symmetrical features.

"His *girl?*" she replied, annoyed. "I guess you could call me that."

"Oh, sorry. Naomi, right?"

"Yes."

He reached out a hand for her to shake, something she wasn't used to from her own age group. None of them were so formal.

"I'm Damien, Brad's roommate if he decides to come to Berkeley this fall."

She took his hand, suddenly recalling Brad's mention of him awhile back—some friend of his she had never met. He had graduated three years ago, and if she remembered right, was supposed to be a great photographer.

"I'm sorry," she exclaimed sheepishly. "Brad told me about you, but he didn't say you'd be here tonight."

His grip was strong as he looked through his glasses into her eyes. "Yeah, I'm visiting my parents for the weekend. This usually isn't my kind of thing. I mean, the cops'll probably show up in a few hours since everyone here is underage."

She dropped her eyes to the beer in his hand and gave him a half-smile. "And you aren't?"

"I'm twenty-two."

"Oh, right."

"Anyway, Brad's told me a lot about you. Says you're into photography." He smiled—a cute smile with dimples. "I'm always looking for somebody else who enjoys it as much as me. You know, who's actually serious about it."

She was hooked.

They talked for ten minutes, halfway through which she wondered where Brad was, but kept talking anyway. That was when she learned about the fog.

"This will be a great spring," Damien said with a toothy grin. "Nice and cold. Perfect for fog. You know, so thick you can barely see through it? If you catch it right when it's rolling in, you can get some eerie-looking shots." He took a drink. "We'll do anything for a great shot, right?"

Chuckling, she lifted her wrists to her nose. The smell was faint, but revolting.

"What's the matter?" He laughed. "You look like you're gonna hurl."

She lowered her hands. "It's just … I hate the smell of fish, and I was digging around in this tide pool yesterday to straighten out a starfish. You know, for that perfect shot? Well, I got my sleeves wet and now they reek."

"What? Tide pool water doesn't smell like fish."

He chuckled and dropped his eyes to her hands now lying in her lap. "May I?" he asked, reaching to touch her fingers. Before she could answer, he slipped her hand into his and lifted the cuff of her sweatshirt to his nose.

His touch was gentle, but persistent. His thumb caressed her skin as he looked into her eyes. He slid the cuff up her arm and turned the underside of her wrist to his lips. What did he think he was doing? Every move made her jumpy and hot, like the flames a few feet away.

He breathed slowly, practically kissing her pale skin with his lips. Excitement wound its way through her. How would those lips feel against her mouth? Those sweet caresses on her neck? She tried to shove the thought away as he took a deep, sensual breath that sent heat all the way down to her chilled toes. Finally, when she thought her heart couldn't beat any faster, he let go.

"You're crazy," he said softly, and then with an elegant smile, "I couldn't smell fish at all. Only you."

"Me?"

"Yeah, you smell incredible. Like lilies."

She wasn't sure if he was trying to flirt with her or not, if the confident, dimpled smile and the way he had touched her was supposed to make her knees weak and her hands warm, or if she was imagining it all. Either way, she was shocked at how he made her feel; at how easily a complete stranger could sweep her off her feet when she was already in love with Brad.

Where *was* Brad?

She looked up to see him standing ten feet away, carrying a plate of food and two open beers. He was stopped in his tracks, frozen next to the fire with fury scorching his face. Embarrassed to see him watching her, she pushed down the cuff of her sleeve as he shot an angry glance at Damien.

"I didn't know you'd be here," he snapped.

Damien smiled and shrugged, apparently oblivious that Brad looked like he might deck him. "Yeah, me neither. I'm in town for the weekend and saw Naomi sitting here." He took a long drink from his beer. "I recognized her from the picture you showed me last summer, remember?"

Brad shifted his weight across the sand. "Yeah, I remember." He stepped forward and sat down on the other side of Naomi. His thigh pressed against hers. "So I guess you two found a lot to talk about while I was gone?" He leaned forward and shoved the two beers into the sand. His irritation was thick and intense. Naomi could have felt it a mile away, but Damien wasn't reacting to it. He was either extremely imperceptive or he simply didn't care. She was inclined to think the latter. All she wanted to do was disappear, but she grabbed one of the beers instead and took a long swallow. Maybe it would take the edge off everything.

Damien leaned forward to look at Brad. "Sure, we found a lot to talk about. You know we both like photography." Then with a heavy sigh, "So have you decided where you're going to school yet? Should I count on you for the other half of my rent?"

Naomi watched the orange flames of the bonfire shimmer off his glasses before she took another swig of beer and turned to Brad, who was staring down at the plate of food in his lap.

"I don't know yet," he mumbled, and leaned forward to snatch the other beer from the sand. He took a long, deep swallow before wrapping an arm around her waist. He squeezed her tightly. So tightly it hurt.

"Baby, are you hungry?"

She looked at the plate in his lap and nodded. The hot dog he handed her was charred, topped with lots of mustard. That was just the way she liked it.

"Looks good," Damien said and stood. He smiled down at her. "Guess I'll talk to you later. See how those night shots go, huh?"

"Wait a sec." Brad set his plate on the ground and stood up to face Damien. Of the two, Brad was more daunting despite his younger age. He worked out nearly every day and was proud of his sculpted biceps and six-pack abdomen. He said he did it for Naomi. He thought she liked his strength, and when she ran her hands across his smooth, muscle-taught skin, she was thinking *protector, intimacy, safe*—when what she was shamefully thinking lately was *pain*. Sometimes he was just too rough with her.

"Listen," Brad snapped into Damien's face, "I don't want you anywhere near her, understand? There's a reason I've kept her away from you, and you damn well know why."

"Sure, whatever you say. Let me know when you're moving in, all right?"

Damien gave her a brief smile and walked away before Brad could say anything else. He whipped around to face her with clenched fists at his sides.

"I swear," he hissed as she shoved her beer back into the sand and shakily ran a finger across her wrist, "if you ever look at somebody like that again ...."

"Like what, Brad?"

She tried to ignore the sweat breaking out on her palms as his fists tightened. He had never hit her before, but that look in his eyes was all too familiar. She was sure he could slam one of those fists into her face without a second thought. Worse than that, he might make her do something in bed that might hurt more than usual. She twisted her trembling hands together at the thought. A fist might be better, but the problem with that was she would have to hide the bruise under makeup, and if someone noticed, she would have to explain it away with some stupid excuse. There was no way she would risk getting Brad in trouble, and he knew it. It was in that moment that something shifted inside her head, like a puzzle piece moving into place.

His fists unclenched and he softened his expression and sat back down next to her. "I shouldn't get angry with you because of him. He's a great friend, but he's a regular player. That's the main reason I don't want him near you. Somebody like you ... he's always looking for an easy—"

He stopped and ran his hand up her back. "Don't talk to him anymore, okay?"

She spotted some mustard on her thumb, eerily bright in the glow of the fire. "Okay," she answered softly.

The food wasn't appetizing anymore as she imagined Brad actually hitting her. For the way she was feeling about Damien, she probably deserved a swift punishment.

VI
March

NAOMI SPENT A LOT OF TIME IN THE SHOWER. SHE took at least two a day, sometimes three. If she was extremely bored, she took four. Maybe it was because she liked the tile walls. They turned slick and dark under the water and reminded her of moss-covered cave walls or smooth stones at the bottom of a river. Safe, enclosed places.

There was a spot between two of the tiles where the grout had turned soft. With her fingernail, she had scratched a mark for every day she was kidnapped.

Twenty-seven so far.

She stepped out of the shower and faced the foggy mirror. She wanted to wipe away the condensation to look at herself, but she knew it was a bad idea. She didn't want to see her short hair. She wanted to forget the motel room. In her mind, it seemed so far away from this isolated bedroom. She was beginning to feel safe for the most part.

Her stomach growled, indicating it was time for dinner. Evelyn would be up any moment. Opening the bathroom door, she stopped dead in her tracks.

Jesse.

He was leaning against the dresser and looked up from a book in his hands. She wanted to run back into the bathroom and lock the door, but she was so shocked to see him—to see anybody besides Evelyn—that she couldn't move.

He smiled, closing his book before he set it on the dresser. It was *The Great Gatsby*. She noticed a new stack of books next to it.

"Evelyn sent me up here," he said, struggling to keep his eyes on her face. They kept drifting to the edge of the towel wrapped around her chest. He shifted his feet. "Get dressed and I'll take you downstairs for dinner."

Heart pounding, she clutched the towel even closer and stepped back. The way he was looking at her invaded her space even more than when he had touched her face and told her she was beautiful.

"I'm sorry," he said with a half-smile. His cheeks were red. "I didn't know you'd be undressed."

She stepped back "You're not going to watch me, are you?"

"Of course not. I'll be right outside the door."

When he was gone, she rushed to the closet. Her breaths were fast and panicked. She looked at her naked body when she dropped the towel and imagined a stranger's hands on her skin. Sick. Sick. Sick. She shuddered, dressing as fast as she could before heading for the door. But something caught her eye. The stack of books Jesse had left on the dresser. He had brought her fantasy novels, even some Mercedes Lackey. God bless him in spite of everything else.

There were classics too, one in particular that made her breath catch in her throat. *The Awakening.* It was the same book her mother had given her in the library at home. The thought of even touching it made her look away. He couldn't possibly know about that, could he? What were the chances?

Slipping through the doorway, she let him lead her downstairs to the dining table where the others were already eating. A lump formed in her throat. The table was set with prepared bowls of chicken Caesar salad, something she always avoided because most Caesar dressings tasted fishy. She hated fish. She had told Evelyn weeks ago that she hated it, but maybe she had forgotten.

Jesse pulled out a chair for her and she sat down. Of all things, the salad frightened her the most. What if she couldn't eat it? This was the first time they had let her downstairs since Eric had slapped her. She didn't want to upset him again—or offend Evelyn, who was watching her from across the table.

"It's all right," Evelyn urged with a glance at Eric. "You can eat."

"Um, sure," she whispered, and picked up her fork.

Eric swallowed a mouthful of food and smiled. "Is it nice to be out of the bedroom?"

Barely nodding, she tried not to narrow her eyes. He had no right to be nice to her. She squeezed her fork in a death-grip.

Eric rested his elbows on the table. "This is how it will be. If you do exactly what we say and don't try to escape, we'll let you out every evening for dinner. You can eat down here with us, walk around if you need, watch TV, read a book, whatever. Jesse spends a lot of time upstairs in the den. He'll keep an eye on you if you want to spend time in there. He's told me you like to read."

Jesse smiled and she nodded. "Yes, I do."

"Evelyn told me you like photography. Is that what you were doing the night in the parking lot? Taking pictures?"

Her fingers shook. "I was in the park," she answered carefully. She was certain he already knew what she had been doing that night. "I was taking night pictures. I didn't see anything you were—"

"That's not what I asked." His voice was firm, but gentle. "I've looked at the pictures on your camera. It's obviously a talent you enjoy very much."

She nodded. That was right. They had her camera bag from the night they had taken her. She had everything in there, including her phone. Brad had probably tried to call her two-hundred times by now. There was also her camera card. What was on there? A storm a few weeks ago, the tide pools, the fog, but why would Eric care? Why would any of them care? They were all looking at her now. She lowered her eyes to the salad and tried to control her quickening breaths.

"I hope you have other interests." Eric's voice drifted through her spinning thoughts. "I can't give you your camera back, but we're willing to consider other things you might like to do. We want to …."

He paused, probably waiting for her to look up, but she couldn't look at him as his intentions became clearer.

"We'd like to make you happy."

Her lips smashed together as she gathered her courage. "You mean so I won't want to leave?"

He blinked. Steve cleared his throat and looked down at his newspaper. Evelyn leaned into the back of her chair. Jesse smiled through a mouthful of food, apparently amused.

"Yes, so you won't want to leave," Eric mocked, glancing at Evelyn with an expression that said, *I told you she wasn't stupid.* "I don't want you here as much as you don't want to be here. It was a mistake to take you—one huge, damn mistake, and if you're not going to appreciate the fact that we're willing to make the best of it, then we can handle things … differently."

The scent of Caesar dressing drifted up to her nose. The sharp garlic and Parmesan was mingled with something fishy. How could she possibly eat it? How could she swallow anything they were going to feed her? Forced kindness, insincere affection, cruel threats.

She stood up from her chair. She couldn't stay here. It was crazy. *They* were crazy. She looked at the front door and tensed her muscles when Eric's voice slammed into her.

"Sit down!"

She turned back to the table. They were all halfway out of their chairs, ready to grab her if needed. Eric's eyes were dark, and as she sat back down in her chair, she watched the trembling in his fingers subside.

"Don't ever try that again," he snapped. "You'll sit there and eat and you won't move until I tell you to. Another move like that and you'll never leave that bedroom again. Got it?"

Evelyn hissed something unintelligible in his direction, but everyone else remained silent as Naomi lowered her eyes and nodded. She stabbed a piece of chicken in the bowl and lifted it to her mouth, determined not to gag and reveal her weakness. She had to remain strong and think clearly. Submission might be all right for the moment, but there had to be a way to outthink these people and escape. Something they would eventually overlook.

The chicken was good, but the dressing tasted exactly as she imagined. She reached for her water and swallowed half the glass.

"What's the matter?" Evelyn asked.

She stabbed another piece of chicken, but wasn't sure she could bring it to her lips.

"Anchovies," Steve mumbled. He peered at Evelyn over the rims of his reading glasses. "The dressing you make has anchovies in it. You said she doesn't like fish."

Evelyn set down her fork and turned to Naomi. "I'm sorry. I didn't even think—"

"It's all right." She lowered her hands to her lap.

"Is there something else you can get her?" Steve asked, turning back to his newspaper. Naomi caught a glimpse of the front cover and saw *The Denver Post* printed across the top. So she was in Colorado. That was just great. Nobody would ever find her here.

"I'll get it, Evelyn," Jesse volunteered before Evelyn could get up from her chair. He stood and went into the kitchen.

"There's leftover lasagna," she called out to him as he opened the fridge. "Is that all right, Naomi?"

Whatever. She wasn't hungry anymore, but even without an appetite, she was still willing to eat. It was the only reliable sensation she didn't have to question. She would do whatever they told her because she was weak and they were strong. It was a familiar place, even comfortable if she settled in far enough.

Jesse took her back upstairs when she finished eating. He opened the door and gave her a pleading stare. There was red stubble on his jaw and an indent on his nose from a pair of glasses. "I won't ever hurt you," he said, leaning close to her.

Confused, she backed into the room.

"I'm not like that," he continued softly. "I'm sorry if I've scared you, that's all."

She nodded. She had to admit he did creep her out on a lot of levels, but then again, he wasn't the first guy in her life to make her feel uncomfortable without any hope of escape.

VII

HER KIDNAPPERS LEFT FOR WORK THE NEXT MORNING, but when Jesse returned he came straight to her door. Naomi lowered her book when he stepped into the room.

"Would you like to go into the den?" he asked. He was dressed in tan slacks and a button-down shirt. His hair was neatly styled. She wondered what he did all day to have to look so nice.

"Yeah," she said with a relieved sigh. "This room is getting small."

"I'll bet."

She followed him down the hallway into a long room lined with bookshelves. In the middle of the room was a pool table, but what caught her attention were the French doors leading out to a balcony. She could see the backyard and hints of the rest of the neighborhood. It seemed like only older people lived around here. She had seen hardly anyone out her window during the day, and she hadn't heard any children or loud noises at all. Lights were on inside the houses. Were the people eating dinner? Watching TV? Here she was in the middle of their neighborhood, a prisoner. It was weird. She stared down at her hands, grateful she wasn't tied up at night. She might scream her head off if it came to that.

"I like to play pool," Jesse said as he motioned for her to sit on a sofa by the table. "You can read if you like. Do you want a drink?"

"A drink?" She sat gingerly on the edge of the sofa, trying not to look uncomfortable. Why was he asking her if she wanted a drink? He was too nice to be a kidnapper. It was all wrong.

"Yeah." He walked to a refrigerator at the back of the room where a weight machine and treadmill were tucked into the shadows. "Water? Coke? Sprite? Juice? What do you like?"

She stared down at her hands. "Uh, Coke, I guess."

"My favorite." He opened the fridge and pulled one out for her. When she had it in her hands he took a cue stick from the wall. "Do you like to play?"

She turned the can in her hands and looked away. The truth was she loved to play pool; Brad had taught her how.

"Well?"

"Uh, I think I'd rather read."

"Be my guest." He nodded to the shelves. She stood and walked to the shelves with the most fantasy titles. A little gasp left her mouth. They had some of the best books. She touched the spines with a trembling finger—classics and newer titles too, mostly hardbacks. It seemed odd that they bought and read fiction. She remembered all the books stacked downstairs and wondered if Eric read fantasy, if he liked all those made-up worlds. Evelyn seemed more the type to love dragons and princes and long, epic journeys, but as she was discovering, these people weren't predictable.

Gradually, she became aware of Jesse's eyes on her back.

"You sure don't talk much," he said.

She turned around to see him leaning against the pool table, his arms folded as he waited for her to answer.

"What do you mean?"

"Don't you miss your family? Your boyfriend? Evelyn says you never talk about any of them."

"What does she want me to say?"

He shrugged. "Don't you miss them?"

Clamping her mouth shut, she considered the question. It should have been easy to answer, but it wasn't. Out of pure habit she rarely thought about her parents, and Brad only entered her mind when she forgot to focus on something else. She imagined her emotions and memories trapped inside a tiny box she was too afraid to open. Her eyes started to sting.

"I'm sorry." Panic crossed Jesse's face as he unfolded his arms. "I didn't mean to make you uncomfortable. I—"

"I-I can't think about them," she said as the box started to open. Now she was going to fall apart. "I think more about the tiles in the shower than I do about my parents. They went to work only *one* day after they found out I was gone, and Brad …."

Her voice trickled into a sob as she thought about his arms around her in his bed. The first time she had slept with him she had panicked that her parents would find out, but they never did. They wouldn't have cared anyway, and that's what hurt. Brad wanted her more and more until it was a regular ritual, and now she missed his lips on her skin, his tight embrace and whispers that he would keep her safe forever. He was so wrong.

Jesse approached her and she backed away. The last thing she wanted was him trying to comfort her. They wanted to make her believe they cared about her, and she couldn't allow that.

"Don't touch me," she whimpered. "Please." She backed into a bookshelf and watched him come closer. He was the same size as Brad, just as strong, but leaner. She could see his firm muscles defined under his shirt. He definitely worked out, but she wondered why—if it was for a girlfriend. Why was he even here? He didn't seem related to the others in any way.

He came closer. Naomi held her breath. She would not freak out. She could handle this, but tears spilled down her face. Something about him tipped her over the edge. It was something strong, like in Brad, the hard glimmer in his eyes pushing her into submission, the way he moved as if nothing could shake him. A part of her yearned for it, and the other part cowered.

He touched her cheek to wipe away a tear. His hand was warm and gentle. "The news reports say you're shy. You have no close friends except for Brad."

She couldn't tear her gaze from the freckles on his cheeks. They weren't nerdy like some of the boys' freckles at school. She could see he was proud of the way he looked, the way he held himself.

He tilted his head. "How can someone so smart and beautiful be so lonely?"

More tears. She couldn't keep them back. She felt behind her, but there were only books, nothing to defend herself with as his hand wrapped around her arm and pulled her away from the bookshelf. She remembered how firmly he had held her in the motel room when he had helped her up from the floor, how he had smelled of stale cologne and sweat—a sweet, almost comforting scent. He smelled like that now, like Brad, like everything she loved and hated.

With a heavy sigh, she gave in and let him gather her into his arms. She rested her cheek on his shoulder, embarrassed that her tears were already soaking through his shirt. It was gross, but he didn't seem to care.

"Shhh," he whispered, tightening his hold on her. It was tighter than it needed to be. He lightly caressed a spot on her back. "You must still be scared to death, even after a month here, but we haven't hurt you, have we?"

"N-no," she whimpered. An odd feeling swept over her, like she was floating in water. She remembered months ago trying to straighten the starfish in the tide pool so she could take a picture. It had velvety, bumpy skin. It clung to the rock for dear life as she tried to pry it away.

"The only reason Eric will hurt you is if you try to get away," he said in a steady voice. "You won't do that."

"I won't." She had no idea if she meant it. They couldn't possibly expect her to give in so easily. She was trembling now. Jesse loosened his hold and nudged her away enough so he could look at her.

"Let's play a game." He nodded to the pool table. "I'll teach you if you don't know how. It'll get your mind off things."

"I don't think so," she said through a sob. Her mind was spinning around thoughts of Brad and the starfish and that night on the beach with Damien as she ate a hot dog with mustard. The only thing she thought about her parents was them driving away to work in the morning, and that made her feel guilty for some stupid reason. The last thing she wanted to do was play a game.

"Naomi, calm down."

She looked up and realized she was sobbing uncontrollably. Little hiccups escaped her mouth. Her nose was starting to run. Fantastic.

"I'm sorry," she spluttered and turned away to wipe her nose with her hands. She didn't want anyone to see her like this, a complete wreck. Even her knees felt weak.

"What's the matter?" he asked. "I had no idea mentioning your parents would—"

"You're right," she interrupted, wiping her snot on her jeans. "I don't even think about them. That's not normal. None of this is normal."

"No, it isn't." He cleared his throat. "But you don't exactly come from a normal family."

She looked at the books on the shelf in front of her. The word normal had never described her, even now. All she had done for the last month was sleep, eat, and read. She obeyed every order. She was their perfect puppet. Her mind was in a rut like a song stuck on repeat. She was getting so sick of it she wanted to curl up and die. Had she felt like this her entire life, or did she only notice now because the situation was more intimate?

The worst thing was she was too scared to do anything to fight back. Jesse wanted her, but what kind of a girl threw herself at her kidnapper just to see if it opened a door? What did that say about her? Was it worth trying to get back to Brad? Her heart ached for him in spite of the bruise he had left on her cheek. She wanted his protection again. He had always helped her feel better about her uncaring family. His own parents were divorced, and he was constantly reminding her that at least hers were together. At least she was taken care of in a lot of other ways. It was only in those brief moments that her resentment melted away. Nobody but Brad had ever given her such stability to lean against, and she would do anything to get back to him so she could feel those solid walls once more. She needed him.

She turned around.

"I'll play a game with you," she said as she glanced at the pool table and then back to Jesse. He had folded his arms, waiting. She lowered her eyes. "You'll have to teach me."

VIII

KAREN KNEW FLYING ALL THE WAY TO MAINE TO BE with her sister was a bad idea, but Jason practically forced her onto the plane. "Elizabeth needs you right now. It's spring break for the kids, and you know how crazy that gets for her."

"Actually, I have no idea how crazy that gets for anyone," Karen had told him. "I can't afford to take time off work right now, and neither can you. The merger is in its most critical—"

"I left all of that in capable hands, and you have Anna to smooth things over while you're gone. We both need this."

Those words played through her mind as she stood in her sister's kitchen on the third night of their stay. It was past midnight and she couldn't sleep. It was obvious now that Naomi wasn't coming back. The counselor Jason was making her see had finally pushed that into her head. Naomi was gone. Missing. Maybe dead. And the only thing she could do was keep breathing and pretend she was strong. Her career would see her through this, just like it had seen her through everything in her life, but now Jason had dragged her away and she had no idea what to do with herself.

She stepped over a pile of toys and made her way to the coffee maker. Elizabeth's house was a hazard zone of dried noodles on the floor, crumbs across the counter, and dirty dishes piled so high in the sink that Karen wasn't sure there was a clean mug for some coffee.

Elizabeth had four children, all rambunctious, little balls of energy. They made Karen wince every time they were around. Elizabeth never bothered to wipe off their sticky faces or hands. She let them run wild, and her messy house was the result. Why didn't she hire a housekeeper? She could surely afford it with her husband's healthy salary.

In the moonlight spilling in from the windows, it took Karen five minutes to find a clean mug. She turned on the coffee maker and leaned down to look at it. How did this work? How did any coffee maker work? She hadn't used one since college. Somebody always made the coffee at work, and Mindy always made the coffee at home, but it couldn't be that hard. This machine seemed more complicated than most.

"You awake?"

Karen spun around to see Elizabeth standing in the doorway. Her hair was pulled into a high ponytail that made her look like a teenager. Karen was once again reminded how different they were from each other. Elizabeth was younger and sported flirtatious curves that let her get away with wearing clothes her nine-year-old daughter thought were cool.

"Yeah, I can't sleep," Karen muttered, and turned back to the coffee maker.

"Aren't you taking those pills Jason said would help you sleep?"

Karen let a loud sigh escape. "Yes, I'm taking them, but they obviously aren't working, are they?" Before Elizabeth could answer, Karen turned around. "Anyway, why are you up?"

"Sara was screaming about monsters under her bed."

"Again?"

Elizabeth shrugged. "It's a phase—it'll pass." She entered the kitchen and nudged Karen aside to start the coffee maker. "Are you sure you want coffee at this time of night?"

"I'm not sure of anything anymore." Karen slammed her mug onto the counter and walked to the sliding glass doors leading to the back porch. With tears forming in her eyes, she focused on a string of dark clouds floating across the moon. What she really wanted was for someone to knock her out for a week so she could get some rest. Jason wasn't sleeping well, either. Sometimes he held her close and she felt his tears sliding onto her chest. So far she had avoided crying.

"Karen, talk to me, please."

Elizabeth was standing with her arms folded across her chest. She looked just like their mother, Karen thought. Or at least how she wanted to remember their mother, strong and healthy, but no matter what she did she would never forget her in that hospital bed, her sallow skin and vacant eyes. The lung cancer had taken over quickly. Too quickly.

"It's over," she finally said, squeezing back her tears. "I've lost Naomi just like we lost Mom. I spent my entire life wanting that woman gone, and then when it actually happened ...." Her voice cracked as she fought back more tears. She wouldn't cry. She had to be stronger than Elizabeth because what she was about to say made her feel weaker than she had felt in a long time.

"Things weren't good between me and Naomi before this. I kept meaning to get closer to her, but how do you do that when your child has shut every door between you? She didn't *want* to let me in, and there was no way I was going to force her to do anything— not how Mom used to poke and pester and worm her way into our lives."

"She only did that because she cared," Elizabeth said quietly. "In her own way."

"But it was too much. She was lazy and stuck in a life she hated. I never wanted that for Naomi."

"Then what did you want for her?"

The clouds slid smoothly across the moon like oil spilling across glass, and something dark stabbed Karen's thoughts. She remembered making the decision to go back to work after Naomi was born. She remembered how easy it was to let nannies take over. Sometimes days went by without her even seeing

Naomi. But she loved her daughter. Didn't she? How could she doubt that?

"I've given Naomi everything you and I never had," she said, touching the glass doors in front of her. "A clean, beautiful home, private schooling when she was younger, the freedom to choose whatever she wants to do. I had to fight hard to get where I am. So did you. Naomi will never … would never have had to … struggle like we …." Her voice died, and silence filled the kitchen. Tears were coming, and to keep them away she rubbed her fists into her eyes.

"You said Mom was stuck in a life she hated," Elizabeth said. "Do you think you're any different?"

"What is that supposed to mean?" Karen turned to face her sister, her heart pounding. The reporters had already made her feel like a failure. The last thing she needed was to hear it from her own blood.

"I'm just asking if you're happy."

"Well I'm not now. Naomi is—"

"Forget about Naomi. Have you *been* happy?"

"Of course I have. I've accomplished everything I've set out to do. I love my job. You know that."

Elizabeth turned back to the coffee maker, but she didn't say anything. Her silence created bubbles of anger in Karen's stomach. It wasn't right for her own sister to judge her like this. Even Jason looked at her funny lately. She needed an escape. She needed some fresh air.

"I'm going for a walk," she muttered and unlocked the sliding glass door. She slipped onto the deck and pushed the door closed behind her. Making her way down the steps, she fished out her cell phone from her pocket. She kept the phone on her at all times just in case the detective or police called—and sometimes she liked to call Naomi's number. Jason had told her to stop trying, but she couldn't help herself.

She glanced up at the deck to see if Elizabeth was following her. Not so far. Turning back to the darkness, she walked to a grove of trees on the borderline of the property and sat down on a rock. The March air was cold, but calm. She pulled her knees to her chest and hit the speed dial she had set up a few weeks ago. Naomi's number. She had never had that number in the phone before, but lately it was the only one she dialed. She put the phone to her ear and listened.

It went straight to voicemail, as usual. Karen listened to Naomi's message. Her voice was clear and happy. It was almost musical with a slight undertone of deepness to it, like Jason's. Listening to her made Karen's heart beat so fast it felt like it might leap from her chest. She had never missed Naomi before, but now she did. It was a sharp ache in her stomach that wouldn't go away. Maybe it was guilt, but she suspected it was more than that.

The voicemail ended. The beep sounded, and Karen waited for a moment as the machine recorded her breaths. She wanted to say something. She always wanted to say something, but nothing ever came. She ended the call and dialed the number again just to listen to Naomi. Then again.

"That won't solve anything." Elizabeth's voice came out from the dark.

Karen jerked with surprise and ended the call. "Damn it, Lizzy, don't surprise me like that."

"Sorry. You don't think I'd let you wander out here all by yourself, do you? Not in the state you're in."

"What state am I in?"

"Shock."

"That's not true." It couldn't be true. People in shock didn't fly out to stay with their sister. People in shock didn't keep working and functioning like a normal person.

Elizabeth shrugged and sat on the ground by Karen's feet. She looked up. "I just want you to know I'm here for you, but I'm not going to pretend nothing is wrong. You can keep denying how you feel or you can do something about it."

Karen stood and grabbed a thin tree branch above her. She snapped it off and threw it into the underbrush. Elizabeth's face was blue in the shadows and a patch of light from the kitchen made her eyes glow.

"There is nothing I *can* do." Karen snapped at her. "Nothing. The police will only investigate for so long, and the detective I hired has already run out of leads. All anyone found was some glass from a broken taillight in the parking lot by drops of Naomi's blood."

"Yes, you told me about that earlier. Have they tried to match the taillight with a car?"

"I think so, but that isn't much to go on. They're going to give up."

"But they've barely started. I haven't seen anything about it here in Maine yet. You should get this on national television. The more people who know about it, the better chances of her being found. You have the money and means to do something like that."

Karen gritted her teeth and squeezed the phone in her hand. "It's hopeless. Why can't you see that? People disappear every day. This isn't any different."

"But it should be!" Elizabeth stood up just as the sliding glass doors opened on the deck and little Sara stepped outside.

"Mommmmy!" she wailed, tears streaming down her face as she clutched a tattered, stuffed kitten to her chest. "I need you. Please, Momma, please."

"I have to go," Elizabeth said with a dark glance at Karen. "But I just wanted to say it should be different. She's yours. You've spent your entire life trying to shove her out of your life. Maybe you didn't mean to, but now it's time to change. It doesn't matter if she's gone."

Karen watched her sister jog back to the house and scoop Sara into her arms. She couldn't remember scooping up Naomi like that or drying her tears in the middle of the night. Did she deserve to miss her? To her, the answer was clearly no.

She sat back down on the rock and looked at her phone again. She didn't have any pictures of Naomi to look at. The only thing she had left in the entire world was Naomi's voice over the phone. She dialed the number again, only this time she spoke after the beep.

IX
April

NAOMI'S KIDNAPPERS KEPT THEIR WORD AND LET HER out every evening for dinner. It was weird sitting with them night after night, pecking at her food like a bird. She was hungry, but her nerves put her so much on edge she could hardly swallow. When Evelyn asked her if she would rather eat in her room, she thought for several minutes, but finally answered no. If she was going to get on their good side, the best thing to do was spend time around them. Eric was nice to her now, and she didn't want that to go away. Sometimes he still looked like he wanted to slam her against the wall and scream at her, but that was rare now. Still, she reminded herself of that darkness, of how easily he might hurt her again.

"Isn't Evelyn's food great?" Jesse asked her one evening as he took her upstairs to the den. "She's Italian, you know. She lived in Italy with her grandmother. She must have learned all her secrets there."

"Her cooking is really good," Naomi answered softly as they approached the pool table.

"You think so? You never eat very much."

She shrugged and wrapped her arms around herself. Jesse turned to her, waiting. Lately, he always waited for her to answer his questions, an unbending look in his eyes that said he wouldn't accept silence.

"It's weird down there with all of you," she stuttered. It was the only explanation she could think of. "Eric tries to make small talk with me, and you're all so nice to each other, even to me. It's weird, that's all. I mean, who eats dinner together every night like that?"

A soft smile played on his lips. "I get it. Everything inside of you expects us to hurt you, and we're not doing anything like that."

She shifted her feet. "Only because I haven't tried to get away. If I did that, you'd—"

"Eric would kill you." He stepped closer and took hold of her arm. "You know that. I see it in your eyes, the way you hold your breath around him, the way your face goes white as a sheet. He sees it too. If you give him a chance, I promise you'll see a different side of him. It took me a long time too."

She looked away. She already saw the other side of Eric—the nice side—and she wanted it to stick. The mean side made her want to punch something—or run into a corner and hide. She hated the way he made her feel. Jesse was different, more in control. Steady.

He released her arm and walked to the wall where the cue sticks hung, grabbing two and handing her one. "Chalk up and we'll get started. Maybe one day I'll let you win."

She smiled and took the cue stick. In a lot of ways she liked the way he treated her. He didn't try to hide his emotions or ignore her situation. It didn't seem to make him as uncomfortable as it made the others. He had an odd sense of humor she connected with, and she didn't feel like he would seriously hurt her no matter how much he invaded her space. Things were stable so far. Of course, that could end any second depending on her actions, and right now all she could manage was the lame flirting idea. She was such a coward.

She chalked her cue stick as he did the same. "Can I break?" she asked.

"Sure."

He stepped aside and she acted flustered for a moment before bending over. She hit the cue ball with a soft nudge, barely breaking the rack.

"That won't do," Jesse chuckled. "I'll let you try again if you like."

She laughed inside too. For weeks she had pretended stupidity when it came to pool. She wanted chances for him to be close to her, and so far teaching her pool was giving her exactly that. The whole idea might seem lame, but at the moment it was the only way out she could see. It was quiet and deliberate and almost felt safe. "I'm sorry," she said with a frown. "I'll do better."

"You just need to hit it harder. You're not balancing it right, either. Remember what I showed you last time?"

She lowered her eyes. "I guess I forgot."

"Let me show you again." He smiled, stepping behind her. His chest touched her shoulder blades as he leaned closer, loosely wrapping his arms around hers. He moved the cue stick into place and balanced it next to her thumb.

"Like this," he explained near her ear, his breath moving across her skin. Then he folded her forefinger over the smooth grain finish of the cue stick. "Or like this. The key is to feel comfortable."

He could have pulled away at that point, but he didn't. She tried to imagine herself wanting him, breathing in the clean, peppery scent of his cologne. It wasn't a hard thing to imagine. Maybe she really did want him. He was wrapped around her, a pocket of warmth. The soft material of his sleeves pressed against her bare arms as his breath caressed the side of her face. Time stood still for a moment. She leaned a fraction of an inch against those strong muscles. Her breath almost stopped.

"I can show you a few more ways," he said, clearing his throat. His hands still rested lightly against her fingers on the cue stick.

"No, I think I'll try again."

He stepped away. The air grew cold again as she leaned over the table and sent the cue ball into the rack—probably too soundly since she hit the one-ball dead on and with more force than she ever managed with Brad.

She straightened and Jesse grinned as he waited to see if any of the balls fell into a pocket. They didn't, and he walked to another end of the table. "Good job, but it's still an open table, so now it's my turn, okay?"

"I remember that rule, yeah."

He pocketed three striped balls and then missed an easy shot, either because he was too busy darting his eyes back and forth between her and the table or he wanted to give her another chance. Either way, it made her heart race. Maybe, just maybe, this could work.

She flashed her eyes a few times in his direction, missing what should have been an effortless shot. Straightening, she rubbed her arms. Her dreams still swarmed with dragons, and they lingered in her waking hours too, circling over the burning valley like scavengers. Shivering, she watched her body split in half as she hit the rocks.

"Are you cold?"

She trembled when he walked to her and ran his hands up her bare arms covered with goose bumps. Why did his touch have to feel so good?

"I-I guess so."

"Do you want me to get you something warm to put on? Didn't Evelyn give you a sweater? Pink?"

She nodded and tried to relax the tension in her body. The dragons in her head flew away. "It's in my closet," she said. "On a hanger."

He tightened his grip, the attraction in his eyes completely obvious. She remembered him in her room, his hand on her face, how he could take whatever he wanted and she wouldn't be able to stop him.

"I'll be right back, okay?"

She nodded and watched him leave the room. There was the clatter of Evelyn washing dishes downstairs.

Then she looked up and noticed the balcony.

It was already dark outside, but she could see the yard in the glow of the house lights. She caught sight of tall, sprawling trees meshed with others leaning over from bordering properties. A white vinyl fence surrounded the entire yard. There were lights on inside the surrounding homes.

She looked for stairs leading down from the balcony, but couldn't see any. The only thing that appeared remotely promising was a nearby tree with thick, twisted branches close to the railing.

Walking to the doors, she reached for the handle.

She was barefoot.

"Naomi?"

She spun around. Jesse stood in the doorway, her pink sweatshirt tucked under his arm.

"What are you doing?"

"N-Nothing."

His face was stern, but not upset. She expected him to yell at her or at least yank her away from the doors, but he just stood there, disappointment shadowing his eyes. She withered inside at that look.

"Let's finish our game." He walked to the pool table and carefully draped her sweatshirt over the edge.

The room shrank. He was leaving it up to her what to do. She could turn and try to run or she could put on her sweatshirt and finish the game. The answer seemed obvious. If she ran, he would catch her and Eric would kill her. End of game. Now was not the time to escape. She was back to playing the lame coward card.

Relaxing as much as she could, she walked to the pool table and grabbed her sweatshirt. Jesse folded his arms and smiled. "I think it's your turn."

"No, it was yours." She put her sweatshirt over her head, surprised to see him closer when she pulled it down.

"The hood's all twisted." Reaching around her, he pulled the heavy material straight. "There's something about you," he whispered, lowering his arms to her waist, squeezing her softly. "So innocent. I love that about you."

He looked into her eyes, a soft smile playing at the corners of his mouth. She thought she might panic, but she was relaxed. He might mean freedom if she saw this through. She would use him to her own advantage if she could keep her courage long enough. Stay focused.

"Are you all right?" he asked, still pressing her to him. She could feel his heartbeat now. She remembered crying on his shoulder weeks ago, how her tears had soaked his shirt. There were no tears now.

"I'm okay," she said, unable to tear her focus from him.

"Something's different. Tell me." The stern look came back into his eyes. His hold on her tightened.

"I don't know," she whispered, her voice like a foreign thing in her throat. "Every time you touch me it's not as … scary as before."

His expression relaxed as he released her. Coldness enveloped her and she shivered.

"I'm a nice guy," he said and chuckled. "Just like Eric—you should give me a chance." He turned and picked up his cue stick. "Let's finish."

That night Naomi buried herself under the covers and thought about the balcony and the trees she might be able to climb to escape. She thought about Jesse's arms around her and how guilty he had made her feel for looking outside. It didn't seem fair how he pushed her emotions around like the balls on the pool table. At the same time it was a familiar situation, one she could sink into and forget everything else. She liked that feeling. It was what had made her cling so tightly to Brad, the reason she still ached for him when she was falling asleep. She always cried before sleep took over, but she did it quietly enough that nobody would hear. She didn't want them to think she was too unhappy in case it might upset Eric and put him on edge.

Burying her face in her pillow, she let the tears come. Pathetic. Weak. It was what she was and she couldn't back away from it no matter how hard she tried. Her eyes drooped, but just as she started to drift away, the locks on the door turned. Great. Evelyn was coming to look at her again.

She tried to relax, sinking as far under the covers as she could. Why did they have to do this? It was creepy. Evelyn saw her all the time now, so it didn't make sense that she would sneak in at night anymore. This time something was off. The footsteps were different. Then she smelled him, that familiar, spicy scent of his cologne. Jesse.

She froze.

What was he doing here? For a moment she thought about sitting up to ask him, but before she could decide what to do, she felt his hand brush her wet cheek. She looked up and his eyes fastened on hers.

"Are you all right?"

Realizing she must have made more noise than she thought, she blushed and backed away. She didn't know what to say. More tears came and she couldn't stop them. She curled into a ball and turned on her side so her back was to him. She didn't want him to see her like this. He had already seen her cry too much.

"Please go away," she mumbled.

"No, I won't do that."

Before she could stop him, she felt his weight on the bed beside her. He stayed on top of the covers and wrapped an arm around her, pressing his chest to her back.

The world stood still. Her heart made a whooshing sound in her head as she waited for him to do something else—touch her wrong, put his lips to her neck, anything. He didn't. Minutes ticked by. She relaxed as his warmth seeped through the blankets and slid around her. Her tears stopped.

"I'll stay until you're asleep," he whispered, keeping his breath away from her skin, his arm around her only tense enough to make her feel secure. "Then I'll leave. You don't have to worry about anything. I just want to be here for you."

Against a million warning bells going off in her head, she believed him.

X
May

NAOMI PULLED THE CURVED MASCARA WAND through her eyelashes. She hated her eyelashes. They were thin and brittle, light brown and practically invisible. She had worn makeup since she was thirteen. Her last nanny, Patricia, had helped pick out her first makeup during a trip to the mall. She drove Naomi to the department store, showed her the most expensive name-brand makeup in the display, and sat her down on a tall stool where excited women in pressed white shirts and five-inch heels showed her how to apply the makeup to make herself look older.

It was all very glamorous and very stupid. She was excited to try to attract boys like the rest of the girls in school, but even with the makeup nobody looked twice at her. She was too shy and timid and soon gave up until Brad started talking to her in history class the day she turned fourteen.

Now she was eighteen. Today, the first day she had worn makeup in three months, was her birthday. She knew only because Evelyn had told her the makeup was a gift for turning eighteen today. She didn't ask how they knew it was her birthday. It didn't feel like her birthday. It didn't feel like anything. She looked down at the beautiful case full of eye shadow, blush, and lip gloss. It was new. Everything they gave her was new.

A knock on the bathroom door made her jump.

"You in there, sweetheart?" Evelyn asked.

Nobody had ever called her sweetheart before. She wasn't sure if she liked it or hated it. There wasn't anything to hate about Evelyn, except that she was a freaking kidnapper. Still, she had never directly done anything to hurt Naomi. None of them had lately.

"Yes, I'm in here," she said and cleared her throat. "I'm putting on the makeup you gave me."

"That's wonderful. Can I see?"

"Sure."

She unlocked the door and turned the handle. Evelyn stepped in, smiling. She had a book tucked under her arm. It looked like a fantasy, but Naomi couldn't see the title.

"You look perfect!"

Naomi pulled out an angled eye shadow brush. "I don't know why you say that. I'm not going anywhere. Why did you even give me this?"

"I told you—for your birthday. That, and I know you want to look nice for tonight."

"What's so special about tonight? I'm not going anywhere." She swept the brush across a shade of light brown and began applying it to her eyelids. She looked at Evelyn. "Am I?"

Evelyn laughed. She was wearing a deep purple sweater. She looked good in purple. It made her skin luminous. "We're letting you go out into the backyard," she said with a sly smile. "I thought you'd want to look nice for Jesse. We know you have feelings for him."

Naomi struggled to keep her lips from turning up into a smile. Her plan was working. Maybe she wasn't so much of a coward after all. She remembered the night Jesse had held her while she fell asleep. He had told her she didn't have to worry about anything, and he had been right. He had only wanted to comfort her. She finished her right eye and moved on to the left. "I think he's nice," she said, shrugging.

It was true. He was very nice, but it was more than that. She liked the crispness of his shirts over his muscled chest, the way he tied his shoes in perfect bows. He had the warmest smile of anyone she knew, and every minute she spent with him was beginning to feel more relaxed. Those things made it easier to pretend she was falling in love with him. She was sure it was what they wanted. She would twist their game to her own needs. She imagined Brad's face. She could almost feel his arms around her again. He must be missing her like crazy. But in a way, that thought seemed shallow.

Then she realized what Evelyn had said. She dropped the makeup brush and it clattered across the counter. "Did you just say you're going to let me into the backyard?"

"Yes, I did." Evelyn laughed and set down her book to pick up the brush. She ran her finger across the bristles. "You'd like that, wouldn't you?"

"Yes!" Her heart beat so fast she thought it might burst. She would give anything to breathe fresh air. None of them ever opened any windows. They seemed nervous that she might start screaming for help in hopes someone would hear her. She just might.

"Calm down, sweetie." Evelyn handed her the makeup brush and Naomi glanced at the book on the counter. It was something she didn't recognize, but definitely fantasy. Why did Evelyn have to be so cool? Was cool the right word? It was just that she loved yoga and good food and reading. She was beautiful and nice. Why did she have to be a criminal?

"It's only the backyard," Evelyn said. "It's entirely fenced in, and if you make any move to scream or run, Eric will—"

"I know." She looked down. "I know."

"Eric's going to grill some steaks when he gets home. The weather is finally nice enough, and I know how much you've been dying to get outside. This is the closest we can give you. I hope you understand."

She nodded. "Thank you."

"You're welcome." She reached up to sweep a lock of hair from Naomi's forehead. "Are you all right?"

"What do you mean?" She held her breath and stared at Evelyn's reflection in the mirror, at her perfect hair and clothes, at the scar beneath her makeup.

"It's your birthday. Aren't you upset at all? Memories and everything?"

Naomi tensed and took a step back, closing her eyes. Her life was this house now. She read books Jesse let her choose from the den. She slept and ate and pretended to know nothing about pool so Jesse could keep teaching her how to play. She stared out the window and watched the elderly neighbors take walks with their little white poodles. If the house was empty, she screamed at them, but no amount of noise ever made them look up.

"I'm fine," she said as a lump formed in her throat. "I'm definitely fine. My mom and dad never did anything for me on my birthdays, and Brad—"

She lowered her eyes to the makeup palette. The colors blurred. Brad always gave her roses on her birthday. She had dried them all and kept them hanging upside down in her closet. Sometimes she found dusty petals on the floor.

"I'm fine," she repeated as she straightened her shirt with trembling hands. "Really."

"Uh-huh." Evelyn folded her arms again. "I don't believe you. There are always tear-stains on your pillow cases. You cry every night and don't let us hear it. Why? Why are you hiding all your pain from us? We want to help you."

What the hell? Were they completely stupid? They were *kidnappers*. She tensed the muscles in her arms and then relaxed them as she counted to twenty. She reminded herself that Evelyn wanted her here probably more than anyone.

"If you want to help me, then let me go." She opened her eyes and glared at Evelyn. "I didn't see anything in that parking lot. I don't even know your last names. How can I lead the cops here? I'll deny everything, I promise." She took a deep, shaky breath. So much for building up trust. She was the completely stupid one.

Evelyn's jaw tightened. She blinked fast and snatched her book from the counter. "I've got to go to the grocery store. Eric will come up to get you in a few hours."

Eric came home early. Naomi heard the garage door open and slid off the bed to see the black sedan pull into the garage. It was only three o'clock. He had never come home early before. She had tried to figure out what they did for work, but could only guess Evelyn was a hairstylist and Jesse was an architect who worked for Steve. The two were constantly talking at the dinner table about projects and companies who outbid them. That at least explained the shelf of architecture books in the den and the reason Jesse sometimes buried his nose in books with titles like, *Architecture: Space, Form and Order,* and *Building Codes Illustrated.*

Footsteps approached her door. She moved away from the window. Eric had never come into her bedroom before. He unfastened the locks and stepped inside, still wearing his suit and a chocolate-colored silk tie that made his eyes stand out. They were bright today. She backed up until she reached the bed.

"What's the matter?" he asked, stopping halfway across the room. "Are you all right?"

"Sure." An obvious lie since her mouth was dry and her hands were trembling. She didn't know why.

He crossed the rest of the room and stopped in front of her. "You look like you think I'm going to hurt you. I thought we were past that stage."

She stared at the floor. "I'm sorry."

"Look at me."

She obeyed. He must have nicked himself while shaving that morning. She stared at the tiny spot of dried blood on his jaw and wondered if he would notice it later and get angry that he had gone the whole day with it there. Reaching into his pocket, he pulled out what she quickly recognized as her diamond earrings. Her heart skipped a beat.

"I know it's your birthday today," he said, looking down at the earrings. "These aren't a gift or anything, but I thought you should have them back." He reached out to take her hand. His touch was gentle as he tipped the earrings into her palm. "They must mean a lot to you."

Her entire body ached when she looked at them sparkling against her skin. "I guess they should," she said softly, and bit her lip against the tears stinging the corners of her eyes.

Eric let go of her hand. "I didn't mean to upset you. I thought you'd be happy to have them back. Evie told me you've been more concerned about your appearance lately. I thought—"

"No, no, it's fine," she stuttered, and turned away from him. "Thank you."

"You're welcome, but tell me why you're upset."

It was more of an order than a request. It reminded her of the time he had made her tell him she didn't love Brad. She still didn't know if she had lied about that. "My parents bought them for me."

He folded his arms. "The earrings remind you of them? You miss them?"

She blinked in surprise. He didn't get it. She couldn't explain how she had felt that day in the jewelry store two days before Christmas. Her mother kept urging her to hurry up and choose something.

Squeezing the earrings even tighter in her hand, she focused on Eric. "I don't think I miss them. These earrings, they remind me of—" She stopped and shook her head, unable to go on.

"How much they don't love you?"

He waited for her to answer, but she had nothing to say. How did he know that? She remembered choosing the earrings as fast as she could, and as soon as the jeweler put them in a box and handed her mother the receipt, it was over. Her parents were late for a company party. They asked if she could walk home since it was only a few blocks away. She nodded and left the store, the box clutched tightly in her hand.

"It must be true," Eric said. "You have a right to be upset about a lot of things. But I think your parents ... I think when you feel that way, it's ...."

She had never seen him so hesitant before, stammering his words. Finally, he looked her in the eyes and unfolded his arms. "Let's just say I understand."

She doubted he did, but nodded anyway.

"You don't have to wear them," he continued. "I thought you might want to, but that's not the reason I'm giving them back. It was impossible to sell them with the rest of the jewelry that we—"

His eyes widened in surprise at the slip.

The pieces came together. The jewelry store. How had she not figured it out before? They had robbed the jewelry store! The very one where she had chosen the earrings now squeezed tightly in her hand. She always passed by it on her way home from Brad's. It was part of a strip mall and the only business worth robbing in that area. Eric had mentioned something about gold in the motel room when she was drifting off. It was the only explanation.

She tried to hide the horror spreading across her face, but Eric didn't miss a thing. He blinked away a surge of anger and stepped forward. "You honestly didn't see anything that night, did you?"

She shook her head, no longer feeling the need to cry, but to scream. He had kidnapped her to keep her quiet about a bunch of jewelry? Could anything be more stupid? She lunged forward with a raised, clenched fist aimed at his chest. She wanted to pound him until he was nothing but a bloody pulp.

Her fist smashed against his hard chest and she raised it again for another blow, but he grabbed her wrist and yanked her close. His eyes were dark. His jaw clenched. For some reason all she could do was stare at that spot of dried blood on his jaw. He smelled like cologne and garlic. He always smelled like garlic.

"You try that again and I'll lock you in this bedroom with no food for a week." He tightened his hold on her arm and she winced. This was the other side of him she had avoided for so long. This was what made her believe he would kill her in two seconds flat if she didn't watch what she said and did.

She tried to splutter a few words out of her mouth, but he shoved her backward until she hit the wall. Her breath came out all at once, a loud gasp.

"I want this absolutely clear," he said through clenched teeth as he leaned his weight into her. "You will never hit me again. You will never talk back. You will never show defiance. Tell me you understand these rules."

She cringed. She wanted to melt away from his grasp and dissolve into the wall. "Y-yes," she stuttered. "I understand."

"Good." He stepped back and let her go. With a long, deep breath, he calmed himself and seemed to relax. She thought she might be sick. If he exploded so easily, she hated to think what he would do if she tried to escape. Nothing pretty.

"You know I don't want to hurt you," he said softly. "In fact, it's the opposite. Your parents cause you more pain than we do. That's why you're content to stay here."

The earrings in her fist weighed her down like boulders, but she kept herself standing tall, her heart beating fast and hard. She wouldn't think about her parents. She wouldn't. Her heartbeat was so loud she thought she might have to cover her ears. Eric interrupted the noise.

"I've watched your parents on the news reports," he said, softening his expression. "I feel sorry for you, Naomi. We all do." He stepped close enough to lift her face so she had to look into his eyes. "It's too bad I had to frighten you just now, but you have to know I won't put up with that kind of behavior. I just don't know if it's possible to make you happy yet."

She was stone still beneath his touch. The diamonds felt like they would cut right through her skin.

XI

NAOMI FOLLOWED ERIC DOWNSTAIRS THROUGH THE patio doors. When she took a deep breath her body tingled. She closed her eyes. There was sun and a breeze and chirping birds. Birds! She had thought she would never hear such a sound again. She soaked in as much as she could.

"Well, come on."

She opened her eyes to see him motioning her to the patio, his eyes trained on her. She was sure he thought she would try something, but at the moment she only wanted to stand in the sun. She stepped forward. Most of the patio was shaded above by the balcony. She smiled when she reached the patio bricks, warm from the sun. She wiggled her toes and Eric cleared his throat.

"You like this, don't you?"

She turned to him and smiled. "I forgot what it feels like, that's all."

His expression fell into something that might resemble pity. He reached up to loosen his tie and she stepped into the cool grass. This was a dream. She tried to imagine Eric wasn't watching her. She tried to remember sand between her toes, Brad's hand in hers as they walked up the beach. She could smell salt in the air. One day she would be there again.

She opened her eyes. There was a white vinyl fence surrounding the entire yard. It had to be at least seven feet tall with no breaks in the slats or any way to climb over.

Except the trees.

They were mostly maple, aspen, and spruce, the maples the largest. The one by the balcony caught her attention, sprawling its thick, curved branches near the railing and over the fence like a bridge into the neighbor's yard. That tree seemed to call to her every time she looked at it.

Walking to a rectangular patio table made of the same teak wood as her parents' patio furniture, she sat down in a comfortable chair facing the house.

"Stay there," Eric warned her gently. "I can see you from the window, and Evie should be home soon from the store."

He left the doors open and headed into the kitchen, removed his suit jacket and tie, and rolled up his sleeves before pulling on the white apron Evelyn usually wore when she cooked.

She closed her eyes and thought of Brad again. She thought of him more now than she had ever thought of him when she was home. There was no homework here to fuss over, no camera, no Internet. At least she had books. She had read all the Mercedes Lackey novels in the den. Now she was working on a stack of classics because Jesse loved them so much. She wanted to know what it was about them that kept him so fascinated.

Still, she kept re-reading fantasy in between the classics. She smiled at the thought of Jesse. The sun felt good on her cheeks. She could feel his closeness to her at the pool table when he had showed her how to balance the cue stick between her knuckles, his body with hers on her bed as he held her.

No matter how many times he got close to her, he seemed to be holding back.

They ate outside as the sun began to set. Eric cooked her steak perfectly—not too dry, not too pink. When dinner was finished, Evelyn brought out a cheesecake. Naomi didn't like cheesecake, but forced three bites down anyway.

"You look nice tonight," Steve said to her from across the table. "Has Evelyn given you everything you need?"

Sure, she had everything she needed … except for freedom. Duh. She set her fork down next to the unfinished piece of cheesecake and placed her hands in her lap. At least he had acknowledged that she looked nice. Jesse hadn't. He was eating his dessert. He hadn't paid her any attention all evening. It was unlike him not to even look at her.

Remembering that Steve had spoken to her, she gave him a soft smile. He was always nice to her. At the moment his laugh-lines looked like a thousand tiny smiles. He was handsome and kind, and she could see why Evelyn loved him.

"Yes, she has, thank you," she lied.

Eric cleared his throat. "We have a gift for you." He lifted the beer next to his plate and took a sip before turning to Jesse. "Did you get it ready?"

Still working on his cheesecake, Jesse glanced up at Naomi and smiled. Her heart tightened. "Yeah, I did, but it's inside. I'll go get it." He stood and went into the house just as Eric's phone rang. He answered with a quick, "*Buongiorno*," then continued to speak in Italian.

Italian? She didn't know he spoke another language. It made sense, but still it surprised her.

"Is it the house?" Steve asked.

Evelyn nodded and kept her eyes on Eric as he walked farther into the yard, his voice fading. She leaned into the back of her chair and pressed a finger to her bottom lip. She seemed nervous, and that made Naomi shift in her seat.

"Sounds like the tenants still want to bid us out, but Eric will take care of it before we move. He knows the ins and outs."

Before they moved? Where? Down the road? To another state? Naomi shifted even more. She didn't know what to do. Should she ask? A part of her was comfortable with these people, but the normal part of her knew they were criminals. They could turn violent in the blink of an eye. Eric had made that clear a few hours ago. This was probably a good time to keep her mouth shut.

Jesse came back and put a small, wrapped box in front of her. The paper was silver with a pink ribbon tied around it. She wondered if he had wrapped it himself. That made her smile.

"You can open it when Eric gets off the phone," he said. "He wanted to see your reaction, and so do I." He walked to the other end of the table and sat back down. Evelyn had her head in her hands. "What's the matter?" he asked.

She sighed. "The house."

"They're not giving in, huh?"

"No." She picked up her fork and poked at the crumbs on her plate.

"You have plenty of time." Jesse took a bite of cheesecake and looked hopefully at Steve. "Unless you've decided to forget the agreement? Eric said—"

Steve glared at him. "Get that out of your head. You're not getting off that easy. You'll do what we tell you to do." He stopped and glanced at Naomi. She looked away.

That was interesting. He would do what they told him to do? That only confirmed her suspicions about Jesse as the odd one out. Everything seemed fishy when she considered why he was living in the same house as everyone else, as if he was a prisoner too.

Eric approached the table. He put down the phone and took a long drink from his beer. "We'll know by next week," he said, sinking back into his chair. He smiled at Naomi. "Go ahead and open it."

She touched the pink ribbon on her present. She couldn't remember the last time someone had wrapped a present for her. Brad always took her somewhere to buy her things or gave her flowers. She snatched the box and started to untie the ribbon. It was the metallic kind, shiny and slick. She was giddy with excitement. Everyone was watching her, and that made it more special. She couldn't imagine what they might give her.

Then Eric's phone rang again and she stopped to see him glaring at the screen. His face fell and he looked up at Evelyn, his lips forming words that never came out. He had turned pale. Slowly, he pushed a button on the phone and answered. No Italian this time. He stood and headed into the house.

Evelyn gripped the edge of the table.

"What's going on?" Steve asked her. "It can't be your—"

She scrambled out of her chair to follow Eric, and Steve jumped up to follow her. Jesse dropped his fork onto his plate and turned to Naomi. "Don't follow them inside yet," he said with an edge to his voice. "I'm pretty sure it has to do with their father."

"Eric's dad?"

"Yes." He looked down at his plate. "I probably shouldn't tell you, but he's in prison for murder. He's been there for the past eighteen years."

Murder.

She didn't like the sound of that.

Dropping her present into her lap, she stared at the ribbon. It was so beautiful—she didn't even care what was inside. She tried to ignore Evelyn's cries drifting through the open French doors.

"Who did he murder?" she asked, finally looking up.

"Their mother and ten-year-old sister."

A chill ran through her. Evelyn's mother was murdered? Her sister too? She had no idea how to process such a thing. Nobody she had ever known had been murdered. It sounded so unreal, even after being kidnapped. What if her mother or father or Brad died all of a sudden? She would never know unless Eric told her. The thought made her stomach plummet straight to the ground.

"Eric doesn't like to talk about it, so I'm warning you not to say anything. I don't know what the hell is going on right now, but it's bad."

She nodded. The air turned cold as the sun sank lower in the sky and Evelyn's cries kept drifting from the house. Jesse sipped his beer, leaning back in his chair. It was unlike him to look so vacant. There was obviously more to the story, but she wasn't going to ask. She was suddenly tired, and thoughts of sleep wrapped around her. She needed to be alone.

She stood. "Can I go back to my room?"

He set his beer on the table. "Sure, if you want." He stood and she followed him into the living room where the others were sitting.

"Evie, calm down." Eric looked up at Naomi. His eyes were red and wet as Evelyn let out a short wail. She was collapsed against him, sobbing on his shoulder. Jesse paused to ask Steve what had happened.

"It was a heart attack," he answered. "He died this afternoon."

Jesse stared at Evelyn, his expression sad, but relieved at the same time. "I'll take Naomi upstairs," he said, and nudged her to follow him. She squeezed the present in her hands and thought of the scar on Evelyn's cheek. She didn't have to stretch her imagination to figure out where it had come from.

XII

"Do you need anything?" Jesse asked as he opened her door and leaned against the frame.

Naomi looked down at the pink ribbon on her gift. It was half untied. Everything felt unfinished right now. "I don't think so."

"Are you okay? You're pale."

Tears were starting beneath the surface, but she pushed them back with an angry shove. There was no way she was going to bawl like a baby again. She had to get a grip. She could be strong and unfeeling like her mother. The woman hadn't even cried at her father's funeral. "I'm confused," she said boldly. "Wouldn't you be confused?"

He studied her face. "You have a point." He motioned her into the room. "I need to talk to you."

He wanted to be in her room again? A part of her was relieved because she didn't want to be alone. All she would do was cry, and she had done enough of that to last a lifetime. Her heart pounded as she stepped into the bedroom with him right behind. He closed the door and moved close to her. The room was dark, but the window let in enough light for her to see his face. He was familiar now. She knew where his freckles started and ended, the exact color of his eyes, the way he styled his hair, kind of messy but nice.

He gave her a worried look. "You need to know something. Eric and the others are planning to move, and they're going to take you with them."

She had no idea if that was good or bad. It sounded complicated. "Okay," she said, hesitant as she tried to figure out her emotions. Moving might give her a chance to escape. That was what she was supposed to do. Escape. Brad would want to see her again. She wanted to be with him again. She was starting to forget how it felt when he held her. Then again, that all sounded like one huge excuse. When she didn't say anything, Jesse folded his arms.

"I won't be going with you, but it might be a long time before they leave—before I won't be with you anymore."

She raised an eyebrow. "Are you 'with' me?"

He inched closer and laughed under his breath. "I don't know. I've seen you almost every day for the past three months, but I've tried to keep things simple. Eric told me to be careful with you."

So that was why he had kept his distance. Seriously? He had come so close to stepping over a boundary she couldn't define, especially when he had held her on her bed until she fell asleep. Even then he seemed to hold back, and she was starting to want more.

"What does he mean by careful?" she asked quietly, looking into his eyes as he wrapped his hands around her shoulders and guided her closer to him. Her body tensed. He had never touched her with such intensity.

His eyes were burning right through her, making her breathe faster.

"I've been trying to avoid this since we first took you," he stuttered, and squeezed her shoulders so hard it almost hurt. "I keep remembering why I'm here. We took you because of things I've done in the past. I'm the reason all of this has happened to you."

That couldn't be true. Eric was the leader, not Jesse. Everything felt distant. Would her plan still work? It didn't seem as simple. Jesse wouldn't promise to protect her—he would hurt her if she made the wrong move. He had helped kidnap her, for crying out loud. She wanted to pinch her arm to wake herself up, but now his hands were moving down her shoulders and around her back. His touch was electric, turning her on in places she had completely forgotten about.

"I can't wait anymore," he whispered and kissed her hard on the mouth.

She dropped her present to the floor and kissed him back, tasting alcohol on his breath. Beyond that, his mouth was sweet like Brad's—but he kissed way better than Brad. He knew how to make her melt against him. His tongue softly caressed hers, sending tingles all the way to her toes as the room started to spin. He nudged her toward the bed and she stumbled backward. He kept a hold of her so tightly she felt his heart beating. It seemed the only thing keeping her steady. They stopped by the bed.

Jesse pulled back and gazed into her eyes. "Like I said, I've been trying to avoid this, but I can't anymore. You know I want you." His hands fumbled with the buttons on her shirt. Her heart pounded. Brad used to lie with her on the bed and kiss her so tenderly it felt like velvet on her lips. He wasn't usually that gentle. Would Jesse be gentle?

He slipped another button loose, his fingers grazing her skin. He finished the last button and pushed the shirt from her shoulders and arms. It dropped onto the mattress, and fear shot through her heart at her almost-nakedness. Would he be like Brad? He was older, maybe even stronger. A thief. A kidnapper. How could she possibly trust him?

"I'm going to keep going unless you tell me to stop," he said, inching his fingers up her back to her bra. He leaned in to kiss her neck, his presence closing around her like a drug. She closed her eyes and breathed him in. He could take whatever he wanted, whether she liked it or not. The question was did she want him to? She could feel in his touch how much he wanted her, maybe even needed her. His skin was warm and flushed. His lips were hot on her neck.

"You mean you'll stop?" she asked, regretting the words the second they came out.

Moving away from her neck, he had that look in his eyes again—the one that willed her to obey him. He almost looked angry.

"I'll stop if you ask me to, Naomi, but don't push things around the table hoping they'll turn out in your favor. I don't work that way."

"What do you mean?"

His jaw tightened. "I mean you need to stop fishing around for someone else to tell you what to do, how to feel. I know we're keeping you here against your will, but there are still things you have control over—whether or not you let me get closer to you, for instance. I'm not going to force you to do this."

Her breath caught in her throat. He was waiting for her to respond, and she had no idea what to say. She couldn't wrap her mind around anything. Evelyn was crying downstairs because her father was dead. Everything felt wrong. The kiss was still fresh on her lips. His stubble had scratched her skin, tingling. Brad's had never been that rough.

"Do you have any idea how much I've wanted you since the second I laid eyes on you?" he whispered, touching her face. "I've fought with myself for ages to keep away from you, but I think you know by now I won't hurt you. Based on that, it shouldn't be hard for you to decide anything."

The solid look in his eyes intensified. He slid one bra strap down her shoulder, eyeing her hungrily. He reminded her of Brad in so many ways, it made her sick. When she stopped to think about why, she began to understand herself in ways that made her head swim.

The truth was she wanted Jesse to force her.

It was comfortable that way, familiar, just like Brad. It was the only way she knew how things worked, and as he pulled down her other bra strap she felt a small whimper of delight building in her throat. Jesse was the only solid thing she had been able to hold onto for months. She didn't want him to go away. Still, a question burned in her mind.

"Why won't you hurt me?" she asked. "Is it because Eric told you not to?"

"What?" He leaned away. "No, that's not why. I don't hurt people if I can help it. I'm not like that."

"Then why did you kidnap me? That's not normal, you know." Her body stiffened, guilt sweeping through her at the sound of her words. Jesse let her go and stepped away. His warmth melted from her skin, and suddenly she wanted her shirt back on. Her eyes drifted to a stack of books on her nightstand. On the very bottom was *The Awakening,* the book her mother had tried to get her to read. It was always on the bottom, and it would stay there.

She hung her head and closed her eyes. Her mother. Her dad. Brad. Home. She would have graduated high school next week. She would have made a decision about where to go to college. She would have kissed Brad when he gave her a bouquet of roses for her birthday.

Jesse was silent. She looked up to tell him she would rather be alone, but he was already gone.

That night when she went to bed she remembered Brad as she drifted off. College applications were scattered across his bed. They crumpled beneath her shoulders when he pushed her on top of them. His fingers ran through her hair as he kissed her. It was the last time she had been in his room, the last time he had unbuttoned her shirt just as Jesse had. He didn't get far. She muttered that Berkeley was the only college she was willing to attend and his hands froze.

"Then why am I bothering with all of this?" He pointed to the applications on the bed. "You agreed weeks ago not to go to Berkeley. You told me you were thinking about Harvard."

"No, I said Harvard sent me an acceptance letter and that my parents would pay for the tuition if I told them about it. But there's no way I'm going there."

"Yeah, and there's no way I would be accepted even if you did," he grumbled. "Your parents went there. Mine didn't."

"That's not why I was accepted!"

"I know, but I'm sure it helped." He narrowed his eyes. "You'll go to the college we choose together, and that won't be Berkeley."

Oh, she would, would she? She rolled onto her side, turning her back to him, and stared down at one of the creased applications beneath her elbow. The reason she wanted to go to Berkeley was because Brad had told her that night on the beach that it was out of the question. It was because of Damien. It had to be. Brad could tell she was interested and would do anything to keep her away from him. He wasn't stupid.

"That's where I want to go," she grumbled, picking at a thread on the sheets. "You can't change my mind." She couldn't believe she was being stubborn.

He grabbed her arm and pulled her to him. "I thought you would follow me anywhere. You said you would." His eyes were jealous even then, as green and jealous as they were a month earlier at the party. Now they were getting angrier by the second.

"I've been thinking that maybe … maybe …." Her mouth was dry. She had belonged to him for so long, been *his girl* for what felt like forever. Was there more out there? Something she was missing? Somebody better?

"Maybe *what?*"

"Would you be mad if I said maybe we should date other people when we're in college?" Her heart pounded. The anger in his eyes exploded and his grip on her arm tightened so much she was sure a bruise would form, but before she could pull away he slammed his fist against her cheek so fast it took her a full minute to realize what had happened. When she did, her reaction was unlike anything she had ever done before.

She left.

She stumbled off the bed, gave him a horrified glare, and marched out of his room, slamming the door behind her.

She didn't cry until she was safely in her own bed. It wasn't the physical pain that made her cry. It was because Brad's anger was her fault. She had never shown defiance like that before, and it hurt that he hadn't immediately followed after her. But she knew he would find a way to make everything better. Somehow. That was more frustrating than everything else combined.

She woke and realized she was still inside a prison with her kidnappers, sweat dripping down her chest. Brad was gone. He could never hit her again if she didn't want him to. Then again, she missed the way he held her, the way he had come over the next morning and iced the bruise while she cried in his arms. He told her he would never hit her again, and even now a part of her believed him. But it didn't matter if she never saw him again. The night they went to the park to capture the fog, he told her he would take her home as soon as she finished, but she had dared to stand her ground and tell him she would be fine on her own. So much for that faith in herself.

She turned to the stack of books on her nightstand, ready to turn on the lamp and lose herself in a novel. Something new caught her eye. Someone had left her a leather-bound notebook and ballpoint pen.

XIII
June

IT TOOK HER A MONTH TO OPEN THE JOURNAL. SHE didn't want to write about how she had been kidnapped or how scared she had been at first. That seemed pointless. Instead she wrote about her birthday gift. They had given her an iPod. Pink. Jesse bought music for her off the Internet, all her favorite stuff from home. Maybe it was a bad idea to keep those ties to home. Maybe not.

She kept the ribbon from the package and put it in her nightstand drawer right next to *The Awakening.* She didn't want to read it. Everything inside of her cringed at the thought of absorbing words her mother loved, but her curiosity got the better of her. Finally, she opened it and read it in one sitting. Then she read it again a week later. She didn't know why. She wrote in her journal about how it made her think of her mother outside of an office and a courtroom. A real person.

She wrote about the dragons and her dreams.

She wrote about Jesse.

She was sure he was the one who gave her the notebook. If he ever read it, she wanted him to know she wasn't scared of him. She just couldn't wrap her head around opening herself to him yet. She could hardly stand writing on those stiff, white pages, the tangy smell of ink filling her nose. Every time she opened the journal and smelled it, she felt like something inside of her might break.

XIV
July

SHE ROLLED OVER IN BED AND SQUEEZED HER EYES shut. Today was Brad's birthday. Even in Colorado in an air-conditioned house, the heat was beginning to swelter just like it did in California. That always reminded her of Brad's birthday, of humid nights in his car and ice cream after a movie. She wouldn't have remembered his birthday if it weren't for the calendar on her iPod.

She listened to his favorite song and waited for tears to come. They didn't, so she stood in the shower and thought about the bonfire and her sweatshirt that smelled like fish. Brad had thrown it on his floor that night when she crawled into bed with him. His mother was a nurse and worked graveyard shifts. That was why he didn't worry about her spending the night all the time.

"She'll never find out," he said when she told him it wasn't a good idea. "She works and comes home and crashes. She never knows when I come and go. She never even looks in my room. I don't think she'd care, anyway. Hell, we're almost in college." He pulled her into his strong arms and kissed her until she forgot about worrying.

Now she stared at the grout between the tiles in the shower and traced the little lines she had dug with her

133

fingernails months ago. There were thirty-five of them. She had stopped after that because it seemed pointless to count the days. Now she counted months, and even that was starting to seem pointless. They flew by so quickly now, the days blending into one another like spilled paint until only a dark smudge covered the floor. Sleep, shower, breakfast, books, dinner, Jesse, over and over and over. Sometimes she watched a movie with the four of them downstairs, curling herself into a corner of the couch. She lost herself in another world on the television screen until the credits rolled and Eric or Evelyn asked if she wanted to go to bed.

She would be with them forever. She belonged to them.

She got out of the shower and went back to bed.

"You should read Hemingway," Jesse said when they finished a game of pool and settled themselves on a sofa. She picked up the book she had been reading earlier.

"I'm not a big fan," she muttered. "My teacher made us read *A Farewell to Arms* when I was a junior. I hated it."

"You mentioned that your mom liked classics. Don't you think you'd like them more if you gave them a try?"

"I have given them a try. I read a whole stack of them, and then all that Shakespeare, remember?"

He grinned and stretched his arms across the back of the sofa. "I just thought you should try even more. Open your mind."

She tried to keep her jaw from dropping. "Open my mind? What do you mean by that? I read lots of classics before I came here. Stop pushing the issue."

Nobody had ever referred to her as closed-minded before. She had an open mind. She had read what he had given her. Just because she didn't like it didn't mean she had a closed mind.

He shrugged, leaning over to look at the book in her lap. "I mean just that. What are you reading right now?" She attempted to hide her book from him, but he grabbed it and looked at the cover. "Fluffy fantasy again. See? You've already read this one three times. You could at least pick up some serious fantasy."

She tried to grab the book from him, but he held it away from her, laughing. All of this closed-minded stuff was his way of kidding with her. That was his odd sense of humor coming into play again. She softened and let herself enjoy it. He knew which buttons to push, and he wanted to see how she would take it. She would show him.

"*A Farewell to Arms,*" he urged as she kept reaching for her book. "Come on. You'll like it this time. We can talk about the parts you hate."

"I hated the whole thing!" She laughed and leaned into him, still reaching for the book. The feel of him against her made her heart beat faster. She loved the way he smelled. She loved his freckles and red hair. She wanted to kiss him, but she didn't know what he would do if she tried. He had only kissed her the one time. She still remembered the taste of him, and the memory made her all soft inside.

She smiled when she finally got hold of the book. He stopped laughing when she moved her mouth closer to his.

"Naomi, don't."

"Don't what?" Her heart fluttered. The book fell from her fingers.

"I said don't." His eyes focused on hers as he touched the small of her back. He looked upset, but that only made her want to kiss him even more. He leaned closer.

"You've never hurt me," she whispered. "You've been nicer to me than anybody ever has, even Brad."

It was true. He had never hit her, and he had never forced her to do anything except stay in the house. His mouth opened and closed like he wanted to say something. She could tell he wanted her. She could see it in his eyes.

Shaking his head, he moved his hand to her hip and nudged her away. "I'm not … this isn't …." He pushed her away and stood up. "Not yet, Naomi. That's all. That ship sailed on your birthday, remember? You're not ready."

She glared at him. "I don't understand."

"There's nothing to understand. Let's find Hemingway." He turned around and headed for the bookshelf with all the classics. He had told her it was Evelyn's favorite shelf. Most of them were hers passed down to her from her mother. Some of them were in Italian.

Jesse stood in front of the shelf longer than needed. "Did you know Hemingway didn't write it in Italy?" he asked as he bent down to look at the lower shelves. "He was there just prior. He was your age when he was wounded and fell in love with his nurse. I think he was in Milan."

"He was eighteen?"

"I think so." He pulled a book from the bottom shelf and stood. He looked more relaxed now. "You'll probably be older before Eric and the others take you there."

He stopped and looked away and started to say something else, but she interrupted him.

"To where? Italy?"

"Never mind."

"Tell me." She shifted across the cushions. "Jesse?"

He narrowed his eyes. "I said *never mind.* Drop it."

She clamped her lips shut. She didn't like the anger in his face, and moved her attention to the book in his hands. The entire story took place in Italy.

XV
August

NAOMI OPENED HER JOURNAL ALMOST EVERY NIGHT and read through specific passages. She wanted to remind herself where she had been in her weird kidnapping journey. She wanted to see how her emotions were changing. So far it was a growing attachment to Jesse and the others. She saw the attachment; she suspected it was deliberate on their part to get her to want to stay, but there was nothing she could do about it. She could never go anywhere, never talk to anybody except them. She was completely, one-hundred percent stuck.

The dragons kept visiting her dreams. She wrote about them and described their thick, leathery wings and long, vase-like necks. She tried so hard to imagine a bouquet of flowers coming out of their mouths instead of fire, but her imagination wasn't strong enough in her dreams. It was always fire, and it always burned the knight who came to rescue her.

After she read a few passages, she wrote a new one. She pushed the pen so hard into the paper it indented the next page. She wrote the words as small as she could so the journal would last because she didn't know if they would give her another one—if she would even have the courage to ask. For some reason, writing in the journal felt like a big secret, especially since Jesse had slipped up and told her they were taking her to Italy and now she kept writing about it.

Italy.

It was so far away. It seemed like a fresh start, because as she looked back on her life, there wasn't anything spectacular about it. Her nannies had cared about her, but they had never been particularly close. In fact, the more she wrote about her life the more she realized being kidnapped was the most exciting and real thing that had ever happened to her—and not necessarily in a bad way. That thought made her close the journal and cry into her pillow for the first time in weeks.

XVI

September

WHEN KAREN ARRIVED HOME FROM WORK, MINDY told her Brad was waiting on the deck. Confused, she made her way through the house as she shed her jewelry and suit coat and left them on various pieces of furniture. Mindy would collect them later.

Brad's voice was dark and smooth. She heard him talking on the phone as she stepped outside and spotted him shuffling along the sandy paths from the beach. The rain clouds were heavy and black. They looked ready to split at the seams. The tall beach grass swayed in the breeze.

"Yeah, I gotta go. Later." Brad closed his phone and smiled at her as she sat down in one of the patio chairs. He had never smiled at her before. That was odd. He reached the top of the steps, stammering, "Hello, Mrs. Jensen. I hope it's okay I came by. Your housekeeper said you'd be home soon, so I—"

She stood to greet him. "I was at my office wrapping things up with a client. Things took longer than I expected."

His eyes widened. "You're back at work?"

"I never stopped." She swiped a hand across her forehead. "It's been seven months, Brad. You'll be starting your classes soon, moving on with your life. Won't you?" Why was she explaining herself to him?

He cleared his throat and stared down at the phone in his hand. "Yeah, I guess so."

"How is it going for you?"

Still staring at his phone, he muttered, "All right, I guess. I've decided on medicine, but not sure exactly what yet."

"That sounds like a fine ambition."

He looked up and tried to smile. "Nothing like Harvard, though, huh?"

"Harvard?"

"Yeah, Naomi said she wouldn't go, but I always thought she might since she was accepted. I applied after she did. I didn't get in, of course."

Karen sat down. The warm breeze tinged with the smell of rain was suffocating. She looked up at Brad. "Naomi applied to Harvard?"

"Didn't she tell you?"

"She was accepted?" Her voice was shaky now. She grabbed the arms of the chair, remembering her own acceptance letter from Harvard. Her mother was in the hospital then, dying of cancer, and her father couldn't have cared less about what school she attended as long as he didn't have to pay for it. It was a good thing she had won scholarships.

"Even if she didn't tell you, I thought you or Mr. Jensen would find out from going through her mail or something."

She put a hand to her forehead. This was only the third time she had seen Brad since Naomi's disappearance. The first time was when he had come by to tell her and Jason that Naomi was missing. The second time was during the investigation. She looked up at him, confused. "Why didn't she want to go to Harvard?"

"I don't know." He pushed his hands into his pockets and looked away.

He didn't have to say anything else. She could see he was implying that it was her own fault. She tried not to glare at him. "So you're in town to visit your family?"

"Uh, yeah, and I wanted to see if you'd be willing to let me do something for Naomi."

"Oh?"

He looked up at the clouds. He was dressed in khakis and a stiff dress shirt that looked brand new. He had probably dressed up just to come speak to her.

"My roommate's a photographer," he finally said, still staring up at the clouds. "He gave me the idea to get some of Naomi's work and enter it into a contest." He looked back down at her. "You know about her photography, right?"

She nodded. "We gave her a lot of money to buy her equipment, but all of those things disappeared when she did."

He cleared his throat. "I was hoping you'd let me enter some of her work."

"I guess that would be okay." She held her breath as a stiff breeze blew across the deck. It was cold and smelled like salt and seaweed. It reminded her of Naomi's constant treks down to the beach whenever a storm was approaching. She was usually dressed in a jacket with her camera bag slung across her shoulders. It surprised her that she had noticed those treks of Naomi's so often. A lot of things she was remembering about Naomi surprised her. "Do the rules stipulate if the contestant has to be …?" She wanted to say "alive" but the word wouldn't slip off her tongue.

"No, my roommate said it'll be all right if we have your permission."

The rain broke free from the clouds, but neither of them made a move to get out of its way.

"I'm sorry about everything," Brad said as the rain plastered his hair to his forehead. "This is what I can do to try to make a difference —even if it doesn't make a difference, you know? At least for me it will."

Later that evening Karen sat in her home office with a glass of brandy. She stared at her computer and thought of Brad's words. He was determined to do *something*. At least he had taken that step. She hadn't done anything yet. So much time had passed, and yet it felt like only a moment.

She turned on her computer and pulled up Naomi's Facebook page. So far she had avoided looking at it, but as time crept on with no hope of seeing her again, she couldn't help herself. The police and her private detective had already searched through it top to bottom. They said they hadn't found anything helpful.

She scrolled through the dozens of posts her classmates had left asking where she was, and then found the last status update Naomi had written. *Going to Dad's banquet tonight with Brad. So much corporate talk. Maybe there will be fog later to shoot in the park.*

Corporate talk? That was something Karen had never heard her say before.

Brad had written in response, Love you, Baby. That dress I picked out will look smoking hot on you.

A boy named Damien had written, Good luck with that fog! Make sure you post the pics later.

Karen scrolled down farther. It didn't look like Naomi had a lot of friends she interacted with other than Brad and a few girls from a photography class. She scrolled past some of Naomi's photos, surprised at how good they were. Why hadn't Naomi shown them to her? Was she afraid she wouldn't care?

A part of her died when she asked herself that question, and she took a sip of brandy and noticed the glass was almost empty. Good. She needed to cut her edginess with something. Ever since her two-month stay at Elizabeth's, she wasn't the same. Work wasn't the same. Nothing felt right, and it wasn't only because Naomi was missing.

The sound of a car rolling up the drive snapped her from her thoughts. Jason was home. Eight-thirty. He was later than usual. Mindy probably had dinner ready an hour ago. She stood and walked to the front door to greet him, but frowned when she saw that he wasn't alone. Reporters had followed him, which was odd. They hadn't come by for a long time.

Jason stopped in front of the garage and got out of the car. Of course he would talk to the reporters, because he knew they would follow him around the next day if he didn't. She took a deep breath and opened the front door to go stand with him. Lately he seemed worn out, and a part of her ached to lift him up, even though she was a wreck herself. He gave her a shaky smile as she approached him. The reporters' faces lit up like Christmas trees when they saw she was joining him.

There were only two of them, but that was enough to put her on edge. If it wasn't for the brandy in her system she might have ordered them to leave.

Jason slipped an arm around her and pulled her close. He smelled like his office, like ballpoint ink and paper and the green-and-white striped mints he kept in a glass dish on his desk. He was tall and thin and always shaved so close that his face didn't get scratchy until late at night. She loved that about him—loved that feel of his scratchy cheek on hers. Right now all she wanted to do was snuggle up with him in bed and fall asleep. If Naomi's disappearance had done anything, it had made her realize how much Jason meant to her and how much he needed her too. He was almost clinging to her for dear life. His fingers rubbed over her lower spine in little circles, and it was enough movement that her undershirt came untucked from her pants. She shifted against him. He was nervous. It was unlike him to be nervous for something as small as two reporters.

"Are the police going to aggressively pursue the case again?" Reporter number one asked.

"I-I don't know," Jason said with a glance at Karen. He started to fidget.

"Are you two going to push to make this a federal case?"

"That's undecided," Jason said in a voice that seemed to be getting weaker by the second. He opened his mouth to say more, but the reporter on the left—the pushier of the two—inched forward.

"How is this affecting your career, Jason? Your stocks skyrocketed after the merger, but we've heard you might hand over your position to someone else. Is this just too much for you?"

Narrowing his eyes, Jason took a deep breath. "The company is doing phenomenal. Any rumor you've heard about me handing over my position simply isn't true."

The pushy reporter turned to Karen. She almost shrank away, but stood her ground as Jason squeezed her tighter. He had told her months ago to always answer their questions and never show weakness. If Naomi saw them on television or read about them in the papers, he wanted her to know they were not falling apart—that her parents were the rock she could rely on and they had nothing to hide. She had looked at him then like he was insane because they were anything but a stable platform in Naomi's life. They had been nonexistent while she grew up, providing her with everything but their own time—the thing Karen finally realized mattered most.

The pushy reporter leaned forward.

"Some unidentified female remains have been found in Southern California. Have you thought about what you'll do if they match Naomi's DNA?"

Karen balled her hands into fists and gave Jason a look that clearly asked, *How did we not know about this?* But his expression told her that he *did* know about it and had kept it from her to protect her. That was why he was holding her so tightly. He hadn't expected her to come out here.

One more plunge into the depths of this nightmare. It was always something—the blood in the parking lot; the broken taillight; the jewelry store robbery; a girl who matched Naomi's description rescued in Kentucky. Now this. But nothing led anywhere. Karen doubted anything ever would.

As Jason hurried to answer the question, she remembered Elizabeth's words—You've spent your entire life trying to shove her out of your life … but now it's time to change. It doesn't matter if she's gone.

But it did matter if she was gone. It meant everything. Karen straightened her shoulders and looked at Jason. She remembered the day she had told him she was pregnant and how he had twirled her around the room in a waltz. She remembered putting a Band-Aid on Naomi's knee when the nanny was away for a weekend. She remembered handing Naomi one of her favorite books in the library and how repulsed Naomi had seemed by it. There were thousands of these memories, and she was only now beginning to recall them as she faced the possibility that Naomi might be dead. Deep down she doubted Naomi was an unidentified corpse in Southern California, but what did she know? Either way, it didn't matter. Now, more than ever, was the time to make a change.

She turned to face the reporters. It was time she told them the truth.

XVII

NAOMI LIKED THE WAY IT FELT TO WEAR AN APRON.
She had seen Mindy in an apron for six years and had
always wondered what it would feel like to wear one.
Now she finally knew that it felt important. She
couldn't pinpoint why.

She was wearing an apron because she was helping
Evelyn with dinner. It wasn't that she hadn't helped
before, but this was the first time she was actually going
to cook. She looked down at two bowls of what Evelyn
called shiitake and crimini mushrooms and scrunched
her nose. She didn't like mushrooms, but she had tried
this dish a few months ago and liked it. Evelyn told her
it was because the mushrooms were cooked correctly.

"You're probably used to chewy and rubbery," she
laughed as she filled a stock pot at the sink. "That
housekeeper of yours you've told me about must not
have any idea how to properly cook them. When they're
cooked right, they should practically melt in your
mouth."

Naomi threw a stem into an empty bowl. "No, I
guess she doesn't know how to cook them right. Most
of her stuff is good except her eggs and mushrooms. I
asked her once to teach me how to cook. She looked at
me like I was crazy."

"I assume your mother never cooked?"

"Of course not."

Evelyn shut off the water. "Sorry. I shouldn't mention her. I forgot."

"It's okay." She fought the tremble in her fingers and kept working on the mushrooms until the bowl was full of stems. It was weird to talk about her mother with Evelyn. Maybe it was because Evelyn was starting to fill a huge gap in her heart—one she thought could never be filled.

Evelyn handed her a damp paper towel folded into a neat square. "Wipe out the caps, then slice them a quarter-inch thick." She poured oil into a pan with some butter. "I'm not going to heat this up until you're finished with the mushrooms. Don't forget the shallots. You need to chop those up as fine as you can. I'll do the garlic and thyme."

"Okay." She tried to focus on the mushrooms, but the sudden mention of her mother sent her mind into a spin. She slid the knife through the soft flesh of a mushroom cap, but paused as soon as the blade hit the cutting board. Ever since she had read *The Awakening,* more and more thoughts about her mother crept into her head. Eric wasn't helping, either. A month ago he had handed her an article from her hometown's newspaper.

Jensens Rise Above Tragedy of Missing Daughter To Succeed in Business.

She tried to lift the knife from the cutting board, but it weighed two-hundred pounds. Her father's company was capturing global attention and growing fast. There were a few lines about her mother winning a recent case for a company wrongly accused of fraud.

"You see," Evelyn's voice interrupted her thoughts. "You have to boil your pasta in enough water so it won't stick together. Oh, and never add oil to the water." She rolled her eyes and snatched a salt shaker from the counter. "Your sauce will slide right off the noodles. The amount of water is the key."

"Okay." Naomi watched her pour a heap of salt into her hand. "What's that for?"

Evelyn shrugged. "To add flavor. Eric likes it, but I don't. It ruins the dish for me."

"So why do you put it in?"

She pushed a dark curl from her forehead. She had pulled her hair up into a high ponytail, and the spirals bounced against her neck like springs. "Because he's Eric," she finally answered. "If it makes him happy, I'll do it."

"But does he know you don't like it? I'm sure he wouldn't mind if you told him how you felt." Then again, maybe he would just get really pissed off. That seemed likely.

"Oh, no, I would never tell him that."

Of course she wouldn't. Naomi couldn't blame her. She started slicing again. "I'm almost finished with these, uh, whatever they're called."

"Crimini. You can call them baby portobellos if that's easier." She smiled. "If I'm going too fast for you, let me know. This is what you wanted, right? I don't want you to feel like I'm making you help me. That's not why you're here with us. I hope you know that."

"I know." She pushed aside one bowl of sliced mushrooms to start on the next. "I want to learn how to cook. Really."

"I'm glad." Evelyn started chopping garlic. Her knife swished across the cutting board faster than Naomi could follow. The smell of the garlic was hot and spicy in the air, and Naomi breathed it in. She couldn't get the article out of her head. *Succeed in business.* That was all they had ever cared about.

Evelyn stopped chopping and looked up. "You like it here now, don't you?"

She almost dropped her knife. "Sure," she said, getting a better grip on the knife. Part of her loved it here. They were nice to her. They paid attention to her. They were going to take her to Italy to some house that meant the world to Evelyn. But it did seem problematic. How would they get her out of the country? She didn't have a passport. Even if they managed to forge her one with some other identity, there was no way they could let her travel in public. Was there? She stared at the crimini mushrooms. They were pure white on the inside and deep brown on the outside.

"I feel comfortable here," she said slowly. "Is that what you mean?"

Evelyn laughed. "I guess that's a start. I hope it's all right if I'm up front with you. It helps me not feel so guilty." Blushing, she started chopping the garlic again. "If that makes sense."

"It wasn't your idea to take me. It's not your fault."

The chopping stopped. Evelyn chewed on her bottom lip. "I forgot the parsley. I'd better call Jesse and Steve and tell them to pick some up on their way home." She pulled out her cell phone and turned away.

By the time Steve and Jesse arrived home, Naomi had started cooking the mushrooms. They smelled so good she wanted to snitch one right out of the pan. The butter and oil were making them a dark brown. They sizzled as she pushed them around with a wooden spoon, careful to keep them evenly spaced as Evelyn had instructed.

"Here's your parsley," Steve said when he entered the kitchen. Jesse went straight to the fridge.

"Oh, thanks." Evelyn was in the middle of tossing a salad when her phone buzzed. She stared at the screen and sucked in her breath.

"What is it, Evie?"

"We got the house!"

"Really?" Jesse turned around from the fridge where he had found half of a leftover sandwich. Naomi had noticed he was always eating, but he had no fat on his body to show for it. She was the opposite. Her pants were tighter than they had been a few months ago.

Evelyn was jumping up and down like a kid. "See? I told you we'd get it! Now everything's ready. We can leave whenever—"

"We can't just leave yet." Steve put up a hand. "There are too many things I have to take care of first. We have to decide what to do with *this* house, and Eric and Jesse still need to finish the last job. It might not even be the last one depending on how much we get, and I've got to figure out what to do about the firm. Jesse said he might be interested."

"Of course I am," Jesse said through a mouthful of sandwich. He glanced at Naomi, who was surprised at the conversation swirling around her. They had never talked so openly about moving before. "I mean, if you want to sell it to me. If you think I can handle it."

Steve laughed and started to undo his tie. "Of course you can handle it. Better than anybody else I'll ever find. Are you kidding?"

Evelyn spun around just before the mushrooms started to burn. "Sweetheart, you need to pay attention!" She ripped the skillet from the burner and shook the pan. "They're fine. Here, add the thyme for thirty seconds then pour it all onto the plate over there. Don't forget to add the pasta to the water. I've already measured it out for you next to the pot."

Naomi took the skillet from her hands and carefully placed it onto a cool burner. Jesse watched her as he finished his sandwich.

"Is Evelyn teaching you how to cook?" he asked with a smirk. He stepped closer and she inched away. It felt weird to have him so close to her when she was trying to concentrate on something else. The closer he got the more she wanted to ignore him so she didn't miss something and screw up dinner.

"Yes," she answered. Her heart skipped a few beats.

"Do you need me to help you?"

Tearing her gaze from his beautiful eyes, she snatched the bowl of thyme from the island before he did. "No, I can do it." She tossed the thyme into the skillet and dumped the bowl of pasta into the boiling water. His eyes sparkled. He leaned closer. She remembered his fingers unbuttoning her shirt. Her heat beat just as fast now as it had then. He had no idea how much she was trying not to want him. It was a fine balance between pretending to want him and actually wanting him. If she really wanted him, what did that say about her? And did she even care?

"Do you like this, then?" he asked. He reached for a mushroom in the pan and she slapped his fingers.

"Don't!"

He grabbed one anyway and popped it into his mouth. Licking his lips, he inched closer.

She cleared her throat. "Do I like what?"

"Cooking—learning new things. You've been reading more classics lately too. You're opening up."

The smell of thyme and butter rose to her face. She closed her eyes. "I like a lot of things here. I guess you could say I'm 'opening up.'"

He raised an eyebrow and the spoon nearly slipped from her fingers.

"Especially with you," she whispered.

He shifted his weight. That steely look came into his eyes, the one that made her want to melt and say yes to anything. She remembered reaching her hands into the cold water of a tide pool, the bumpy skin of a starfish, the resistance it gave before it let go.

XVIII
October

THE JOURNAL WAS ALMOST FULL NOW, SO NAOMI wrote her words smaller. She liked the way the pages felt when she opened the cover. They crackled as if they were brittle, but it was only because they were covered with ink over every available spot.

She ran her fingers over the words and thought about what they meant. Was it fear that filled them? Or something else? It had to be something else because the dragons in her dreams were gone now. She had written them out of her head and forced them into the journal. In one section she wrote about a dragon opening its mouth to breathe fire onto the knight, but then it stopped and Naomi stood up from the rock where she had shattered. Piece by piece, she pulled herself back together. The knight smiled and offered his hand to her, but instead of taking it she ran to the dragon and climbed onto its neck. Its scales felt like thick paper. It was hot like a sunbathed stone. She wrapped her legs and arms around its neck and it spread its gigantic wings and flew her away into the sunset.

XIX
November

IN OCTOBER THE SUGAR MAPLES HAD TURNED BRIGHT orange. Now, near the end of November, most of the leaves had dropped and curled up into brown scrolls. It was a mild week, and a few of the leaves were still bright in the center, beginning to fade. Those were the ones still clinging to the trees.

Naomi liked to sit on the balcony and look up at the maze of leaves and branches. She could smell winter coming. It was spicy and woody and cold. Today was Saturday, and Eric was bent over three black garbage bags. He pushed the leaves in with his hands and smiled up at her when he saw her watching. She smiled back.

He was still divided in her mind—two pieces shuffling about. One piece was his kindness. The other was him pushing her against the wall in her bedroom. She could never decide which one to attach herself to. The kindness was the best, of course.

Turning back to the book in her lap, she shivered as a cool breeze ripped a few leaves from the branches. They fluttered in spirals to the balcony like bronzed butterflies. She saw them out of the corner of her eye, but was so intent on reading the last paragraph of her book that she nearly jumped out of her chair when one twirled into her lap and covered the last sentence. Annoyed, she flicked it away.

It wasn't that she didn't know how the book ended. In fact, she had read it four times in the past five months. It confused her every time. She looked up and blinked. Everything turned blurry. She didn't want to think about her mother anymore. She tried not to write about her in her journal, but she kept showing up on the pages. Finally, she put the journal in her dresser drawer and vowed not to open it again. She wanted to get rid of *The Awakening* too, put it back on a shelf in the den and forget its existence. Yet here she was, reading it one more time. She was truly insane.

When she turned to look at Eric again, he was almost finished with the leaves. He dragged the bulging garbage bags to the patio and tied the last one closed. His face was sweaty. She squeezed the book in her hands and looked up at the branches. A few more leaves were holding on.

"Naomi?"

Jesse entered the balcony and closed the glass doors behind him. He had been away with Eric for the past week and a half. They had arrived home a few days earlier with bloodshot eyes and rumpled clothes.

"Evelyn said you were out here. There's some lunch downstairs if you're hungry."

"Can I stay out a little longer?"

"If you like." He took a seat across from her. He hadn't told her where he and Eric had gone, but she guessed another jewelry store. She couldn't imagine him doing it. Did he wear a ski mask and gloves and carry a crowbar? The whole thing seemed ridiculous.

"What are you reading today?" he asked, leaning over to look at her book. Confusion filled his face. "I gave that one to you months ago."

"You did." She stared down at the cover.

"Is it any good?"

"It's okay. It's something my mom tried to get me to read once, but I never did until you gave it to me with all those other classics."

He leaned back in his chair. "So the truth comes out."

She looked away, upset at the insinuation in his voice. What did he mean by that? She didn't have to like the classics he gave her. He just kept pushing and pushing. She ground her teeth together and gathered courage to look at him. "You know, you don't have to be such a jerk about the classics thing."

"A jerk?"

"I didn't mean it that way. I just meant—"

"No, I get it. I'm pushing them on you, and that bothers the hell out of you."

She shrugged, trying to act nonchalant. The truth was it did bother the hell out of her, and it was about time he acknowledged it.

"Yeah, it might be that," he said. "My dad wanted me to read his favorite stuff too." He folded his arms, his expression stiff. "Maybe I'm taking it out on you, who knows? I'll stop if you want—I won't make you read crap you don't want to read."

She looked down at *The Awakening.* "It's not crap. It just reminds me of her. I hate thinking about her."

"Then why are you reading it?"

"I don't know." The answer came quickly, but it wasn't the truth and Jesse knew it. He unfolded his arms and focused on her until she looked him in the eyes. There was no way out. She should have gone downstairs to eat lunch when he had given her the chance.

It wasn't that she was afraid of him, or even that she thought he was a jerk. It was how he knew her so well that made her uncomfortable, like walking to the edge of a cliff knowing if she didn't stop she would fall off in a few more steps. He saw her approaching that edge, and he wanted to help her. For months he had seen it, and for months he had gently nudged her away. He had kept her from throwing herself at him. He had given her a journal to record her deepest thoughts. He had given her classics to try to help her understand a part of herself she was trying so hard to suppress.

Her heart melted as she kept her gaze on his eyes, realizing how careful he had been with her, how frightened he might be that she would push him away. She wanted to explain herself. She had to.

"It's hard to think about my mom," she said, the words shaking on her tongue. "It's hard to read something that connects me to her. It feels intimate, and that's something we never had before. It's something I always wanted. My whole life, I needed her and she was never there." She ran her fingers across the cover of the book, tears filling her eyes. "Now, in the weirdest way, she's here with me. I don't know how to explain it. I know it's not real, but I—"

"Sure it's real."

She looked up at his softened expression. "How can it be real? She doesn't even know I'm reading it. She doesn't even know I'm alive."

For a long moment he watched her, and then he looked down at his hands. "My dad is an English professor," he said. "He eats and breathes books. You can imagine what it was like for me growing up. He'd talk forever about stories he loved—things like Camelot and Hobbits and magic rings. It was exciting, but when I got older he started shoving things like Dickens and Faulkner into my hands. I realized he was going to make me read everything on his shelves whether I liked it or not. He has a lot of books—more than Steve and Evelyn own in there." He nodded to the bookshelves in the den. "I've learned to appreciate and understand all kinds of literature, especially the classics. I guess, in a way, I wanted that same experience for you. I got to know my dad so well through those books because they are what he loves to read most. I can't explain it, either."

She lowered her eyes to her book and thought of the ocean and death and what her mother must have thought of the terrible ending. She didn't want her mother in her head. The more she crept in, the more confusing the whole kidnapping situation became. If she looked at Jesse and thought of her mother at the same time, things started to fall apart. Escape entered her mind. The freedom she had constructed around herself began to dissipate. But if she kept her mother distant, everything became solid again.

Another breeze drifted across the balcony. She shivered under her pink sweatshirt. She looked at Jesse and tried to imagine what his father was like. He was probably thin and smart, the old-fashioned type who wore bowties to parties and kissed your hand when he met you. He might have red hair and green eyes. Freckles. A smile that could melt your heart.

"What about your mother?" she asked. "Does she read a lot too?"

His face fell. "My mom left right after I was born. I never knew her."

"Oh."

Brad's father had left his family right after he was born. It made her sad to see families broken like that. When she was younger, she had thought she was lucky to have two parents who loved each other and stayed together. Now she knew better. If they both ignored you, it didn't matter anyway.

"Your dad sounds like he cares about you, at least," she said.

"He does, and I'm lucky for that." He touched her arm and she nearly jumped out of her chair. He was going to kiss her again. He was staring at her mouth.

"Tell me," he said softly. "Are you happier here than you were at home?"

"What?" Her heart seemed to stop. He was still staring at her mouth. Was he going to kiss her or not? The book in her hands felt like a ten-ton brick.

"Tell me."

She looked at the branch reaching over the fence. She had no desire to try to climb onto it. All she wanted was for Jesse to pull her into his arms and kiss her like he had on her birthday. She wanted something steady and strong and reliable to hold onto. Brad was gone forever. There was only Jesse, and every part of her was happy it was him instead of Brad. Maybe that was wrong. Maybe that's what they wanted. She didn't care.

"Yes," she whispered. "I am."

"Good." His eyes were luminous in the sunlight. He leaned forward, practically on the edge of his chair. Fire whipped down her spine as he reached forward and pulled her closest arm to him. Carefully, like handling a fragile piece of glass, he took her hand in both of his. She looked down as he cradled her palm in his fingers, squeezing gently.

"I don't see why you would ever want to leave," he said quietly. "You have more here than you ever had at home. The way the news reports make everything sound, your parents were never there for you. They can't care for you like we do ... like I do."

Her heart thudded. The soft look in his eyes, his touch, the way he held her hand so protectively, but not in a selfish way. She looked up at the stark, exposed branches where the leaves were fluttering in a breeze she couldn't feel. Their color would fade and bring winter, but first they had to let go.

Somewhere in the neighborhood a dog started barking. It was as far away as the waves near her home, pounding and crashing against the shore in ceaseless rhythm. She looked away from the leaves just as Jesse leaned in closer, this time close enough to press his mouth to hers. She kissed him back. She had to kiss him back. She had dreamed about this moment for months. It was even better than she had imagined.

He helped her stand up, and *The Awakening* slipped from her lap. It fell to the balcony, but she barely registered what had happened. Jesse's hands slid beneath her sweatshirt up the bare skin of her back. She leaned into him. She wanted him closer. If he loved her, nothing else mattered. Nothing.

He pulled away and looked into her eyes. "I won't stay away from you any more," he whispered. "I've fought it for so long, but it's hopeless. You want me too, don't you?"

She closed her eyes. The dog's barking grew louder. The leaves rustled in another cool breeze she hardly felt. Jesse wouldn't stay with her forever, she remembered suddenly. Eric and Evelyn would take her away from here, away from him. Italy.

"I thought you said you would be leaving," she said. "When they take me to Italy with them, you're not coming."

He moved his hands from around her waist and planted them on her hips in a tight, sensual hold. "Oh, I'm coming. I've wanted to tell you for awhile, but I was waiting for the right moment. It's time for me to make some changes in my life, and I want you to be a part of that—a part of me."

A knot formed in her throat. She couldn't swallow. "What do you mean? I thought you wanted Steve's firm. I thought you wanted—"

"Not anymore." His heartbeat pounded against her chest. He lifted a hand and cupped her face, peering deeply into her eyes. "Everything has changed. I used to want you for different reasons, but you've changed things in my head, Naomi. You've made me see who I can become. All I want is to be with you—forever."

Naomi kept the word forever in her thoughts every day. She looped it in her mind whenever Jesse kissed her. Things went farther every time, and it made her sweat with excitement. He would lean into her on the sofa, kissing her, holding her, running his fingers through her hair, and she would think *forever, forever, forever.* At night she opened her journal and wrote on the few fresh, clean pages that were left. She had given up trying not to write in it anymore. She breathed in the scent of the ink and wrote Jesse's name with delicate loops and a smile on her face. Paragraphs formed beneath her fingers about how Jesse made her feel, the way he cupped her face in his hands when he kissed her, so gentle, but urgent and strong at the same time. He was perfect. He made her smile even when he wasn't around. Just writing his name made her feel giddy and light-headed.

"That's an awful lot of dessert," Evelyn said as Naomi piled her bowl full of brownies and ice cream.

Naomi blushed and dropped the ice cream scoop back into the carton. "I'm sorry. I thought there was enough for everyone."

"There is, but you don't normally take that much." Evelyn scooped some ice cream into her own bowl, and they both walked to the living room where everyone sat down to watch a movie. Jesse patted the cushion next to him, and Naomi sat down with a happy sigh.

"It's for Jesse too," she said to Evelyn. "We, uh, we...."

"No need to explain," Evelyn said with a smirk as she sat down next to Steve. He wrapped his arms around her and squeezed. Naomi wanted Jesse to hold her like that, but it felt too weird here in front of everyone. They only kissed in private, and never in her room. Jesse refused to enter her room lately. So far she hadn't asked him why. Right now, sitting so close to him was as far as he seemed willing to go in front of the others. He picked up the second spoon from her bowl and scooped up a piece of brownie.

"You want to stay down here or go upstairs to the den?" he asked and slid the spoon into his mouth. He chewed the brownie slowly then licked his lips and looked her up and down.

Naomi tried not to giggle. It amazed her how she felt all hot and tingly inside, like someone had lit fireworks inside of her stomach. It was wonderful and crazy and scary, all at the same time.

"Upstairs," she whispered, nudging him with her shoulder.

"We're going to go read," Jesse announced to everyone, and stood. He offered Naomi his hand. She grabbed it and followed him up the stairs.

"Have fun!" Eric called out behind them.

Naomi stifled another giggle. "What's going on?" she asked when they entered the den.

Jesse took the bowl from her hands and set it on the pool table. "Nothing. I just want to kiss you again, that's all." He pulled her into his arms, and she kissed him in a way she had never kissed Brad. She was sure she would never kiss anybody the way she could kiss Jesse. He was leaving in a few days to spend Christmas with his father, and she had to savor him every moment before he left. He reached inside that secret box, the one she had locked up for so long. For the first time in her life, she wasn't afraid to open it.

XX
December

NAOMI'S MIND FILLED WITH VISIONS OF STEPPING onto the sun-baked stones of a patio and looking across a panorama of rolling green hills stretched beneath a turquoise sky. The hills were dotted with yellow sunflowers, some larger than both her hands put together, even if she spread her fingers wide apart like elegant petals. Olive trees bent themselves across the landscape, some old and some young, some lined in perfect rows. Vineyards were hazy in the distance. She smelled olives and grapes and bread baking in Evelyn's kitchen behind her.

She closed her eyes and listened to the silence. Then Evelyn told her there was a small town ten minutes down the dirt road. At the market they could buy aged cheeses, fresh pasta, and white truffles.

"I don't mean chocolate," she laughed.

Naomi opened her eyes and shook the sunlight from her imagination. All she could see now was the twinkle of Christmas lights in Evelyn's eyes. Truffles? Weren't those mushrooms that grew from the root systems of trees? Would they taste like trees? She scrunched her nose. "Aren't those really expensive?"

"Like you wouldn't believe." Evelyn hugged her knees to her chest, the Christmas lights sparkling around her like a halo of fireflies.

She was happier than Naomi had ever seen her as she sat on the floor next to Steve. He played with the ends of her hair as she sipped from her mug of hot chocolate. Lately, Naomi had noticed they were always touching each other, almost flirting, but in a comfortable, unhurried way. Her parents had never been that way. She couldn't remember the last time she had seen them kiss each other. Something inside of her ached when she watched Steve and Evelyn. She wanted that kind of affection for herself, like some greedy monster starved for raw, pure love. Jesse could give it to her, but he was still away visiting his father.

"They're worth every cent," Evelyn said, referring to the truffles. "Even Eric, the penny-pincher, will tell you that."

Eric smiled as he finished stringing the last of the lights on the Christmas tree. He was on his knees bent halfway beneath the limbs. "Yes," he grunted, "they're good once in a while."

Evelyn winked at Naomi. "Everybody has to try them at least once. We'll have you try a lot of things when we get there." Steam from her hot chocolate drifted around her face. "Doesn't it sound amazing?"

Naomi nodded. She was sitting on the couch adjacent to them with a blanket pulled over her lap, her own mug of hot chocolate warm in her hands. "It does sound amazing," she said with a sigh. She saw the sun-baked patio again, felt it hot under her bare feet, a glittering swimming pool down the hill. The cloudless sky promised her freedom, a kind she had never felt before.

"Don't go dreaming too fast, Evelyn," Steve said with a short laugh. "The tenants still have six more months."

"I know, I know." Evelyn glanced at him. "But she needs to know where we're taking her." She looked back to Naomi. "It was my grandmother's house. I lived with her for four years starting when I was fifteen. It was after our father ...." She glanced at Eric. "After he went to prison. Eric was in college then, and when our grandmother died Eric told me to—"

"I didn't order you to come back here." Eric crawled out from under the tree and wiped his hands on his jeans. "I asked you to. You wanted to go to school here, remember?" He took a cookie from a plate on the coffee table and smiled at Steve. "I'm happy you met somebody better than Mom did. Not that I would have let you marry someone like *him*."

Evelyn gave him a disapproving glare, but remained silent.

Sipping her hot chocolate, Naomi tried to ignore the tension in the air. Her mouth tasted like garlic from Evelyn's roast and potatoes. The kitchen was still a mess, and Steve had turned on some Christmas music playing softly in the background. Everything was perfect. Almost.

Eric turned to her. "Now that Evelyn has told you about the house, do you think you'll like Italy? Nobody's around for miles, so you can go outside anytime you want." He finished his cookie and brushed off his hands. "We'll get you a new camera, and when you're older we might be able to travel. Once people forget …."

His voice trailed off. Naomi squeezed the mug in her hands and tried to smile. She knew he wanted to say once people forgot about her. He was right, but she wasn't sure what to think about it. Her entire life people had forgotten about her, so what did it matter? Her parents had obviously moved on.

"There are oranges on the counter," Evelyn said, breaking the silence. "Eric, go get some." She turned to Naomi. "I've noticed you're quiet tonight. Are you feeling all right?"

"I'm just tired."

Her eyes twinkled. "It's not because of Jesse? He'll be back in a week, sweetheart."

"Well, I … I …."

"It's all right." She glanced at Steve, who smiled and nodded. "Jesse is thinking about coming to Italy with us," she said. "I don't want you to think we're taking you away from him."

Naomi held her breath. Her cheeks turned hot. They obviously didn't know Jesse had decided for sure to go to Italy. How much had he kept from them? Did they know they kissed all the time? They didn't seem to care if it went farther than that. In fact, they probably wanted the relationship to go as far as it could possibly go.

Eric came back from the kitchen, his hands filled with four oranges. He set them on the coffee table and sat back down next to Evelyn. She snatched two from the table, tossed one to Steve, and started slicing through the rind of hers with a long, red fingernail.

"It's tradition," she said to Naomi. "We always eat an orange on Christmas Eve."

Naomi tried to keep a smile on her face. She couldn't recall any holiday traditions in her family. Her mother hired someone to put up a Christmas tree every year, but it didn't matter anymore. Nothing about her parents mattered. Even Brad didn't matter.

Steve finished peeling his orange and held it out to her with a smile. Her heart nearly stopped. She saw thick rinds falling to her father's office floor. His elbows were propped on his desk. His eyes twinkled as he pulled a segment from the fruit and placed it into her eight-year-old hands. Nothing had ever tasted as sweet as those oranges.

"Do you want it?" Steve asked, interrupting her reverie. He was still holding the orange out to her. She took it.

XXI

KAREN SIPPED AT HER COFFEE AND WATCHED THE traffic from her office window. It was midday. She had just eaten lunch with Anna, and now they were both fighting the afternoon lull.

"Why don't we have a siesta like other countries?" Anna asked from her desk. She drank the last of her soda and tossed the cup into the trash. "Afternoon naps should be required, don't you think?"

"Absolutely," Karen said, and chuckled softly. "I think Jason takes a nap every afternoon. He's got a nice, big office, of course, and I think he locks the door and schedules one hour to himself."

Anna's expression turned serious. "We should do that! Really, we could get another couch in your office. There's space. We could both chill out and listen to ocean wave soundtracks or something."

The suggestion was ridiculous, but at this point Karen didn't care. "Sure, we can do whatever we want." She turned and sat in her chair. There were eight new emails in her inbox. She ignored them and picked up a picture of Naomi. It was in a small, silver frame one of her clients had given her as a thank you gift. Finally, she had put it to good use and slid Naomi's picture inside it. Her smile in the photo was natural and sweet—different from the other pictures the press had used countless times in their stories. Karen had kept this one for herself. She thought of the message she had left on Naomi's phone all those months ago. She could hardly remember what she had said—only that she had started crying by the end of it.

"So you're serious? I can black out an hour every afternoon?"

Karen shrugged. "Sure, why not?" She looked up from Naomi's picture. "You know, I've been thinking about what I told the press back in September."

"You mean that story they ran about you?"

"Yes, how my mother died of cancer and I've never been the same since." Karen ran her fingers over Naomi's picture. Her mother's death had affected everything, especially after Naomi was born. Getting close to Naomi was too hard. It was a shame it had taken her so long to realize why. She waved her hand in the air. "Anyway, you watched all that, right?"

"Yes, and you've definitely been happier since then—like a weight was lifted from your shoulders when you explained everything publicly." Anna smiled. "It helped me understand you better, that's for sure. It was really nice to hear you talk about her too, about how much you love her."

Karen laughed. "Yeah, I think you hated me there for awhile. I think everyone did, including me."

"I didn't hate you." Anna looked away and started typing an email.

"You can admit it," Karen said as she put Naomi's picture back in its spot. "I'm glad you understand me better, but there's got to be more than this—more I can do."

"You talked about funding some national things," Anna said over her shoulder. "Remember?"

"Yes."

"So why don't you do it?"

Standing, Karen stepped away from her desk and made her way to the couch. "You know, I think a nap sounds like a great idea."

She stretched herself out on the cushions and grabbed a small pillow to put over her face. She needed to block everything out. She didn't want to see or think about anything. The pillow didn't help, and Anna was right. Why didn't she do more? Jason and Elizabeth had been bugging her, as well. Everybody seemed to think they needed her permission for anything concerning Naomi. Maybe they did. She was her mother. She was supposed to be the closest person to her, right?

She groaned and pressed the pillow more tightly to her face. It smelled of coconut.

"You know," Anna called out from the other room, "I heard about a girl Naomi's age who went missing up in Oregon."

Why did she have to bring that up? Karen focused on keeping her breaths slow. People would forever be telling her about missing children. They thought since her own child was missing, she naturally wanted to relate to every single person on the planet with a missing child. Ridiculous. She decided not to respond.

"Karen?"

With a heavy sigh she pulled the pillow away from her face. All she could think about was Naomi and the way she separated her food on her dinner plate into neat little portions—like a checkerboard. Naomi didn't often eat dinner with her and Jason, but Karen was surprised at how much she remembered from the few times they had been together. The more she thought about Naomi, the less guilty she felt—but then it hurt to think about her so much. She couldn't win.

"Did you hear me?" Anna asked.

"Yes, I heard you."

"Well, the story was that she disappeared over a year and half ago. The police had enough evidence to show she was a runaway, but the parents refused to believe it. The sad thing is they didn't have enough money to keep their own investigation going."

"That's too bad."

Anna came into the room and stood where Karen could see her. Her hair was wild today. The corkscrew curls stood out every which way. Her little button nose scrunched up as she made a confused expression. "Well, don't you think it's obvious what you should do?"

Karen sat up and put her head in her hands. "Yes, I know. You've been hinting at it for weeks. I should start a foundation to help people like that." She looked up. "But don't you think that's pointless since I haven't even done anything extensive for Naomi? I've done more in the past few months, but no matter what I do it's been hard to get her name so widespread without a specific angle that excites people and stands out. It's just that everything has gone cold. It's so unlikely we'd get results from all the effort. Even my private detective has said so."

"But you should push harder anyway, don't you think? You're always talking about stuff. Get out and do it. Maybe that's why you and Naomi had such a hard time connecting, you know? You sure think a lot, but you don't show what you're thinking. You've always been that way. It's great for your job to stay nice and calm in the courtroom, but in the other parts of your life, not so much."

There was a pinging sound from Karen's computer as another email arrived in her box. Her heart plummeted. More work. She used to love her job, but lately it was only stress and pain. Everything was flat now. No excitement. Just breathing. Existing.

"Maybe you're right," she said, running her fingernail over a pattern on the couch cushion. The pattern, she realized, was a red starfish, and it made her think of Naomi's photo Brad had chosen to enter into the contest. Her eyes widened with a sudden realization.

"What do you mean *maybe* I'm right?" Anna asked with an exaggerated huff. "I'm always right."

Karen smiled, her heart beating quickly. "Yes, you are."

XXII
January

ERIC SURPRISED NAOMI WHEN HE ASKED HER IF SHE wanted to watch the New Year's Eve fireworks outside. Dressed in her pajamas, she stepped out the front door and tiptoed down the driveway where Steve and Evelyn stood.

Snow was still clumped in little patches around dead grass and frozen dirt. It had just turned midnight. The sky was clear and black. The fireworks Denver was shooting off in the distance were easy to see above the neighborhood.

"We're on a bit of a hill," Steve explained to Naomi as soon as she reached him, Eric right beside her "So we're able to see the fireworks from here if the weather is good."

She nodded. They hadn't let her come out to watch them on the Fourth of July, but that was months ago. Besides, she might have tried to make a run for it back then. Not now. Now she knew better.

She shifted her bare feet across the icy cement and folded her arms. Eric looked down at her and smiled. "Are you cold?" He wrapped an arm around her as she returned her attention to the black night. Bursts of green and yellow popped in the sky. Seconds later, the sound reached her ears.

Everything was in its place now. Her past was far away like the fireworks, and not even as beautiful. It was nothing more than a memory.

"Do you want to go back inside?" Eric asked. "You're shivering. I can get you one of Evelyn's coats, if you like." He squeezed her shoulders again. "I thought you'd like to see—"

"I'm okay."

She looked down at her toes and smiled. Evelyn had painted them for her. They matched her fingernails.

"I first went to school to study biology," she had said, bent over Naomi's hands at the dining table. "Then I changed my major to English, then dance. This is what I ended up doing." She smiled. "Beauty school. Then I met Steve in the salon where I was working, and he was good friends with the manager of a jewelry store downtown. When we got engaged, he got me the assistant manager job I have now at the jewelry store, and that led to—" She stopped and looked away. Her hand tightened around Naomi's fingers, the smell of nail polish thick in the air. "Well, I love my job and I love Steve, and I'm happy you're here with us."

Eric's arm tightened around her as she stared at the sidewalk. It led to nothing but darkness.

❦

Jesse arrived home a few days later. Naomi knew his flight would land at seven and that it would take him at least an hour to get home from the airport. It was eight now, and she kept looking at the clock as she sat on the couch watching TV with a bowl of popcorn. Eric had let her stay downstairs by herself after dinner. He did that a lot lately.

"Looks like a party," Jesse said when he came in through the front door. He smiled and her heart did a somersault as she blurted, "How was your trip?"

He shrugged and looked around. "Good. Where is everyone?"

"Evelyn and Steve are upstairs, and Eric's in his office." She nodded to the open door by the dining room. If she leaned over far enough, she could see him in his chair talking on the phone.

Jesse was quiet for a moment. He cleared his throat and nodded to his bedroom down the hallway. "I brought you something. Want to see?"

"Yes!" She jumped up and the popcorn flew out of her lap and landed on the floor.

"Happy to see me?" He laughed and set his duffle on the floor before stepping around the couch.

She fell to her knees, cursing when she spotted a butter stain on the tan carpet. "Evelyn's going to kill me."

"Nah, she has cleaning stuff. It's not a big deal." He dumped a handful of popcorn into the bowl.

Naomi shaped voiceless words in her mouth. She hadn't seen him in two weeks. Her heart was pounding at the sight of him, at his clean, familiar scent now that he was only a few inches away. Their hands brushed as they picked up some kernels. "I missed you," she blurted. "A lot."

He smiled and set the bowl on the coffee table just as Eric peeked out from his office.

"Oh, you're home. Good flight?"

"A bit crowded, but it was fine."

Eric nodded. "Come see me in the office when you can. We need to talk about the meeting."

"Sure thing." Jesse stood and offered Naomi his hand. "Follow me."

She stood and followed him to his bedroom, staying in the doorway. She had never seen his bedroom before. Bookshelves lined the walls and in a corner by the window sat a drafting table. One thing she hadn't realized was the fact that both Jesse's and Eric's rooms were directly below hers. Her heart fluttered at the thought of Jesse sleeping right below her.

"During the first weeks you were here I heard you crying at night," he said as he let go of her hand and walked to his bed. "You don't do that anymore."

"Uh, I guess not." She stared at her red toenails. They were bright, just like her fingernails. The color reminded her of Evelyn. Until she had met Evelyn she had never been one to paint her nails or do anything very girlish—except for the makeup thing.

Jesse cleared his throat and she looked up, giving him an inviting smile. She wanted him to take her into his arms. He should at least say something sweet and predictable like, "I missed you too. I could barely breathe I missed you so much."

Instead, he turned around and started rummaging through the duffle he had thrown onto his bed. "They're in here somewhere," he said, pulling out a few paperback books. He tossed them onto the bed, mumbling to himself while pushing aside shirts and pants. "Ah, here they are." He turned around and motioned her toward him.

She approached and looked down at a stack of books in his hands, counting four of them. They were old, cloth-wrapped hardbacks with gilt lettering on the spines.

"These are my dad's," he said, and set them in her hands. They were heavy and smelled like the basement of a library.

She looked up with questioning eyes. "Your dad's?"

"He said you could borrow them for as long as you like." He glanced at the top book in her hands, which she finally noticed was *The Great Gatsby*. Her stomach plummeted as her mom filled her head. She shoved her away.

"They're first edition prints. My dad thought you'd like them. You know, not everybody appreciates stuff like this. I told him you would."

"I thought you said he didn't know about me."

"Oh, he didn't." He turned back to his bag and pulled out a few more paperbacks. "He does now. Well, he knows *about* you." Clearing his throat, he gripped a paperback in his hand. "But he doesn't know who you are. I can never tell him … who you are. I told him we ran into each other in a parking lot. I suppose that's not a complete lie." He cleared his throat again and tossed the book onto the suede bedspread with the others.

She didn't know what to do. Her chest was pounding with more emotions than she could possibly sort through. When he finally turned to her and didn't take her into his arms and kiss her, she thought her heart might burst.

Eric's voice yelled out from the office. "Jesse, you free yet?"

His face fell. "I'll be back. Do you want to wait for me here?"

Her heart retreated to a manageable pace. "Sure."

"Make yourself comfortable." He smiled and ran a hand over his scratchy jaw before settling his attention on the bed. "There's plenty to read. I'll be right back."

She waited until he was gone and set the stack of books on a desk beside the bed.

Her hands froze.

He had left his laptop case on the desk, and her mind filled with a very stupid idea.

Jesse had helped her download music to her iPod countless times, and she had noticed that on his laptop he had a guest account with no password. Emailing Brad would be easy. She could type Eric's full name— Eric Moretti, or Steve and Evelyn Thompson, or even the address she had memorized from the mail she had seen for the first time on the kitchen table a few weeks ago. They were careless about things like that now. They trusted her. It would be easy for the police to find her. None of them would know.

She hung her head and rested her hands in her lap. Could she do that? To Jesse? To any of them?

She couldn't. More than that, she couldn't fathom what it would be like to go back home. She recoiled at the thought.

Positioning herself on the edge of the bed near the desk, she looked at the stack of books. She picked up *The Great Gatsby* and ran her fingers across the emerald green cloth and Fitzgerald's name before opening the cover. The print date said 1925. The paper was yellowed and dull against the shiny, red polish on her fingernails. It was probably worth a small fortune. She had to admit it was amazing, but at the same time it freaked her out just to touch it. Shouldn't Jesse's father keep it in a safer place instead of sending it off with his son in a bag full of dirty clothes?

She set it back on the desk and turned to the clean, white pillows on Jesse's bed. There was no clock in the room. The air was stale and silent, and after a while she pushed Jesse's duffle to the floor and curled herself in the middle of the bed. Tears formed in her eyes. Was she making the right decision? Her mother's voice echoed in her head. *Don't judge him too unfairly in the beginning.*

Her throat tightened. Had she judged her mother too unfairly? She was eighteen now—old enough to decide who to live with and what to do with the rest of her life. It was her decision to stay here. As crazy as it was, she wanted to stay. She buried her face in Jesse's pillow.

❧

She dreamed of flowers, a whole garden of them. One in particular caught her attention—white and ample, like a magnolia unfolding beneath the sun. It reminded her of a painting in her mother's room.

"Naomi?"

Her eyes fluttered open to see Jesse leaning over the bed. "I'm sorry," she stuttered, sitting up. She focused on his messy red hair and bright eyes.

"Why are you sorry?" He leaned closer and glanced at his watch. "I've been gone for over an hour. I was afraid you might head back upstairs."

She returned her head to the pillow, but kept her eyes attached to his. "No, you said you would be back."

He looked at his watch again. "It's getting late and you look tired. You should go to bed."

"No!" She shook her head and raised herself from the pillow. "I don't want to leave. I want to be with you. I missed you so much while you were away."

If he made her go back to her room, she might scream at him. She needed him.

He smiled. "I missed you too. I wanted to talk about you all the time with my dad, but I couldn't say very much without giving away my ... secrets." He leaned down close to her mouth. "You were the first thing I thought about when I went to sleep and the first thing on my mind in the morning."

His lips touched hers. Finally. She wrapped her arms around him as he crawled onto the bed next to her. "Let's not wait anymore," he mumbled, moving his mouth to her neck. He paused along her collarbone, breathing heavily, and slid his hands up her back. Then he peeled her shirt up her body and over her head.

She was surprised at how natural it felt to be with him like this. On his bed. With her shirt off. It wasn't awkward or scary. Smiling, she wrapped her arms around him and pulled his shirt off too. There were freckles across his shoulders and chest. She ran her fingers over them. He was warm and strong and beautiful. She wanted him so badly her entire body ached.

"You won't ever hurt me," she whispered, staring into his eyes. Then she moved her attention to her red fingernails. "Not like Brad."

She gritted her teeth. Brad was the last person she wanted to think about right now, but no matter how hard she tried, he still hovered in her mind like a lonely shadow.

Jesse's fingers tightened around the button of her jeans. "What do you mean? Did he hurt you?"

She tried not to cringe. She supposed it depended on what he meant by hurt. "Not exactly," she said, thinking carefully. "I wanted to the first time ... so much. I swear I was the last girl my age at school to have sex. Maybe that's what I wanted to believe, I don't know, but it didn't seem like it would be a problem. It was fine, I guess, but that first time ... it hurt. I guess that's normal. After a while, he sometimes ...." She choked on the next words and looked away.

"Yes?"

"It's nothing. Most of the time I didn't want to and he made me feel like I had to ... and always his way. That's all."

That really was all. As far as she could remember Brad had never truly hurt her—except for the one time he had hit her, of course. He was simply overbearing, insistent, persuasive, demanding, and a hundred other things she didn't want to think about right now. Jesse was none of those.

"Oh." He pushed away from her. "So is that the problem, then? Brad?" He leaned closer to her face. "I know you want this as much as I do."

She did want him. She wanted a commitment with him more than she had ever wanted with Brad. Her body was begging her mind to shut off and leave her alone.

"I'll be gentle," he whispered, unbuttoning her jeans. He pulled the zipper down. "I won't hurt you, Naomi. You must know that." He searched her face, and when she didn't react to him tugging her jeans down her hips, he stopped. His eyes hardened. "Are you still in love with him?"

"I was never in love with him." She was surprised at how fast she answered the question, and shifted beneath his weight. Why did her heart feel like it was being ripped in half? Why were her fingernails digging into her palms like daggers? She was sure they would draw blood any moment as he leaned down to kiss her cheek. He lifted his hands from her waist and curled them around her face.

"I've already told you I'm going to Italy with you. I'll stay with you because I've never felt this way about anybody."

Her heart swelled. She focused on the weight of his body, his skin on her skin. His heart was pounding almost as hard as hers. Something was opening up between them, letting in more light to the darkness that had surrounded her for so long. She knew if it shined brightly enough she might see him for who he truly was, if he let her. She had already let her own secret box open to all those raw emotions that still haunted her sometimes. This made her shrink away.

Like so many times before, she tried to imagine him dressed in black, head to toe, picking a lock, cutting wires, whispering to Eric that everything was going as planned. This image was more of an annoying shadow than her thoughts of Brad.

"You have to tell me," she whispered, breaking the silence.

"Tell you what?"

"Why do you steal jewelry? Are Steve and Eric making you do all of that?"

He sat up, the hard look in his eyes again. "How do you know about the jewelry?"

She cringed at the change in him. "Well, I ...."

This was exactly the part of him she didn't know, the darkness she sensed beneath everything else. She was too afraid to admit that a part of her was drawn to it, craved it, maybe even turned on by it. He was dangerous, but he controlled that danger, and she knew he was the type of person who would never let it harm her. It made him strong and powerful and mysterious, and that was something she had always wanted. She hurried to answer him. "Eric let a few things slip a long time ago. I figured it out."

His bare chest rose up and down with heated breaths. "You don't need to worry about it. It's going to end. All of it. That's some of the shit I'm trying to change about myself." Moving off her, he grabbed his shirt. It was clear he didn't want her anymore. She had destroyed the moment.

Suddenly cold, she wrapped her arms around her ribs. It was January. She would have been in college by now, probably wherever Brad was because she would have followed him anywhere. Harvard? Forget it. She wasn't capable of standing on her own two feet. It was almost laughable. She stared at Jesse with pleading eyes.

"What's all this about?" he asked, getting off the bed. He glared at her, his expression darker than she had ever seen it. "You're not thinking about trying to leave, are you?"

Sensing the anger in his voice, she chewed on her bottom lip and stared at *The Great Gatsby* on the desk.

"Naomi, forget it. You belong here. I've told you before—there's too much at stake and Eric will kill you. That's not even a question in my mind." He pulled his shirt over his head. "You know, you're the hardest person I've ever tried to read. You're like a box I can't open, and it's driving me crazy. I've tried everything with you. I've been patient, but I can only go so far." He curled his hands into fists.

She cringed. A box he couldn't open? If he felt that way, maybe she was mistaken about her own emotions. She thought of Brad's fists, a bonfire, Damien's glasses, then her journal and the countless pages filled with thoughts of her mother—things she never would have remembered otherwise. She remembered *The Awakening* on her nightstand, of the dragons she never dreamed about anymore.

"I don't know if I belong here," she said softly, turning away. "Sometimes I can't stop thinking about her. Sometimes I wonder if I've made the right decision."

There was a long silence.

"I should have known," he said, his voice sharp. "I thought you wanted to be here with me. I thought I was the reason you haven't tried to leave—not because of your mother. Your mother thinks you're dead. Everybody thinks you're dead. Why the hell would you want to go back?"

She turned to look at him as he left the room. She stared at the open doorway, confused. Everything about him confused her. She wanted to be with him, but at the same time she wondered how much of that had to do with her situation. If she had met him in college, would she have been attracted to him? A part of her knew the answer was no. She was smart enough to know that, but her heart was oblivious to it. No matter how hard she tried to move her emotions to a normal space, they resisted. She could barely recall freedom from the walls of a house, from rules set up by someone else. The worst part was it didn't feel any different from before she had come here.

It only seemed like yesterday that she had put her hand in the tide pool to straighten out the starfish. She was like that starfish. She needed a rock to cling to, a protected space where she could live. Brad had been these things, and now there was Jesse. He had twisted her in directions she was too weak to resist.

Putting a hand to her head, she sat up and held her breath. She was half naked. She needed her shirt, but she couldn't see it anywhere. Everything was blurry behind her tears. Jesse had left her because he thought she might try to escape again. He didn't think she cared about him, but she hadn't tried to escape once the entire time she had been here. What more did he want her to do?

She shivered. Glancing at the stack of books on the desk made her think of the painting in her mother's room—a white magnolia opening to the sun. She remembered one of the times she had been in her mother's room. It was a large space with huge windows overlooking the ocean. There was white carpet and billowy curtains and seashells on the walls. Her mother leaned down and smiled.

"Can you pull up my zipper, honey?"

She nodded and took the zipper in her fingers. She must have been nine or ten. As she pulled it up her mother's back, she looked at the painting on the wall. She thought of her mother as a flower in her smooth, white gown and honeysuckle perfume.

Years later she saw that painting again. It had started with Brad. The morning after she had first slept with him she stared at the ceiling in his room, clutching the sheets to her body as she asked herself a million questions about what she had done. Was her body supposed to hurt? Should she sleep with him again even if it scared her? It was normal and healthy to have sex. All the popular girls at school slept with their boyfriends. It was crazy she had waited so long.

Still, questions nagged at the back of her mind. Her mother might get angry with her if she knew what had happened, but a part of her desperately wanted to talk to her about it.

Finally, three days later, she knocked on her mother's bedroom door. When it opened she saw the painting on the wall and felt sick inside. That was when she remembered her mother was raised in a time and place where having sex before marriage wasn't talked about, let alone done with any amount of approval from others. Her mother was as pure and clean as that flower. She would never understand.

"Never mind," Naomi had muttered and walked away.

She looked up just as Eric entered the bedroom, his eyes growing wide when he spotted her half naked on the bed. She covered herself. She still hadn't found her shirt. Jesse had tossed it somewhere.

"Where the hell is Jesse?" He looked around the room. "I heard you crying. What happened?"

She touched her face and felt tears. How loudly had she been crying? "Nothing happened," she whimpered. "I just need to find my shirt."

He bent down and picked it up from a dark corner, then held it out to her as she wiped away more tears. She was a complete mess. She couldn't look him in the eyes.

"Get dressed," he said softly. "I'll be right back."

As soon as she pulled on her shirt she heard yelling from the kitchen. She slid off the bed and crept down the hallway, her entire body trembling with fear and adrenaline. She peered around the corner just as Eric slammed a fist into Jesse's face. She jumped back as if it had been her who was hit.

They were both standing by the refrigerator. Eric's back was to her. Jesse stumbled and cupped a hand to his nose. "You told me—"

"Get the hell out of here. Get your bags and leave right now."

Jesse tensed his shoulders. "This makes no sense. You told me to do this with her!"

Her breath stopped in her throat. She wrapped her hands around the corner of the wall, heat swelling in her chest. Eric had told him to seduce her? It was something she had suspected, but kept pushing away. It couldn't be true.

"If it made her happy," Eric growled. "That's not what I saw. If you've hurt her, I swear I'll knock your damn head off."

"Hurt her? I will never hurt her."

"Then why the hell is she so upset?"

She wanted to step around the corner and tell Eric her tears were mostly over her mother, but how could she explain that? If she said anything of the sort he might freak out on her instead.

"Because she's changed her—I mean—hell, I don't know. I didn't hurt her. I swear to you I would never hurt her. I told you that already." He placed his hand to his nose again. It was starting to bleed. "You know me better than that."

Eric's shoulders slumped and then tensed again. "I thought I did, but you've forgotten what I told you before. I don't want anybody harming her. Ever."

Jesse's eyes narrowed. "I didn't hurt her." He leaned forward, squaring his shoulders. "Ask her."

"I don't need to ask her." Eric squared his own shoulders, towering over Jesse who still stood his ground. Blood streamed from Jesse's nose and down his lips, but he didn't move a centimeter away from Eric. They stared each other down until Naomi thought their faces might break.

Finally, Eric grabbed Jesse's collar and pulled him close. "I saw her face, and that's enough to convince me. You're supposed to make her happy, and if you've got her crying like that the first day you're back, she needs more time. Now get out."

Naomi held her breath. He couldn't leave! He had barely gotten home. The heat in her chest burned hotter. Jesse grabbed Eric's hand and ripped it away from his shirt. "You know, if it weren't for Evelyn, I wouldn't put up with any of your shit. I'd punch a hole right through your face."

Eric glared. "It's a good thing you haven't tried. Now I told you—get out."

"Fine. When the hell do you want me to come back?"

"When I call you and tell you to come back. Don't even think about disappearing. I want to hear from you at least once a day."

"Whatever you want." He brushed past him and headed toward the stairs where Naomi stood, Eric right on his heels. They both stopped when they saw her. Jesse's eyes went wide. "Naomi!"

She glared at him. "You've been doing all of this with me because Eric told you to?"

"What? No, it's not like that." He turned to Eric. "Tell her."

Eric glared at him, his face bright red with anger as he reached out to grab Naomi. She backed away.

"Go up to your room," he ordered. "Now!"

She remembered how fast he could hurt her, how his anger might spiral out of control. She sucked in her breath and raced up the stairs to her room. Ten minutes later she stood at her window and watched Jesse drive away into the darkness.

XXIII

SHE HARDLY SLEPT THAT NIGHT. WAKING FROM A light doze, she saw dark clouds outside her window. That was perfect. She needed a nice gloomy day to finish off her misery. As far as she knew, she wouldn't see Jesse for weeks. She didn't care that Eric had told him to play with her emotions. All she wanted to do was talk to him and figure out how he really felt. Whatever had happened between them wasn't all an act. It was too real, gone on for too long. Brad's affections for her felt more forced than Jesse's ever had.

A knock on her door made her jump. She groaned when Evelyn undid the locks and stepped inside. It was Saturday, and that meant she could eat breakfast downstairs with the others. She usually enjoyed that far more than eating alone in her room. Today was different.

"I'm not hungry," she said when Evelyn approached the bed.

"I didn't ask if you were hungry."

She rolled over to see Evelyn dressed in her yoga clothes. Her hair was pulled into a tight ponytail. She wore no makeup, and the scar down her face was bright pink. For the five-billionth time Naomi wondered how it had happened, if her father had given it to her or if it had been Eric.

"I don't want to do yoga, either."

Evelyn put her hands on her hips and glared. "You're the one who begged me to start exercising with you." She patted her own thigh. "All your sitting around is going to ruin your figure. Don't you want to look great in Italy?"

Naomi rolled her eyes and covered her face with the blankets. "I don't *care*. Jesse won't be coming anyway. Eric kicked him out. Didn't you hear?"

"Yes, I did. He'll come back. They'll work it out."

"That's not it at all." She clenched her teeth and breathed heavily against the blankets. Her breath smelled of garlic from yesterday's dinner. "We were in his room last night," she mumbled. "We were on his bed. I thought we might finally, you know ... but I ruined it and Eric thought it was because Jesse hurt me and I need more time away from him. He didn't hurt me. He would never hurt me."

"You almost slept with Jesse?" Her voice was edged with surprise.

Naomi pulled the covers down. "Eric didn't tell you that?"

"No." She folded her arms and twisted her expression into disapproval. "You should have told me things were going that far."

"I thought you wanted me to be with him like that. Isn't that what Eric wants?"

"What on earth gave you that idea?"

"Jesse said so when they were arguing last night. I know why, but it doesn't matter." She turned her back to Evelyn and heaved a deep breath into her pillow. "You want me to fall in love with him so I'll never leave."

The room fell silent. Evelyn sat on the edge of the bed and started pulling her fingers through Naomi's hair. It was soothing, and she didn't move away. She analyzed the weight of what she had just told Evelyn. They were words she could never have said to her mother, or anybody else for that matter. That made her heart sink lower than it already was, and as Evelyn combed through her hair she thought about when Damien had kissed her wrist and looked into her eyes. That small, intimate gesture had been one of the most memorable moments of her life. Damien had reached a part of her she hadn't known existed—a part constantly reaching out for a connection nobody else had tried to grasp until she had come here. It was lame that she loved and hated it here at the same time. It left her in no-man's land, a place where she avoided making any sort of firm decision. She just wanted to ride things out and see where they went on their own.

"It's true we want you to choose to be here," Evelyn said gently. "All Eric told Jesse was that he was free to pursue you if he wanted. It wasn't always like that. At first we didn't want anything like that going on. We wanted you to have as much control over your choices as we could give you, but then we saw how much you were attaching yourself to Jesse, so Eric told him it was okay."

Naomi stayed silent. She closed her eyes and concentrated on the fingers moving through her hair.

"Do you understand what I'm saying?" Evelyn asked.

"Yeah, I think so, but that's not going to bring Jesse back any faster."

Her fingers stopped. "Maybe not, but what's the rush?"

"I don't know. I miss him. He's been gone since before Christmas."

Evelyn was quiet for a moment. "You're in love with him, aren't you?"

Love. It sounded heavy and serious, but it was what she wanted more than anything in the world. She remembered how much Steve and Evelyn cared for each other. It was so *real.* She couldn't even imagine what that must be like.

"I don't know," she mumbled. "Maybe." What else was she supposed to say? That she didn't think she could breathe without him? It sounded ridiculous.

Evelyn moved her hand to her shoulder, stroking gently. "It takes a long time to understand love. Nobody says you have to figure it out now or tomorrow, or even in a year. I hope you don't think we're trying to push you into anything. I'd never want that. The truth is," she said with a catch in her voice, "I've never been happier in my life than I have been with you here."

Turning, Naomi looked up at her. She thought of that night in the darkness when Evelyn had whispered to Steve that she couldn't have asked for anything better. Confusion gripped her. "I don't understand how I make you happy."

Evelyn's expression fell. Her fingers froze. "A lot of reasons," she said softly. "I was hoping I could help you understand it someday—if you give me a chance. A girl can get awfully lonely with all these men around. That, and I've always wanted someone I can talk to like this. Steve doesn't get it. He doesn't do yoga, either." Her face brightened and she winked, making Naomi laugh.

Naomi sat up and stretched. Leaving her room was sounding better. "I guess yoga sounds good."

Twenty minutes later they were in the living room stretching their bodies into positions she wouldn't have been able to accomplish a year ago. Now she was limber, like Evelyn. It felt good to breathe in rhythm with her. It almost took her mind off Jesse. Almost.

"How did you know you were in love with Steve?" she asked as they started another position.

Evelyn bent down to the floor. Her ponytail grazed the carpet. "It might sound strange to you," she said as she stretched. "I've never thought of myself as ugly, but my scar is something that once someone notices it, they kind of stare—a lot. Steve never looked twice at it, not once, even after we went swimming and I had no makeup on. He looked at me like no other man had ever looked at me, and I knew."

Naomi's frame shook as she fought to hold her position. "That's cool. It must be nice to have someone like that." She wondered if Jesse could ever be like that, but then she realized he was already. Her heart nearly stopped at the thought.

"It is."

They both stood from their positions and started the next in the series. Naomi glanced at Evelyn's scar as they turned toward each other. "Can I ask how ... how you got it?"

She winced. "I knew you'd ask eventually."

"I'm sorry."

"It's okay, really." She stretched her arms above her head and entwined her fingers. Naomi mirrored her movements and tried not to look at the scar. It was difficult.

"You don't have to tell me."

"My father cut me with a kitchen knife. That's how he murdered my mother and my sister. Stabbed them. I'm sure Jesse has told you about that, at least."

"A little bit." She tried to focus on her position to keep herself from shuddering. Goose bumps popped up on her bare arms. A kitchen knife. It sounded awful.

"My father intended to kill me too, but Eric stopped him. He saved my life."

For some reason, that surprised Naomi. She couldn't imagine Eric rushing in like a hero. "Wow, how old was he?"

"Nineteen—barely in college." Her eyes glazed over. "He happened to be home that weekend. I had never seen that side of him before—the violence, the absolute madness in his eyes, just like our father's when he got angry. When he saw what our father was doing, something inside of him broke. He's never been the same since, especially after I told him everything that had been going on for years."

Naomi looked at her with questioning eyes.

Evelyn took a deep breath. "I had decided to tell my mom about what my dad did to me and my sister whenever she was gone. Eventually, I had to tell Eric about it too. I'm sure you can guess what it was I had to tell them—what kind of twisted abuse I had to endure from my own father."

"Yeah," she said with a lump in her throat. "I heard about that kind of stuff happening to people I knew in high school. They were seriously scarred for life. I can't even imagine." She couldn't, either. Her parents ignored her, but she suddenly realized how much worse things could have been. Then there was Brad. No, no, she had to try not to think about Brad.

"Yeah, I'm unable to have children because of it. He used to beat us if we resisted him, and I wanted it to stop. It was a bad idea. When he found out I had told our mother, he went after all three of us. He was drunk. He was always drunk. I'm lucky all I got was the scar."

Sick to her stomach, Naomi lowered her arms and sat on the sofa. "I didn't know about any of this," she said as her eyes glazed over. "Brad hit me once, but I never realized how bad he used to treat me until I came here. I never saw it before."

"You didn't know any different. I know exactly how that feels." She lowered her arms. "My dad is dead now. It finally feels like it's over, but I'll never be free until we move away from here. Italy was where I was happiest, and I'm dying to go back."

"That's why we're moving there?"

Nodding, Evelyn motioned her to stand up and finish the yoga. She did, but she could barely concentrate on the positions. Her heart beat fast as she thought about where things might have gone with Brad if she had never been kidnapped.

Two weeks later she was still thinking about it, but it had moved to a quieter place in her head as she lay sleepily on the loveseat in the living room. Mostly, she wanted to see Jesse again. The scent of red peppers and bacon was thick in the air. She pressed the pause button on her iPod when Eric walked in from the kitchen. He kneeled so she could see his face.

"Do you want two or three eggs?" he asked sweetly, and tucked a piece of hair behind her ear. She stared blankly at him.

"Three." She tried to breathe in the smell of Jesse from the couch pillow, from anywhere, but he had disappeared from everything.

Eric nodded and took his hand away from her ear. "Toast? Anything else? I'm cooking some bacon, and Evelyn bought some strawberries."

She looked into his caramel-brown eyes. Not one spark of anger. They were so kind now, so concerned for her all the time, especially the last two weeks. He was trying his best to smooth over Jesse's absence.

"If you put sugar on them," she said, wondering if she should still be angry with him for kicking Jesse out of the house. She missed him. Wildly. She missed him sitting next to her at dinner, his smiles across the pool table, his voice when he talked about books. She wanted his arms around her again. Right now she felt like she was in limbo waiting for him to come back so they could work things out. Eric might have urged him to pursue her, but the longer she thought about her relationship with him, the more she was convinced he really did care for her. Maybe that was Eric's plan all along, but she didn't care. Nobody could plan emotions. Nobody could plan for a person falling in love, could they?

He curled his fingers around her wrist. "Sure thing. I'll put lots of sugar on them." He leaned closer. "Try to cheer up, okay? I know you miss Jesse, but you'll see him again soon. I promise."

"Really?" She sat up. "He's coming back?"

He puffed out his chest and smiled. "Yes. He's been staying with a friend, but I've told him he can come back now. I think both you and he needed some time away from each other to sort out your emotions. Everything's going to be fine."

Naomi nodded. He was probably right, but it didn't make the separation any easier. She watched as he stood and switched on the television before heading back into the kitchen. Right now the weather report was on.

"The high today will be forty-seven with a low of nineteen. Low pressure could bring some snow later in the week."

She hit play on her iPod and tried to drown out everything but the music. She was listening to a playlist Jesse had made for her the last time they downloaded music together—a strange mix of Mozart and Chopin, some heavy metal bands, and one band that combined the two genres.

Just like him, she thought, concentrating on the hard, driving beat of intense guitars and drums layered against an ethereal mix of piano and female vocals. Everything mysterious about him suggested violence, but it was hidden from her beneath everything beautiful she craved about him, especially the way he touched her—as if nothing else in the world mattered but her. The violence was so hidden, in fact, that she didn't care about anything he had ever done wrong—or was doing, for that matter.

She settled farther into the loveseat and readjusted her earphones. The smell of cooking eggs drifted through the room. She knew Eric was doing everything he could to please her. They all were. She liked being fussed over. She liked the attention. She liked that she didn't have to worry about anything else going on in the outside world. If Jesse returned, life would be perfect again. She could get back to a place where she didn't think about her mother and father anymore. Brad was only a shadow now. Her parents could be too.

The song on her iPod ended.

"Yes, but is there any truth to the reports given at the beginning of your daughter's disappearance? You have both admitted—"

Another song began, loud and suddenly annoying. She slammed her finger on the pause button, sat up, and stared at the TV with wide eyes.

There she was, sitting on a sofa under the bright lights of the *Today Show,* dressed in one of her cream colored suits with her hair twisted into an elegant knot at the nape of her neck. Her hands were folded gently in her lap as she stared at the male host asking her a question. Naomi could tell she was irritated, a certain little twitch at the corner of her mouth before she spoke. Naomi hadn't realized she knew about that twitch, how ingrained it was in her memory. She couldn't recall making a note of it before.

"Of course there's truth to the reports," Karen answered calmly, professionally. "There has been a little more pressure about Naomi's disappearance than other missing children because ...." She paused, narrowed her eyes and twitched her foot with one short jerk before glancing at Naomi's father next to her on the sofa.

"We are both constantly in the public eye," she continued. "We're successful, isn't that right? It leads straight to your question if we neglected our daughter or not, and all I can say is that yes, because of our careers, we did." She leaned forward. "That doesn't mean we don't love her, and it doesn't mean we can't try to correct the mistakes we've made in the past."

The host acknowledged her answer with a brief smile and gestured to both of them. "Hence the reason you're here with us this morning. We'll talk about the foundation you've started in a few minutes, but let's discuss Naomi's photographs first. We wouldn't be speaking with you if they hadn't garnered so much attention."

Naomi's stomach churned. Her vision blurred. Her mind reeled. She could hardly focus on the TV now that the reality of what she was seeing hit her like an explosion deep in her heart. It finally burst, exactly like the green and yellow fireworks a few weeks ago. Only this time there was one loud, deafening boom that shook the entire center of her being.

That doesn't mean we don't love her.

Her parents were a distant memory suddenly rushing back—surreal, candid, and tangible. Was it true? Were they on national TV telling the world how they felt about her? Had they done this before? Was Eric lying to her every time he handed her an article and told her with saddened eyes that they were hopeless, inadequate, irredeemable?

No, he hadn't lied. She remembered him seeming very surprised, even upset.

The TV screen faded to a picture of a bright red starfish clinging to a craggy, black rock. Her starfish. Her picture. Something about a contest and a national magazine. It hadn't won, but then her mother kept entering more and more photos into contests, and this one finally won. Then one of the judges found out she was missing.

As the screen faded back to her mother, Naomi hardly saw her sitting under the lights. She could only see her in her bedroom in a white gown, eyes sparkling when she bent to kiss Naomi on the cheek. "Thanks for helping me with my zipper."

Naomi never saw her eyes that way again—until now, as she began to speak.

"The foundation is something we've started to help families with missing children. Many families aren't in a financial situation to continue searches on their own once the police or FBI stop investigating—when there is no more evidence or leads. The foundation we've started—Naomi's Hope—allows families to keep searching when all other hope is lost." Her face practically glowed with something Naomi had never seen before—pure happiness. Jason, grinning next to her, put a hand on hers.

Naomi couldn't believe what she was hearing. A foundation? Something outside of her father's company and her mother's law profession? Something completely unselfish?

She had always seen her parents as selfish beings, like two gluttonous creatures reveling in their work as she suffered in the background. Now that melted away.

"Have you continued the search for you daughter?" the host asked.

"Oh, yes."

"With any luck?"

Jason's expression crumpled and he fought to put it back to a smile. "No luck yet, but we won't stop trying."

The host nodded. "If you could tell your daughter anything right this moment, what would you say?"

Karen glanced at Jason, silent words passing between them. She smiled. "I would tell her how much I—"

The TV turned black. Naomi glanced at Eric now standing behind the loveseat with the remote clenched in one hand and a sugar spoon in the other.

"You don't need to see that," he growled. "Your breakfast is ready."

Her chest heaved as she struggled for breaths and fought to hold back the nausea rushing through her. "I'm not hungry," she stuttered as she scrambled off the loveseat. Her iPod slipped from her panicked fingers and fell to the floor.

"Naomi, calm down. We can talk through this. I didn't see what you were watching until it was too late. I didn't hear it all the way in the kitchen. If I had known—"

"Why didn't you tell me about them!" she screamed, surprised at her outburst and even more surprised at her accusation. "You knew they were doing this, didn't you? You knew they were still looking for me—that they *care.*"

His face turned bright red, but he remained calm. That was good, because she knew her outburst was cause for severe punishment. "I only knew a few weeks ago," he said stiffly. "None of this changes anything." He raised the sugar spoon. It trembled in his fingers. "They're only saying those things for the public. It doesn't change why you're here."

"Th-that's not true." The room spun around her so fast she thought she might fall down. Eric came closer and started to wrap his arms around her, but she yanked away.

"Don't touch me." She looked up at him through her tears, hoping to find a shred of peace in the world crumbling around her. He looked like he might be trying to sympathize, but mostly it seemed he was trying to contain his anger. His jaw was clenched, his eyes dark. He reached for her again, but she backed away as panic swirled her vision.

"Let me help you," he said, still moving toward her. "*We* care about you. Doesn't that matter?" His face softened in true pity, but it didn't help her.

"Turn it back on. I want to see them again."

She had gone too far. The pity in Eric's face melted into rage. "What have I told you before?" he growled, stepping closer. He threw the sugar spoon and remote onto the floor so hard that they bounced. "Don't ever yell at me again and don't ever tell me what to do or I'll hit you so hard you'll bleed for a damn week. Your parents are nothing. *Nothing.*" He moved closer, every muscle in his body ready to hit her.

She backed away, trembling. "No," she whispered.

In a burst of energy, she raced past him to the stairs and up to her room. She slammed the door and ran into the bathroom, locking the door behind her. Her entire body shook. He couldn't get to her in here. He couldn't tell her what to do. She had to be strong now that she knew the truth—and that truth was bitter. It came up her throat as she dropped to her knees in front of the toilet and fell apart at the seams.

XXIV

EVELYN POUNDED ON THE DOOR FOR THIRTY MINUTES.
Naomi didn't answer. She tried to plug her ears, but the
words still got through.

"Honey, please come out! We have to go to work,
but we need to know if you're all right. Eric said you
saw your parents on the TV. Sweetie, we can talk about
this. You're very hurt. You know you can talk to me
about anything."

Naomi curled herself into a ball on the cold
bathroom floor and squeezed her eyes closed so tightly
that no tears could escape them. She didn't want to cry
anymore. It was stupid to cry.

"Naomi! Open the door!" Evelyn pounded harder.
"Honey, please."

She curled tighter. Her body trembled. All she
could see was a red starfish and her mother's eyes,
twinkling with what had to be love. They loved her.
They had started a foundation in *her* name. They had
changed. It was all over their faces, and no matter how
much she didn't want to believe it, she couldn't get it
out of her head. She wanted to throw up again, but
nothing was left.

"I'm leaving," Evelyn said with a heavy sigh. "If
you don't open the door when I get back I'll have Steve
force the lock open. You can't stay in there forever."

Naomi repeated those words in her head all day long as she stayed on the floor, trying not to cry. After several hours, she took off her clothes and stepped into the shower where she finally let the tears come.

Then Steve got home from work and forced open the lock to let Evelyn inside.

Only, it wasn't Evelyn.

"Jesse, you can't go in there!" Evelyn's voice yelled out. "She's in the shower. She might not want—"

"I'll handle this," Jesse growled and slammed the door. When he pulled open the shower curtain she backed into the farthest corner, covering herself the best she could. He kept his eyes on her face and held out a towel. He looked sad.

"You can't stay in here forever."

"That's what Evelyn said." The water was turning cold. She shut it off and snatched the towel, hurriedly wrapping it around her naked body. She was sure Jesse had caught glimpses of everything. Part of her didn't care.

"She's right. How long have you been standing here under the cold water?" He folded his arms.

Her teeth chattering, she whispered, "I don't know." Then she knotted her brow. "When did you get back?"

"Thirty minutes ago. Eric called me from his office and told me I had to get here to calm you down."

She looked at her towel and considered the heavy emotions in her heart. "I don't need to calm down," she muttered. "Look at me—I'm not screaming or anything. I'm perfectly fine."

"I don't believe that." He narrowed his eyes and stepped closer. "Evelyn said you saw your parents on TV. What happened?"

Her teeth were still chattering. She wrapped the towel closer just as Jesse gave her his hand. At least he wanted to help her and he was being calm about it. She had to admit she was happy to see him, even past all the drama in her head.

She took his hand and stepped out, allowing him to pull her into his arms. He held her tightly. It was only natural to rest against him, a sigh of relief escaping her mouth. He was safe to her. Through all of the crap she was feeling, he was the only one she wanted to help her.

"Tell me, Naomi. I'm here."

"I don't want to talk about it." She was surprised at the monotone sound of her voice, as if something inside of her had died. She felt weak from hunger and crying.

"Try," he said, and put a finger beneath her chin to lift her face up to his. When she looked into his eyes she saw no impatience, no frustration. He wasn't going to make her answer his questions this time. Something inside of her opened, and any doubt she had felt for his affection melted away. She took a deep breath. She could tell him.

"They were on the *Today Show* talking about a foundation they've started. They're still looking for me. They're different. They've … changed." Fresh tears welled in her eyes. She tried to keep them back, but it was impossible. Jesse pulled her close again, stroking her bare shoulder blades, but not in an erotic way. Every movement he made was filled with concern.

"I had no idea about any of this," he said. "We haven't been keeping an eye on any recent news reports about you. We got lazy."

"Would you have told me even if you had?"

Silence. She knew the answer. They would never have risked telling her about the foundation or her parents' altered feelings. She closed her eyes and held her breath. Maybe their feelings weren't altered. Maybe they had loved her all along. That thought hurt most of all.

"Come on," Jesse said, releasing her. "Let's get you in some clothes so you can rest."

Nodding, she watched as he turned and opened the door. She had expected Evelyn to be waiting, but the room was empty. She followed him to her dresser where he opened a few drawers.

"You don't have to do everything for me," she said as he searched through the drawers. "My pants are the third one down."

He pulled it open and looked over his shoulder. "Just let me help you, all right? You're a wreck. Go sit down."

"Are you going to search through my underwear drawer, too?" She walked to her bed and sat on the edge, wrapping her arms around herself.

He turned around and waved a pair of panties at her. "Already did. Does that bother you?"

"No." She took the clothes he handed her. He had picked one of her favorite outfits, and she realized how much attention he paid to things like that. At any other time she might have stood and hugged him, but right now all she wanted to do was curl up under the covers and cry herself to sleep. She couldn't get her parents out of her head. They buried everything else.

"I'm staying here until I know you're okay," he said as she stood to put the clothes on. His eyes met hers before he turned around. "Get dressed."

Staring at his back, she dropped the towel. She knew he wouldn't turn around. He had already seen her naked anyway, so what did it matter? Her heart beat fast at the trust she felt for him, at how he had never forced her to do anything and she knew he never would.

"I'm finished," she said softly.

He turned and nudged her to the bed. "Lie down."

She didn't fight him. She knew he wanted to hold her again like he had so many months ago. It was exactly what she needed. When she was on the bed she turned her back to him and waited for him to crawl beside her. He pulled her close.

"Now tell me why seeing your parents on TV was so upsetting."

She closed her eyes and took a shuddering breath. She would not cry. She wouldn't. "Don't you understand?" she whispered. "I haven't seen them for a year. You and the others made me believe they didn't care, and now it's obvious they do."

With his other hand he smoothed her wet hair away from her face. "I don't think we made you believe anything," he said. "We only built on the truth—on what you told us yourself that night Eric slapped you. Don't you remember?"

"Yes, I do." She clenched her jaw.

"I don't know what's happened with your parents," he said, still stroking her hair. She was sure his shirt was soaked by now. "All I know is that I've seen you happy here—happier than you've probably been anywhere else. Isn't that right?"

She concentrated on his warmth and inched closer to him, if it was possible to get any closer. He spoke the truth, but she still ached inside. Now that she knew her parents loved her, something felt unresolved. A door had opened, and she didn't know if she could ever close it and walk away.

Jesse was quiet for a long time. He didn't urge her to answer his question. She relaxed against him and her eyes began to droop.

"Naomi," he finally said, a slight tremble in his voice.

"Yes?"

"I have to leave again for a few days. There's something I have to do."

Her eyes popped open. "Leave again? You just got back. When are you finally going to stay?" Twisting, she looked him in the face. He appeared defeated somehow, as if he had been punched in the gut. That made her hurt too. "I don't think I can handle you leaving again," she said. "Seriously, I really, really don't. Please, Jesse …."

"Don't worry," he said, and nudged her back onto her side. "Get some rest. I'll be here when you wake up."

He left the next day, promising her he would be back soon. From her bedroom window she watched him drive away in Steve's car just as Evelyn came in with her cleaning supplies.

"Bathroom-cleaning day," she said in a happy voice. "You want to do yoga when I'm finished?"

Naomi turned around, her shoulders drooping. "I guess so."

"Oh, honey, he'll be back soon."

"I know."

She raised her bucket of supplies. "Want to help? Get your mind off things?"

"Sure."

As she sprayed the tiles down with a cleaner that smelled like mint, Naomi thought about how much time she had spent in the shower during her first few days in the house. She ran a cloth over the grout where she had etched the thirty-five marks and wondered what Evelyn had thought when she first saw them. She must have noticed.

"Thanks for helping," Evelyn said as she climbed onto the counter to reach the top of the mirror.

"I don't mind. It's my mess, after all."

"Not much of a mess." She laughed. "You used to be messier."

"Really?"

"Yes, but it was never bad, I promise." Evelyn winked.

Then Naomi remembered how she had never cleaned a bathroom before she had come here. She often helped Evelyn, and it made her appreciate Mindy's job back home. She was forgetting what Mindy looked like, but she could remember her mother, especially now. Seeing her face on the TV made it seem like only yesterday that she had last seen her.

"Are you all right, Naomi?" Evelyn stopped wiping the mirror and lowered herself off the counter. "Jesse said he smoothed things over with you, but I'm worried."

Finished with the tiles, Naomi turned and stepped out of the tub. "I'm not going to try to leave," she said with a deep sigh, and shrugged. "There wouldn't be any point."

"I suppose not." Evelyn pulled her into a hug. "Eric's going to be with you this evening while Steve and I go out. Remember that opera I've been talking about for months?"

She nodded. Evelyn had been looking forward to the opera forever, and now it was finally here. "Did you get that dress?" she asked, remembering the dress Evelyn had shown her online.

"I did. It fits beautifully, but I need to decide on a necklace. Will you help me pick one later?"

"Sure."

That night she stood in front of Evelyn's dresser. Staring down at four necklaces spread across the cherry wood, she ran her fingers over the diamonds and pearls and stopped at a gold chain studded with two rows of diamonds. Rubies sparkled in the center.

Her fingers trembled as a sudden thought entered her head. Had Jesse stolen this jewelry?

She looked up to see Evelyn standing in the bathroom applying her makeup. She was stunning. The bodice of her gown was fitted and laced, the skirt suddenly full at the hips. Gathers cascaded all the way down the back, falling to the floor in a waterfall of brilliant red. She blinked her brown eyes and smiled at Naomi in the mirror.

"Choose one yet?"

"I think so." She turned back to the necklace and picked it up, the stones cold and smooth in her hands. She imagined Jesse snatching it from a safe with gloved hands, his eyes glowing green through a mask. She set it back on the dresser.

He couldn't have stolen it. They weren't that stupid. They didn't keep anything they took, except for her. They sold all the jewelry so they could live in Italy, wealthy, free and happy for the rest of their lives. She knew they hadn't spent a dime of jewelry money, not yet. She had overheard them say it was to live on once they were in Italy. They would never have to work again, and that suited Naomi just fine. No temptations to ignore her for a career. No getting up to leave every morning. Together and happy all the time, free to do anything and go anywhere they wished. It sounded divine. Perfect.

At least, that's what she was trying to convince herself, but thoughts of her mother kept interrupting the dream.

She lowered her gaze to a small, gold-framed photo on the dresser. It was the house in Italy. That much was obvious. It took her breath away.

Situated on a hill overlooking the countryside, it was built mostly of stone with panoramic windows and manicured trees shading the upper yard. She could see a hint of rustic furniture through the windows, and a wide patio surrounded by lattice work.

"Evelyn," she said quietly, "why are there people living in it right now?"

Evelyn turned away from the bathroom mirror. "Oh, you found the picture of the house. I should have shown you that before." Turning back to the mirror, she continued her makeup. "There are people living there because my grandmother sold it to a business that rents it out to temporary tenants. That's when we moved to an apartment in Arezzo, near Florence."

"You wanted to buy it back?"

"Of course. It's where my mother grew up, but she never had the time or money to go back after she moved here to the States." Her shoulders dropped. "I don't think she would have liked that my grandmother sold it."

"But it's yours now, right?"

She shoved a bobby pin into her hair. "Oh, yes. It's what I've always wanted most—to raise a family where I remember being so happy. It was my dream to adopt a child once we were there for a few years, but now we have you, and Steve and Eric made sure to—" She stopped, lowered her hands from her hair, and turned to Naomi with a relieved smile. "They installed a swimming pool last year. You'll really like it there. I promise."

A child. She figured that's why Evelyn was so attached to her, but it was all right. It felt good for someone to want her that way.

"A swimming pool sounds nice," she said, her voice distant. She imagined swimming under a hot, blue Italian sky with Jesse next to her. She could feel his hands caressing her waist as he pressed his lips to hers. They tasted of garlic and wine from the dinner they had eaten on the sun-drenched patio. He would read to her in the evening before bed, and hold her through the night as she dreamed about growing older. She would forget what it felt like to be a child, even at seventeen when she thought Brad was her future, when he held her in his fist like a bird with broken wings, squeezing so tightly she didn't know what was sky and what was ground.

Now she knew. Now she could see the sky unfolding before her, the color of sapphires in Jesse's open palm, his eyes telling her, *I'll stay with you because I've never felt like this about anybody.*

"Oh, the rubies," Evelyn exclaimed as she walked over to her and noticed the necklace Naomi had chosen. Smiling, she lifted it from the dresser. "It was my mother's." She pulled the chain around her neck and her fingers fumbled with the clasp. "Naomi, could you?"

She tore her eyes from the picture and reached up to fasten the necklace. She caught a glimpse of herself in the mirror, small and plain next to Evelyn's magnificence.

It was a familiar vision, Naomi thought bitterly. It was how she felt about her mother, how she would never be her equal, never be as beautiful, successful, or happy with what she had chosen in her life. She was nothing but a pale, silvery imitation trying to follow in her footsteps. Forever.

Her fingers slipped from the unclasped necklace as she realized that she had, in fact, never resented her mother. It was the exact opposite. She wanted to be just like her. That happy. That sure of herself.

"Oh!" Evelyn said as the necklace fell to the floor with a metallic thud.

"I'll get it." Her body breaking into a sweat, Naomi stepped around the full red skirt of the dress.

"Oh, thanks. I can't bend over in this thing. It has a corset. I can barely breathe."

Strange, Naomi thought as she scooped the necklace into her clammy hands. It was difficult for her to breathe too.

XXV

THAT NIGHT ERIC LET HER WATCH A MOVIE IN THE living room while he worked in his office. Halfway through the movie she went into the kitchen to fix herself a cup of hot cocoa. Evelyn bought the kind she liked with the little marshmallows in the packet. Jesse liked that kind too, and as she stirred the mix into the hot water she thought about how he had held her until she fell asleep. He was there when she woke up in the morning. He hadn't moved an inch. Then he left.

With a sigh, she sat at the table and put her head in her hands. How many times would he leave? She felt the strongest connection to him, like a string stretching to the breaking point every time he was away. One day it would snap If he didn't knock it off. What could he possibly have to leave for again? Eric hadn't ordered him away.

She lifted her head and took a sip of cocoa. She could see Eric sitting at his desk in his office. He was on the phone and smiled when he looked up at her. He mouthed "Pizza," and pointed to the phone receiver.

She nodded. Pizza sounded good. Then again, so did some fresh air. She hadn't been outside in so long. She envied Jesse's freedom to leave the house and drive away.

Lowering her eyes to the table, she studied the newspaper Steve had left sitting by his reading glasses.

Then she froze.

A magazine poked out from beneath the newspaper, an article partially visible. She read what she could of the title: *Revealing the Mysteries Behind Abusive Emotional Bonding: A Closer Look Into—*

Somebody had gone through the article and highlighted specific sections in bright yellow, like a homework assignment. Her stomach sank. Slowly, she reached forward and pulled the article out from underneath the newspaper. A part of her wanted to ignore it, forget she had seen it, but the other part of her couldn't stop. She had to see what it said. Yellow highlighted paragraphs. She made herself read one of them. Her fingers started to go numb.

Further research has shown that the largely accepted idea of consistent positive treatment is perhaps not the strongest way humans secure attachment to others ... hostages often bond to their captors most strongly when those captors consistently reward good behavior and severely punish bad behavior (often physically or with threats of death). This also occurs frequently in romantic relationships where abusive control is prevalent.

Naomi swallowed and pushed the article away. There were a lot more paragraphs highlighted. She wondered why they would highlight them. It was sick and wrong. Was it because they were studying better ways to gain her loyalty—to get her to bond to them more strongly than before? Standing, she met Eric's eyes and swallowed.

It wasn't that she had never realized what they were doing to her, but seeing those sections highlighted made her want to throw up. It made their actions seem shallow. Fake. Did they really care for her or was it only for their own benefit, their own safety, to keep her freaking mouth shut?

She left her mug on the table and headed upstairs to her room. She had to think. She went straight to her bed and grabbed her journal from the nightstand. When she opened it, the smell of ink drifted to her nose. She scanned passages about Jesse and her mother, noticing that she sometimes talked about Evelyn and the others, but not often. The entries progressed from mentions of escape and thoughts about home to nothing but Jesse and occasionally her mother.

Then, in one entry near the end, she stopped and read a line that made her hands shake.

When Jesse comes home we can talk about what happened.

She thought of this house as her home now. They had made sure she saw it that way, even if the rational side of her brain told her exactly how they had done it. Was it wrong? She saw herself standing in front of an open door, blue sky and the ocean on the other side. That door had opened when she saw her parents on TV. Could she really turn away?

She had already turned away, she realized. Now she had to turn back. A knock on the door made her slam the journal shut and throw it under the covers. Eric stepped inside, confusion on his face. "Are you all right?"

"Yeah," she said with a shrug. "I just came up to get a book. It must be in the den."

"I was heading there anyway. Come on. You can read while we wait for the pizza."

Nodding, she followed him down the hall and into the den. She tried to keep her eyes away from the double glass doors where the night was already cold and black. Her heart pounded as she imagined swinging herself over the railing of the balcony—right onto the tree branch. She sat in the armchair closest to the balcony doors. Her shoulders slumped.

Eric raised his eyebrows. "Didn't you want a book?"

She shrugged again. "Not really, I guess. I'm just hungry."

"Well, I ordered your favorite." He headed straight for her. "Pepperoni and olives, right?"

She looked up at him as he stopped in front of the armchair. He was dressed the same as the first time she had seen him—jeans and a black T-shirt. He was clean-shaven.

"Thank you," she mumbled, sliding her trembling fingers beneath her thighs.

He kneeled and put a hand on her knee. "Jesse's coming back soon. Everything will be okay." His hand tensed. "Nothing has changed."

She nodded, but her mind was a million miles away, focused on her journal. She hadn't noticed before how her handwriting was just like her mother's. It had the same feel, the same personality.

"Do you want me to get you anything?" Eric interrupted her thoughts. "Do you want a drink before our dinner comes?"

She shifted beneath the weight of his hand on her knee. He would have to leave when the pizza came to the front door. She would be alone for at least three or four minutes while he paid the delivery boy and got plates and napkins. Her eyes glazed over.

"Naomi?"

"Oh, sorry." She changed her stupid expression to a sloppy grin. "Sure, a drink sounds good, if there's Coke."

She hoped there wasn't. The last time she had looked, the stash of Coke in the fridge was gone. Eric knew as well as she did that Evelyn kept more in the pantry downstairs. The longer she could get him out of the room the better.

"Sure." He stood and headed for the fridge. She waited with frozen breath, staring at the bookshelves. She had read so many books in the past year.

"No Coke up here," he muttered. "There might be some down in the pantry, but it'll be warm. Sure you don't want anything else?"

"I can drink it with ice."

The refrigerator door closed. "Okay. I'll be right back." He was halfway across the room before he turned around and walked back. "I thought you might want your iPod. I brought it from downstairs." He fished it out of his pocket and handed it to her.

As he left, she clenched her jaw and thought about the painting in her mother's room. A white flower. Innocence. What would her mother think if she knew she had never tried to escape this prison? She would be hurt. Her father would be hurt. Brad would be hurt. Her entire life led to this moment, this decision. She squeezed her hands into fists as fear gripped her heart. It wasn't fear for what she was about to attempt. It was fear at what she was, at the cowardice she had let consume her. It was selfish. It was wrong.

For the first time in her life she understood how ugly her weakness had become. She didn't understand how Jesse could care for her, how any of them could.

She stood and paced in front of the bookshelves and glanced at titles Jesse had given her to read. Her heart sank at the thought of him. If she managed to escape, would she ever see him again? Would she want to? She had a hard time imagining what her life would be like outside of these walls, what doors would open, how her mind might break free. She had shaken herself free of

Brad; it was time to wake up. The article had made it clear she still had some sense left in her head. If she didn't hold onto that and at least attempt to leave, she might never have the chance again. It was more about finally choosing something brave than anything else, and it made her sick inside to continue on as she was, the girl stuck in a box, the girl who wrote in her journal about everything except herself because she had never known who she was or what she really wanted.

Tears filled her eyes. It had to be now.

Stuffing her iPod into her sweatshirt pocket, she walked to the balcony doors. She saw her reflection in the glass, the girl she had become, and she wanted nothing more than to walk beyond that girl and finally grow up. Her hand shook as she turned the handle and stepped out into the frigid night.

XXVI

THE FIRST THING SHE SAW WHEN SHE HOISTED HERSELF
onto the branch was a stone walkway on the other side
of the fence. It looked like a fifteen-foot drop. She was
insane. If she had stopped to think about how far it was
to the ground she might never have stood from the
armchair.

Now it was too late.

Wincing, she pushed her bare feet against the tree
bark as she held tightly to the branch overhead. She
took two more steps forward and inched her fingers
across the branch. The bark was cold and icy in the
chilled air. She glanced over her shoulder through the
glass doors. He was still gone.

She took another step, her breath rising in thin,
misty clouds around her face. There was no grass where
she could land, only stone. Crap. She had to keep going.
For once in her life, she had to do something brave. Eric
wouldn't catch her. No way in hell. She would jump
and get to her feet and run so fast he would never see
her.

One more step. She slipped. Gasping, she clutched
tightly to the branch above and righted herself. A
weight shifted in her sweatshirt pocket. Looking down,
she saw her iPod slip out. She let go of the branch with
one hand and caught the iPod in her trembling fingers.

"You idiot!" she hissed as she swayed. She had to get to the edge and jump. Eric would be back any second. The iPod was heavy in her hand. She stared at it and thought of Jesse. So much of his music was on it, but she couldn't think of him. Not right now. If she did, she would turn around and settle right back into the armchair. She couldn't think about any of them. She had to keep going. This was the only way to escape that reflection in the glass, the weakness she had let overtake her.

One, two, three steps.

She swayed and straightened as she pushed the iPod back into her sweatshirt pocket. One more step and she would be clear of the fence. She could jump. She could finally make a choice.

She shut her eyes and tried not to feel the cold air biting through her clothes. She was leaving Jesse forever. The police would make her tell them everything, but how could she? How could she hurt him? Any of them? Maybe *that* was weakness.

Shaking her head, she cursed. How could she do this? Which was the right choice?

It didn't matter. She had to keep moving forward. One more step and it would be too late to change her mind. She felt ice beneath her feet just before she slipped one last time. Down, down, down. Screaming, she grabbed for anything solid and caught hold of the branch where she had been standing, her bare feet dangling in the air as she watched the iPod slip from her pocket once again and plunge to the ground. It shattered into pieces that skittered across the stone walkway. Pink plastic and metal, a cracked screen, headphones flailed out like a white snake.

Jesse had warned her not to try to escape. He knew what would happen. He knew she was weak.

Her fingers slipped. Tears stung her eyes. She tried to imagine her mother's arms holding her close, pulling her tighter as her fingers finally lost their grip. Angry pain stabbed through her ankle. Twisting her body, the stones were cold through her pants and against her cheek. She had to sit up. She had to run!

She scrambled to her feet in a rush of adrenaline. With one last look at the broken iPod, she ran as best she could through the neighbor's front yard and down the sidewalk. Her ankle felt like it might break and she gasped in pain. She pretended not to hear Eric's footsteps behind her. She didn't look back. Maybe one of the neighbors would answer their door, but most of the houses were dark. One looked like someone was awake. Past the stop sign. She had to get there.

He rushed up behind her near an empty intersection, right next to the stop sign, and grabbed her arm, swinging her around to face him. Silent words formed on his lips. Disappointment clouded his eyes.

Still pumped with adrenaline, she tried to yank free from his grip, but he wrenched her close to his body and kept her there as he forced her back to the house. A scream built up in her throat, but he clamped his hand over her mouth before it escaped.

In a calm voice he whispered, "As soon as we get back inside, I'm going to kill you."

She wasn't sure if he was serious, but he had to be. This was the last straw, the last time he would put up with her defiance. Still, she fought with herself to believe he would actually end her life after all the time she had spent with them. Evelyn loved her.

He dragged her inside and headed straight for his bedroom.

"I'm sorry," she whimpered the moment he shoved her in the room and let go of her arm. "I don't know what I was thinking. I promise I'll never—"

"Shut up!" He slammed a fist into her face so hard she almost fell over. Stumbling backward, she caught her balance and touched her cheek. It hurt worse than the first time he had hit her, only this time there was no blood. Not yet.

"Eric, I—"

"I told you to shut up!" He grabbed her shoulders and slammed her into a shelf. Books tumbled to the floor. He glared into her face and ground his teeth. A scream rose up her throat, but she swallowed it back down. He let her go. "You'll stay right there while I get my gun or I'll hit you a lot harder."

Crying, she fell to her knees and wiped away hot tears. She had to stay calm. She knew he could be reasoned with. Maybe. He pulled a thin, black box from the top shelf of his closet.

"Damn lock," he muttered, slamming the box onto a clean desk next to the bed. He fiddled with a combination on the front and glanced at her to make sure she was wasn't moving.

She wasn't. She bit her lip and gave him a hopeful expression. "Eric, I'm so sorry. It's just that I saw my parents. I swear I wasn't going tell anybody about you. I could never—"

"I told you to shut up!" His lips curled around his teeth. "I trusted you." He fumbled with the lock. His hands were shaking. "I promised I'd kill you if you ever tried to get away. I'll have to take you out to the garage where a mess won't matter." Opening the lock, he lifted the lid and picked up the gun. It was silver with a black grip—larger than she would have expected. Her heart dropped to her toes. He was really going to kill her.

She wouldn't waste any more time.

Scrambling to her feet, she bolted out of the bedroom. She passed Jesse's room and rounded the corner, heading straight for the front door. Her ankle buckled. Right behind her, Eric growled and shoved her to the floor. He grabbed a handful of her hair and smacked her head against the tile. Pain sliced behind her eyes. This was it. She had gone too far, pushed him over the edge. She gulped down a scream. Everything inside of her hurt. Her ankle throbbed.

"I didn't think you were this stupid," he growled, forcing her to look at him. "Why are you doing this? *Why?*"

She stared into his eyes, black and angry, and blinked away a fresh set of tears. She tried to think past the throbs of pain on the side of her head, but nothing came.

He tightened his grip. "Answer me!" It was almost a plea, his voice strained.

"You were going to kill me," she whimpered. "Of course I'm going to run!"

"But you've never tried to get away. Not once. Why the hell would you do it now?"

What was he getting at? She couldn't possibly explain how she was beginning to see herself as someone who could decide things on her own, how trying to escape was more about something inside of her than anything else. Could he understand that? It didn't matter. She saw the impatience in his eyes and knew she had to say something fast.

"I thought you cared about me." She tried to make it sound as pathetic as she possibly could. "You told me you do."

His grip loosened. Silence gathered around them, nearly tangible as she focused on what she believed were tears in the corners of his eyes. He blinked them away and tightened his grip once again. She gasped.

"If you're going to change your mind about us," he said through gritted teeth, "then I don't have a choice. I can't allow you to do this again. I've risked too much, made too many promises—to myself and Steve, but mostly to Evie." He leaned closer. "I have to be able to trust you."

Her breaths came in spurts. She was on her side, twisted awkwardly to face him as he clutched her hair. Something in his expression spoke to her. He cared for her. She had seen it before, but never so raw. He was fighting it.

Her heart softened and slowed as she understood that he wouldn't kill her if she made the decision to forget about her parents and stay—*really* made the decision to stay. He would know if she was lying.

He released his grip on her hair and carefully helped her sit up. She glanced at the untied laces of his tennis shoes. He must have put them on just before bolting out the front door to chase her down. She had forgotten what it felt like to wear shoes.

He peered into her eyes. "Can I trust you? You have no idea how badly I want to trust you. I did trust you, and Evie loves you. You've made her so happy. If I kill you, she'll … she'll …." He paused and cupped her face in his hands. They were steady. "Please tell me you won't do this again. Promise me."

Her heart pounded. He was looking at her with such desperation, but how could she possibly promise him such a thing when all she wanted now was to feel some tiny measure of freedom inside her own heart? She had thought she was free in so many ways, but now that she had seen her mother and couldn't reach her, she was starting to see freedom differently.

She closed her eyes. It was clear to her now why it frightened Eric to kill her. He was afraid to lose her—to lose anybody he cared for. As long as he had someone with him, he didn't have to face himself or the reality of how much his own father's mistakes had hurt him—and changed him. His father had murdered his mother and sister, and it was clear now how deeply that ran inside him. It was as deep and painful as her feelings for her mother. If he killed her, Evelyn might not forgive him, and he would face even more of the loneliness that frightened him so much.

For the first time, she looked into his eyes and saw a glimmer of the real person behind the anger and pain. He was kind and compassionate. He was hurt. He had been hurting for years.

"Naomi?" he asked, almost pleading. "Can you promise me?"

The doorbell rang. It had to be the pizza.

He let go of her shoulders, but didn't move. He was waiting for an answer. She looked up and saw the baseball hat of the delivery boy silhouetted through the beveled glass. The brief thought of what might happen if she stood up and yanked the door open raced through her mind, but instead she looked back at Eric and chewed her lip. She had to give him an answer.

"I promise," she said quietly, hoping it didn't sound too hollow.

He studied her face before helping her stand. She cried out in pain. "My ankle's broken. It kills!"

"I'll bet it's just a sprain. Let's get you on the couch." He helped her to the living room where she sat down with a heavy sigh and then watched him open the door to pay for the pizza.

Later, as she nibbled at a piece of pizza and held an ice pack to her ankle, she mumbled repeated apologies for betraying his trust. He watched her from across the room, but didn't say anything.

Jesse came home two days later. She rushed into his arms. Seeing him clicked her feelings into place. She had made the right decision. Staying with him was her choice, the best choice, the only choice now. He was all she needed, because with him she could be strong.

"I missed you so much," she whimpered into his shoulder as he pulled her tightly to him.

"I missed you too, Naomi." His voice was soft and fragile, as if it might break.

Everything about him made her heart melt—the way she knew every detail of his face but could see there was more underneath, more to discover. The smell of him wrapped around her once again. His arms were protective. When he kissed her, she knew he was in love with her. He had to be in love with her, the way he looked like he might kill someone when he spotted the bruises on her face.

He left her sitting on the couch and went into Eric's office. As soon as the yelling started, Evelyn pulled her upstairs and told her to wait in her room.

"I'll make sure Jesse comes up to see you." Before turning to close the door, she gave Naomi a gentle hug and kissed her on the cheek over the bruise from Eric's knuckles. The kiss was soft and smelled of roses from her perfume. Eric's yelling drifted up the stairs.

"Evelyn, what if he tells Jesse to leave again? I don't think I can handle that." Panic started in her heart and rippled through her body. "I can't, I can't, I can't." She squeezed her eyes shut. "If he leaves, I'll have nothing left. Nothing. I can't—"

Evelyn touched her face and she opened her eyes.

"Sweetheart, please calm down. Jesse will be fine. He's not going anywhere, I promise. I'll make sure they talk through things without killing each other." She turned and closed the door behind her without fastening the locks.

Burying herself beneath the bedcovers, she trembled from the excitement of seeing Jesse again. Despite Eric's attempts to keep her ankle iced and wrapped, it still throbbed. It hadn't broken, but it was a terrible sprain. It didn't matter now. She held onto her pillow and looked at the stack of books on her nightstand. Her mother's book was at the bottom. She looked away.

When Jesse let himself in an hour later, she looked him in the eyes. "Are you angry with me for trying to leave? It wasn't that I wanted to leave *you*. It's just that I saw how bad it was not to try. I don't know if that makes any sense."

He approached the bed. "I'm not sure I understand completely, but you don't seem like you're too eager to try again."

"No," she said and lowered her eyes. "I want to see my parents, but a part of me knows it would be awful. It would be pointless, and if I have you it's okay that I don't see them." She looked up. "It's just that I found an article on the table, and there were these highlighted paragraphs in yellow about abusive behavior and emotional bonding. It made me realize how I've been— I mean how you've manipulated—I mean … so you're not angry with me?"

"No." He tightened his jaw. "I'm angry with Eric, but that's over now."

"Really?"

Nodding, he sat down and curled a hand around her cheek. "I'm so sorry," he whispered. "I'm sorry for everything I've done to you—for any pain you've felt while we've kept you here."

She held her breath and looked at him in the dim light from the lamp. Her breaths turned into quiet, excited gasps.

"I know you've never meant to hurt me," she answered carefully. "I could never be angry with you."

"I think I already knew you would say that." He inched closer as his smile faded to a frown. "Nobody will ever hurt you again." He sat on the edge of the bed and leaned in to kiss her. She melted against him, pulling him on top of her.

XXVII

THE SUN WAS SHINING THROUGH THE WINDOW WHEN she woke. Jesse was next to her, his arms wrapped tightly around her bare middle. She let out a happy sigh and snuggled into him.

"Good morning," he said, squeezing her tighter. "Did you sleep all right?"

"You have no idea," she said, laughing as she twisted around to look at him. "I didn't know it could be that good. Brad never ...." Her voice faded away.

"Brad never what?"

She forced herself to shrug as if what she had realized was nothing. Only, it was everything.

"He was never like you," she said, thinking about how her body didn't hurt like most times she had slept with Brad.

Jesse's eyebrows knotted. "You haven't told me everything about him, have you? He hurt you more than you let on."

She looked away. Her body tensed as she remembered Brad's bed and the smell of his cologne on the pillows. His quilt was old and fraying on the edges. She used to wind the strings around her fingers as Brad told her to hold still so he could do whatever he wanted to her. He claimed it was to please her, but it never did. Not really.

"He liked things a certain way, is all," she said. "He thought pain was what I wanted—what turned me on. It turned *him* on, but I ... it was too much, and I was too afraid to tell him because I knew he wouldn't stop. I know this sounds crazy, but I thought it was how sex was supposed to be. I thought it was normal. I just ... I never knew any different." Cold seeped into her toes and crawled up her legs, creeping toward her heart.

"Keep going. Get it out." He stroked her face.

"I never saw it until now," she stuttered, keeping her eyes on his. "Last night with you was perfect. You didn't hurt me. You didn't force me to do anything." She shuddered as the iciness in her heart filled her head. She felt like she had been dunked in water and couldn't breathe. "It wasn't all about you." She focused on his hand stroking her face. It was the only warm thing on her body.

"Of course it wasn't all about me. Naomi, I've waited a long time for this, but I have to admit it used to be for selfish reasons. Now it's not."

She waited for him to say the three little words she longed to hear. Instead, he kissed her.

When they went downstairs, hand-in-hand, Evelyn looked up from her cereal, her eyes widening. "Good morning," she stuttered.

Jesse smiled. "No jokes, Evelyn."

"Didn't cross my mind." She went back to her cereal.

"Good." He squeezed Naomi's hand. "I'm going to take a shower. You get some breakfast, okay?"

"Sure." She went straight for the cereal cupboard and poured herself a bowl.

"Sugar's over here," Evelyn said from the table. She grinned as Naomi sat down across from her. "So, was it good?"

Blushing, she snatched the sugar spoon from the bowl. "Uh, yeah, it was." She didn't know how it was possible to feel so confused and satisfied at the same time. She had never felt that way with Brad.

Evelyn reached forward and touched her hand. Her eyes were troubled, but happy too. "Please let me know if you need anything. If you have any questions or problems, I'm here for you, okay? You need to make sure you're being safe. We don't want you to get—"

"Jesse's taking care of all of that." She shifted in her chair. "I'm all right."

Nodding, Evelyn smiled. "Do you think you're in love with him now?"

She took a big bite of cereal and shrugged. "I don't know what it would feel like," she said through her chewing.

"From the way you're glowing, I'd say you are."

She swallowed and took another bite. To say she was glowing sounded cheesy, but at the same time Evelyn wasn't far off the mark.

For the next two weeks Jesse spent every night in her room. They stayed up late, talking about Italy and what they would do when they got there.

"I've only been there once," he said as she relaxed in his arms and looked into his eyes. She couldn't get enough of them. "When we've traveled everywhere you want to visit, we'll go to other countries. I like Ireland the best."

She giggled. "Why? Because you're Irish?"

"My ancestors are Irish, yes." He squeezed her. "Do you know where yours are from?"

"No."

"We'll find out." Pausing, he brushed her cheek with his hand. "Unless that would make you uncomfortable. You might not want to think about your family."

"It's okay. I knew both my grandpas when I was little. I remember my mom's dad used to give me M&Ms. He always picked out the green ones for me. I like green."

"M&Ms?"

"The color. Your eyes are green, you know."

"I know, believe it or not." He laughed and she snuggled into him. She was almost nineteen. She didn't feel nineteen. In a lot of ways, she still felt small and childish, but Jesse helped that go away. When he held her, she was strong and happy at the same time. He was the only person who had ever made her feel that way.

With a heavy sigh, she traced her fingers over his lips. They were soft and smiling. She touched his eyes, his delicate lashes, his freckles. "Who are you?" she asked softly. "Will I ever know?"

His smile faded, but not from anger. He was contemplating an answer. "You'll know me better in a while," he finally said, and shifted across the mattress. "There are things I want to tell you. I've been trying to build up the courage."

"You know you can tell me anything."

"I know."

When he leaned in to kiss her, she wrapped her arms around him and thought about sunflowers beneath an Italian sky.

The next night she woke up at one in the morning. Jesse's side of the bed was cold, and she twisted around to see him standing by the window. In the dim light, she made out his expression. He looked confused.

"Are you okay?" she asked.

He glanced at her and folded his arms. "I've had my car packed up for two days now."

"You have a car? I thought you always drove one of Steve's cars or took a cab."

"None of them know about it. I bought it while I was away. It's parked down the street."

She stirred beneath the sheets. So that was why he had left again. He was dressed. His hair was ruffled from when she had run her fingers through it earlier. She glanced at the clock for the third time in a row, and a sick dread fell over her. "Why did you buy a car?" she asked. "Why is it packed?"

He turned to her and frowned, his eyes filled with pain.

"I need to tell you some things. I've put it off for too long, but it's time." He unfolded his arms. "There's some stuff that might make you see me differently."

She pulled the sheets closer to her, suddenly feeling vulnerable. "Is it about you stealing?"

"Yes, and it's about Evelyn too." He took a step forward, his face eerily solemn in the dim light. For the first time she believed the vision in her head; dressed head-to-toe in black, he wouldn't make a sound, because she knew that was how he would pull off something like that—noiselessly, steadily, and with great precision.

He glanced at the clock and turned back to her.

"You see, I hired someone to … no, you wouldn't understand. I have to go further back."

He turned to the window again. "By the time I was your age—almost nineteen—I was most of my way through college. My father wanted me to be a professor of English, just like him, but I chose architecture instead. I finished school, but had to find an internship before I could get licensed, so I started looking around. I had several offers, but Steve's was the most promising. He owns his own firm, as you know— prominent and respected, very accomplished. I was thrilled to work with him. It was a fresh start far away from ...."

He trailed off, folded his arms again, and continued to look out the window.

She leaned forward. "Far away from what?"

"From things I wanted to stop doing. Stealing, as you put it." He looked down at the floor and took a deep breath. "I had a group of friends. We liked to test our skills, I guess you could say, and we found ways to get whatever we wanted without getting caught. I was caught once with a good friend of mine, back when I didn't know what I was doing, but it was only a minor offence."

He let out a short laugh filled with sadness. Naomi rested her head on the pillow. "I've heard Steve say you're very good at what you do. Architecture, I mean. Didn't he say he was going to sell the firm to you? He doesn't want anybody else to have it."

He smiled. "I guess so."

"What about literature and all the things you know?"

His smile faded. "Like I said, I want to focus on other things now, but none of that fixes ... you."

"Me?"

"Yes. Look at you. You're the most beautiful thing I've ever laid eyes on. You're perfect, Naomi. So innocent. So willing to please everybody. You've decided to stay with me, and I honestly think you might be in love with me. Nobody's ever felt that way about me before, and until a few hours ago I was convinced all of this might work—Italy and everything."

She sat up. She felt like she might snap in half. She couldn't bear to lose him. Not now.

"What do you mean?" she stuttered. "You're not coming now? I thought we were going to stay together. These last few nights we've been so close. I thought it was your way of telling me you love me—that you're going to stay with me forever. You said you would."

He let out a sigh and lowered his eyes. "When Steve took me on as his intern, I thought my life was changing. It was, I think, until an old friend of mine called six months later. I hadn't talked to him for a long time, but he'd been a good friend and I owed him a lot. He needed my help to pull off a jewelry heist. I couldn't say no. He needed some fast money, so I guess he was in some sort of trouble. He wouldn't tell me what it was. Since he couldn't pull off the job himself, it had to be me."

"Why?"

"Because that's what I'm good at." His words came out snappy, and Naomi backed away as he continued. "The point is I decided to help him. I found out Steve's wife—Evelyn—worked as the manager of a jewelry store. It was too easy. My internship didn't pay well, so I told my friend yes. I shouldn't have done it, I know, but it was too tempting. I was living in a shitty apartment with barely enough money to buy a few groceries and pay my rent. It was a no-brainer to get some extra cash until my internship was over, but it was the first time I'd be pulling off something so risky on my own. That's why I decided to use Evelyn. It made things easier—one less security measure I'd have to figure out. I never intended for her to get hurt. I had no idea."

"You hurt her?"

He looked up, his jaw clenched. "*I* didn't hurt her. It was that damned idiot I hired to steal her keys who stabbed her. I told him not to threaten her. I mean, hell, she was my boss' wife. It was supposed to look like a random purse snatch. He was going to knock her out, steal her wallet, and replace her existing store keys with a matching fake set, but she was stronger than he'd planned. When he pulled her into an alley on her way to her car, she fought back and he threatened her with a knife. I guess she still fought back, and that's when he stabbed her in the chest, took her purse and ran. Complete idiot. He gave me the purse and told me what happened, but I had no idea it was so serious until I stopped by Steve's firm a few hours later. I had to do the job that same night, because I knew as soon as Evelyn reported her stolen keys, the locks and other security devices would probably be changed the next morning—if they hadn't already been changed. I was willing to take the risk, but then I ran into Steve. I'd left some stuff I needed in my workspace, and I passed him on my way out of the building."

He shook his head. "That's when I said the dumbest thing I've ever said in my life. He told me his wife was in the hospital. He'd been with her all day, but had come into the office to grab some things. He was beside himself, saying he had to get to her as fast as he could because she'd taken a turn for the worse. So, not even thinking, I looked him in the eyes and told him I couldn't believe she'd been stabbed. I knew what I'd done the second the words came out of my mouth. How the hell could I have known she had been stabbed? He hadn't said a word about that to anyone—only that she had been mugged and injured and was in the hospital."

Naomi sat up. "He couldn't have known what you were up to, though. He couldn't have known It was you who—"

"No, but it sure got him thinking. You know Steve. Well, maybe you don't; even I hardly know him. He's so quiet, always thinking and scheming in the back of his head. He knew something was going on and that it had to do with me. I could see he was suspicious, but I didn't have time to think about it right then. I had work to do, and it couldn't wait. Everything was planned and ready, so I left as fast as I could."

"Did you do it? Did you get into the store?"

"No, I didn't."

"You mean Steve called the police on you?"

"No, he didn't call the police. I think he made sure Eric was with Evelyn, and then he followed me. I still can't believe I never noticed him. He waited until he saw what I was doing, and stepped around the corner to tell me if I made one more move he'd turn me in."

"Why would he do that? Why wouldn't he call the police right away?"

"Because he wanted to see what I was doing before landing me in jail. He's always liked me. I'm sure deep down he didn't want to have to turn me in."

He glared in her direction, but she was sure it wasn't intended for her. "He's like me, always looking for a way to get ahead. I think that's why we've always gotten along. He made me get into his car and tell him everything. He was mad as hell that I'd hurt Evelyn, and told me I was in for it, that Eric might kill me. I didn't even know who Eric was, but I found out soon enough."

Naomi stared at him in shock. The whole story was crazy. "That's how you met Eric?"

"Yes. Steve made me stay here at the house until Evelyn was stable and Eric came back from the hospital. That's when we struck a deal."

"Because you hurt Evelyn?"

"Mostly, yes. You see, I didn't realize at the time how much I had actually hurt them, what with Eric and Evelyn's past—knives, you know, and losing their family. Eric wanted to kill me, but Steve brought him to his senses. Then they started asking me about my past and my special skills, and that's when they got it in their heads to use me."

"You actually agreed?"

"Yes, I mean, what did I have to lose? We never robbed Evelyn's store, of course, but Eric works as a broker and has access to information about other stores that are easy to take down. You know, whenever a property is built or sells in the jewelry market, security systems are always put in or redone, and he knows exactly which brands and how to ... well, you get the idea. They said I could live here with them and I could keep a percentage of what we made. Eric was even willing to help me pull off the jobs. I thought they were crazy at first, but everything fell into place. It was meant to be. I felt so guilty for what I'd done to Evelyn, especially after I met her. I still do. I mean, she almost died. It would have been completely my fault."

His shoulders dropped as he stepped closer to the bed and looked down at her with teary eyes. It was the first time she had ever seen him come close to crying.

"She's part of the reason you're alive, Naomi. Eric was going to kill you while you were still unconscious. First he wanted to kill you in the parking lot. He thought it would be easiest to end it right then and there in case you'd seen something."

"Why didn't he do it, then?" She imagined Eric aiming that silver gun at her head and pulling the trigger. She wondered if her parents would have cried when she was found.

"He didn't want to. He was scared senseless, but he honestly believed it was the only way out. I finally picked you up and put you in the back seat. I had delayed the store alarm, so we only had a few minutes before it went off. We said we'd figure out what to do with you later, and we fought back and forth from the moment I put you in the car until I finally told him to call Steve and Evelyn and let them decide what to do."

"What happened?"

"Evelyn begged him to keep you alive, and I mean *begged*. She was bawling. Screaming."

"Why?" She shook her head and looked down at the floor. "I mean, I know why Evelyn wouldn't want Eric to kill me—kill anyone—but why did you take me in the first place? You really thought I'd seen you?"

"We had no idea. It was so foggy. We had no clue what you might have seen or how long you had been there. Maybe you'd memorized our license plate, our faces, our car, who knows? Either way, Naomi, I never leave evidence behind, and you were evidence. I told Eric we couldn't shoot you right there. Even a bullet is evidence. So we took you. It was spur of the moment. It was stupid."

"Then why didn't you just kill me later? Evelyn couldn't have swayed Eric that much—to change your entire lives just because of me. It would have been easier to get rid of me."

He sighed. "That's what I've been trying to explain. You must know by now that we're not like that. Not really. Eric might have considered it, but deep down he doesn't want to hurt anyone."

"But you steal."

He stepped closer. "Murder is a lot different from stealing, isn't it?"

Yeah, that was an understatement. "I guess so," she muttered.

Shaking his head, he turned back to the window. "I'm not happy with who I've become. I decided to help them because I wanted to fix what I'd done to Evelyn. I know they've played on my guilt this whole time, but I always figured it was my own fault. The plan to help them didn't sound bad at the time. The only drawback I could see was the risk, of course, and all four of us had to keep out of relationships until I finished helping them. That way no women Eric or I dated could ever have the chance to get nosy or suspicious. It keeps things simpler."

Goosebumps prickled her skin. She cleared her throat. "So is that why you've always wanted me? Because you couldn't get laid somewhere else?"

She regretted it the second it came out of her mouth, but she did wonder if it was true. She cringed at her own stupid cruelty.

"What!" He spun around to face her. "How could you possibly ... how could you ...?" He gritted his teeth and turned away. "It doesn't matter now. My car's packed. I have to end this."

"End what? Us?" Heat built up in her chest. She felt dizzy. "I'm sorry. I didn't mean to say that. I don't really think that's why you want to be with me. I just—"

"Don't worry about it. That has nothing to do with my decision."

"What decision?"

His eyes widened. "Haven't you figured out I'm leaving for good?" He looked at her again, wiped away a tear on his cheek, and sat down next to her on the bed. He was close enough to take her into his arms, but he didn't. She almost backed away from him.

"Wouldn't Eric eventually let you leave, anyway? Aren't you almost finished helping them? They have what they want now."

"Yes, but that's not the point, is it? You've changed everything."

"You can't leave," she pleaded. "None of what you've told me changes how I feel about you."

He leaned forward and took her face into his hands. "I was hoping it wouldn't, but this can't work. I want to change, but I'm not sure how. I mean, stealing property is one thing, but stealing you—that's completely different. I was okay with it for a long time, but I can't live the rest of my life with someone I'm responsible for kidnapping. We would never be free, Naomi."

Kidnapping. She moved away from him. "No, that's not the way it is now. I want to be here. I'm old enough to decide for myself. I can stay with you if I want."

She looked him directly in the eyes as the words formed on her tongue—those sweet, delectable words she had never said to anyone. "I love you, Jesse."

He looked at her with tenderness, but gave no response. The dizziness worsened. Why wouldn't he tell her he loved her? He had never said it, not once. "I want to stay with you," she whimpered. "It's my decision."

He looked away. "No, it's not your decision. It's never been your decision." Standing, he tensed the muscles in his arms. "I was looking at you a while ago, lying in bed. The only thing I want to do is protect you because I … I …." He glanced at the clock. "I'm getting you out of here."

The air around Naomi turned to stone. She couldn't breathe. She couldn't think. "Wh-what did you say?"

"I'm taking you with me. I wasn't going to at first. I was just going to move out in order to remove myself from the temptation of staying with you, but I can't." He looked at her bedroom door as if Eric might burst in any second. "I'm not abandoning you. This is for you more than anything."

She found air again as she processed what was happening. "But what will happen?" She could hardly force the words out of her mouth as she thought about everything leaving would involve. "How long will we hide?"

"Hide?" His eyes widened. "Haven't you been listening to me? I'm letting you go, not running away with you." He stood from the bed and looked around. "You probably can't take much. The police will confiscate it anyway, so get dressed and grab your shoes and we'll—"

"I don't have any shoes."

He turned to her, surprise on his face. She realized he knew very well she didn't have any shoes, but he must have forgotten. "Yeah, you're right."

"Or did you keep my shoes from when you took me?" She still couldn't say the word "kidnap."

"I'm pretty sure they're in Eric's room, or maybe Evelyn's, I don't know.

"My camera?"

"Same."

Her heart pounded. The whole plan was insane. "Are you really serious about this? Eric will come after you—after me. He'll be furious."

He looked hard into her eyes, his face cold. "That's why I'm turning them in."

"What!" She lowered her voice to a whisper, keenly aware that Steve and Evelyn were asleep in the next room over. Throwing her covers aside, she stood and faced him. He towered over her. "You can't turn them in," she whispered.

"Do you want Eric coming after you? Think about it."

"Do you really think he would?" she asked, double-guessing herself. "Maybe he wouldn't. Evelyn would stop him." Her throat constricted again at the thought of Evelyn in a prison cell. "She loves me."

"She wouldn't stop him from coming after me, the one who started all this shit." He grabbed her shoulders. "No, this is what I've decided, and you're coming with me. Get dressed and let's go."

"Jesse, I—"

"I said get dressed. Now." His grip hardened, and she knew there was no choice but to go with him. For once, he was forcing her.

She dressed quickly, her mind spinning. What would happen to the others? Would the police break down the door? How would Jesse turn them in without incriminating himself? He couldn't possibly be thinking about turning himself in! She looked up at him as she pulled on her jeans. "So you're going to run?"

He nodded. His face wasn't exactly panicked, but she did see fear in his eyes. Somehow, she knew it wasn't for him, but for her.

"I know I should turn myself in," he said with a crack in his voice, "but they are the ones who deserve to be locked up." He motioned toward Evelyn and Steve's room. "I've only tried to do the right thing from the beginning with them, but I'd stand no chance in any case against me. It all looks so bad. I need to get my head in the right place. I need … it doesn't matter. You need to hurry. I want to get out of here fast."

"I know. I'm trying." She pulled on her pink sweatshirt and grabbed her earrings from the dresser and her journal from the nightstand. *The Awakening* was missing.

"Where—"

"Don't worry about it, come on." He grabbed her hand and they left the room, creeping down the hallway like a pair of thieves. Except Jesse didn't creep. He was more like a silent shadow, no noise at all, and for the first time she caught a real glimpse of the dark side of him she had feared to see for so long. Now she desperately wanted to see more of it. She wanted to be a part of it, a part of him, but everything was crumbling around her.

He opened the front door.

Fresh air.

Holding his hand, she walked with him down the sidewalk. When they passed the stop sign where Eric had caught her, she took a deep breath. This was it. A few more steps and she would be free. Could it be that easy? It was almost a full year to the day since she had been kidnapped—the first part of February. There would be fog rolling into her hometown if it was cold enough. It sounded crazy that she might see it again, that her life might fall back to where it was before. But it could never be like it was before. Would she even want it to be? She took one last look at the house. It was dark. She saw her bedroom window, and it felt like a huge, gaping hole in her chest. Guilt swept through her, and she felt herself tugging to go back.

Jesse yanked on her hand. "No, Naomi. It's over."

They walked two more blocks until they reached his car. He held the passenger door open, and with a heavy sigh she got in. The hole in her chest widened as they drove away. She didn't understand why she didn't feel free.

He drove her into Denver, deep into the city, where he parked the car across the street from some large, concrete and glass buildings.

"I have to leave you here," he said softly. He was distant and withdrawn, unlike she had ever seen him before. His hands tightened around the steering wheel as he nodded across the street.

"That's the police station. They'll take care of you. You'll be safe with them. You'll see your parents again."

She stared at the wide concourse in front of the building, at the few lamps over pine trees and benches. She started to cry, muttering something about not wanting to go home, and he waited for her to finish.

"You're going to have a hard time getting over this—over everything we've done to you," he said in a cold voice. "But you will eventually."

She knew he was turning himself off to dull the pain. This wasn't him. Harsh. Withdrawn. He wouldn't even look at her.

"I'll never get over this," she said, staring down at the journal in her lap.

"Yes you will."

The tears started. No way around them. She loved him more than she had ever loved anybody. "You can't just drop me off and leave me like this," she said stiffly. "I know I tried to escape once, but that was different. You were gone and it was my choice. I wanted to prove to myself that I could decide. This is different. You're making me leave you, and I don't want to. I've decided to stay with you. Doesn't that matter?" She stared at him, willing him to look at her.

He shook his head and kept his focus on the buildings across the street. "I have no choice. This is the only way."

"Where are you going to go? I have to see you again." Her tears landed on the journal and rolled onto her jeans. "Jesse? Please."

"I can't tell you where I'm going. They'll ask you, and if you don't know you don't have to lie."

"I'll see you again, though. When all of it's over, I'll see you."

He finally turned to look at her. There were no tears in his eyes. "Get out of the car, Naomi."

"I can't." She wanted to grab onto him and never let go. How could he do this to her? He was ripping her in two and he didn't even care. Anger filled his eyes. It seemed to expand through the entire car like heavy smoke. It made her tears come faster.

"Get out."

This time she sensed that he meant it with every ounce of his being, and her hands fumbled with the handle. Her journal fell out of her lap and onto the floor of the car. She left it there and slammed the door. The gravel of the parking lot was rough on her feet as Jesse drove away.

XXVIII

Sunlight sifted through a pair of white Venetian blinds. They were twisted half open so the light landed on the green-flecked floor tiles in glittering stripes. Naomi blinked once, then twice. The bars of light were amber colored across the bed. She thought they might be warm, but they weren't. She ran her fingers across the bedding, trying to feel any heat at all, but there was only coldness against her already cold fingers.

She longed to be in her room with Evelyn's quilt pulled close over her body, the smell of Jesse surrounding her, the radiance of dreaming about Italy and a future of happiness.

That was impossible now.

Now there was a stiff sheet spread over her, the smell of iodine and bleach, and the beeping heart monitors somewhere outside the door. She closed her eyes and fought back a wave of panic, remembering the moment she had stepped into the police station and told the drowsy-looking woman at the front desk who she was and what had happened. The woman had looked at her with eyes that got bigger and bigger until she called for an officer who immediately took Naomi to a room and asked her a hundred questions. Then they had brought her here to the hospital. It would be the third time in an hour that she was going to relive it all. Only now she was alone. No one was holding her hand, writing down her few awkward sentences, telling her everything was okay.

She pulled her knees to her chest and listened to a conversation through the open door behind her. The woman's voice was irritated but hushed, obviously trying not to bother her. Too late. They had told her they would be right back, but she wished they would leave for good. They were no help at all, asking her to take off all her clothes, pull on a hospital gown, and lie on a table with her legs spread wide open so a doctor could poke and prod and examine her for evidence and her own safety and health. She had told him it was fine and she understood, but she had never been so embarrassed in her entire life, even when Eric had stood in the motel bathroom while she peed. All she could do was sob and whimper. Everybody seemed upset with her.

"It's your classic Stockholm case," the woman said out in the hallway.

"There's the man she keeps mentioning," a gruff man's voice replied. He sounded irritated, and that made Naomi curl into a tighter ball. "The anonymous caller gave all the information on how to find the others, but not him. She must know something about where he's gone, Steph. The longer we wait the less likely—"

"You think I don't know that? Here, sign this, this, and this. I'm going to ask her a few more questions then we need to get going. Amy from the DCCV will be here soon. She's better at this."

Naomi closed her eyes. She would never tell them what was going through her mind. It was none of their damn business. She squeezed her fists so tightly her knuckles grew white. Jesse could hide from them forever, right? She certainly wouldn't help them find him.

She had no idea what the DCCV was. Nobody bothered explaining it to her. She guessed it was some sort of counseling center, and this Amy person was sent over to weasel more information out of her.

"Is it all right if I ask you some questions?"

Naomi sat up in the hospital bed and nodded. People had been asking her that question all morning. Of course it was okay. But it didn't mean she would give answers.

Amy smiled. She wasn't the only one in the room. Nurses occasionally came in and out. One of them took another blood sample. Another checked her eyes for the fifth time. Sitting in one corner was a tired looking Asian man from the FBI.

"Is it all right if Agent Huang writes down what you say?" Amy asked kindly. "I know this is informal, but we'd like to try to understand what situation you were in while it's still fresh in your mind. Does that make sense?"

She nodded again. Amy had spent the last half hour gaining her trust by talking to her in sweet, hushed whispers, telling her why she was feeling panicked, confused, and alone. So even though Naomi wasn't going to give her any more information than she had given the FBI agents earlier, she was more inclined to look Amy in the eyes and try to smile.

"There are some clothes in the bathroom for you to change into when we're finished," Amy continued. She nodded toward the doorway to her left, straight across from Agent Huang. He was dressed in a tan suit and he held a small notebook and pen. He looked bored.

She turned to Amy and tried not to think about Jesse. Amy had red hair. It was brighter than Jesse's, pulled into a ponytail of tight, frizzy curls. It stood out in the white room and glowed in the morning light shining through the blinds. Naomi hugged her waist even tighter, her entire body freezing beneath the thin material of her hospital gown. She missed her pink sweatshirt.

"Why did they take my clothes?" she asked quietly.

Agent Huang looked up from his notebook and narrowed his eyes. "They're evidence," he mumbled.

She tried to control the panicked breaths rising in her throat. Evidence. Although she was sure they believed her story about being kidnapped, she wasn't giving them all the details. The police needed all the evidence they could get.

Amy leaned forward and touched her arm. "Just a few questions, all right?"

"Okay."

Amy fiddled with her pen for a moment then looked Naomi in the eyes. "Who is the person who set you free?"

Focusing on Amy's pen, Naomi gritted her teeth. She couldn't tell them anything more about Jesse than she already had, but she also knew they might find out everything about him soon enough from Eric and the others.

"He was one of my captors," she said, shuddering at the sound of the last word. It wasn't how she wanted to describe Jesse, but no other word sounded right.

"He's the one you've admitted to having a relationship with?" Amy asked with a soft pat on her arm.

Naomi swallowed. Dr. Reed had forced that information out of her as he was examining her. "Yes."

"All right, that makes sense now. You haven't been very clear about who is who, and it's very helpful for us to have you clear things up. Also, that was very kind of him to let you go after all this time. Do you think it's because he cares for you?"

Naomi squeezed her eyes shut and shook her head. "No, he doesn't care about me. He left me. The only reason he's done any of this is to get back at *them*."

"I see. You seem upset about that. Am I reading your emotions correctly?"

Such guided talk. It might be manipulation, but perhaps not. She saw her future spread out before her, filled with counselors and authorities trying to squeeze information out of her. She kept her eyes closed, willing it all to go away. She wanted to be back with Jesse, and that was all. How could he have left her like this? So alone.

"Can you tell me anything about him?" Amy asked.

"Like what? I don't want to talk about him, I really don't."

"Okay, fair enough. Can you at least tell me if it was his idea to initially keep you captive?"

"No! I mean, maybe." She put a hand to her forehead. Had it been Jesse's idea? Was it all his fault? He had admitted that he was the one to put her in the car. He was the one who had convinced Eric to keep her alive at first. He was the one who agreed to steal jewelry. It sounded so bad in her mind when she thought of it in such a light. But she loved him. She couldn't possibly blame him for everything. The others had made decisions too. Eric was the true leader.

"Maybe? Can you elaborate?" Amy asked.

Naomi stuttered for a moment. "I-I can't. I mean, they all kept me there. It wasn't just him. I can't blame him. He only wanted to make everything right."

Patting her arm once again, Amy nodded and kept a concerned expression on her face. The oddest thing of all was that she truly seemed concerned. For a moment Naomi wanted to tell her everything. Nobody else cared as much. She had nobody.

Amy cleared her throat. "It sounds like there is a very complex story behind of all of this, but it's going to take some time for you to be ready to tell it, am I right?"

Relieved, Naomi whispered, "Yes," and fought back some tears. Everything made her cry now.

"Your parents will be here in an hour. Do you want to wait until they arrive before we ask you any more questions? You still seem upset."

"They'll be here in an hour?" Her voice came out as a squeak. She put a hand to her mouth and choked back a wave of panic. Amy helped her lie down and put a hand on her forehead.

"Try to rest for a bit, sweetheart."

She tried not to think about how Evelyn had called her sweetheart. She tried not to think about anything, but Jesse filled her head until she cried out in pain.

XXIX

KAREN AND JASON WALKED THROUGH THE HALLWAYS
of the Denver Health Medical Center as an officer
explained Naomi's condition. Karen glanced at the
generic landscape paintings lining the walls and an old
woman in a wheelchair who looked like she was about
to fall asleep. Everything seemed so calm, but Karen
felt the complete opposite. She was going to see Naomi.
What would she look like? Would she be different?
Angry? Broken? She didn't want this to be a bad
experience for Naomi—to face parents who had ignored
her most of her life. Was it possible to repair such a
thing? She remembered walking into the hospital the
day before her mother died of cancer. The sharp smell
of impending death hung in the air, and Karen knew it
would never go away in her mind. It was soap and
iodine and bleach. No smoke. Too clean to be her
mother, and the smell was made worse by Karen's
anger for the past, for her mother's careless choices and
laziness. Even now it upset her. Would Naomi hold on
to things the same way? Could things really change
after such a long time?

The officer escorting them through the hospital
stopped as a young, red-headed woman came toward
them from down the hall. She reminded Karen of Anna
with her wild hair. She carried a notebook in one hand

and a cup of coffee in the other, but quickly maneuvered the notebook under her elbow and reached her hand out to Jason.

"You must be Naomi's parents," she said with a gentle smile and nod to the officer.

Jason nodded as she finished shaking his hand and moved on to Karen's. Her grip was firm but gentle as she continued.

"I'm Amy Williams—a volunteer counselor from the Denver Center for Crime Victims. I've been helping your daughter this morning."

She nodded for them to keep walking, and they all continued down the hall. Karen felt like she was about to split in two with impatience. She wanted to see Naomi. She was somewhere in this building, and the mere thought of her alone in some cold room made Karen have to catch her breath. She had never felt so much trepidation in her life, not even before a trial. She had to fight to keep her tears back. She thought about the dozens of parents she had met with in the past few months after starting the foundation. So many of them had no hope left, and here she was with her hope completely restored. Her daughter was safe. Alive. But so many things could still be wrong. She had been gone for so long, and there was so much to fix beyond what had happened to her in the past year.

"Is she all right?" she finally asked Amy, who walked briskly by her side. "Is she ... mentally stable, I mean? I've read about what can happen in—"

Amy smiled. "She's surprisingly well, actually, for what she has been through."

"I want to see her right away."

"You will, you will," Amy said with a wave of her hand. "However, it would be best if you know a few things first."

A voice sounded behind them. "Excuse me. Are you Naomi's parents?"

Stopping, they all turned to see a dark-haired physician rushing down the hallway. He introduced himself as Dr. Reed as he shook both their hands. "Please, keep walking."

"You've been taking care of Naomi?" Jason asked as he took Karen's hand and squeezed. They weren't walking slowly, but Karen wished she could break into a jog. Jason must have sensed her impatience, and gave her a look that reminded her to stay calm. She wasn't alone.

"Naomi's doing fine," Dr. Reed explained. "She's been through a lot since the police brought her over here."

"I heard she was found outside your police department." Jason said. "Somebody dropped her off?" His hand tensed. Karen noticed for the first time that day that he hadn't shaved.

"Yes," Dr. Reed answered, slowing his pace. "You haven't been told much, have you?"

Jason shook his head. "Nobody's explained much of anything."

Amy cleared her throat and glanced nervously at Dr. Reed. "You're aware four people kept her captive, right? They must have told you—"

"Yes, yes, we know that much. The FBI took them into custody."

"Yes," Amy answered. "Except for one." She looked behind her shoulder as they turned a corner. "Agent Huang should be on his way back with some others working on the case. They were hoping to be here before you arrived. They'll be able to answer most of your questions, but you should probably know—"

"I've examined your daughter," Dr. Reed interrupted. "It's standard procedure. She's in excellent health, very surprising. No drugs or signs of physical neglect or abuse except for a few bruises on her face and a sprained ankle that's healing. She says both are from her attempt to escape earlier last week, but she's admitted to having a relationship with one of her captors."

Karen stopped and everyone turned to look at her. "What do you mean by relationship?"

Dr. Reed cleared his throat. "Sexual, but she's adamant that any intercourse between her and this man was consensual."

Karen withered inside. "She's not pregnant, is she?" The thought made her sick. She looked at Jason to see if he felt the same way, but he looked calm. His hands weren't trembling like hers. He was handling things better than her, at least. Why did she have to be so weak? She had done so many things in her life, but this one thing made her feel like a brittle shell.

"No, no, she's not pregnant," Dr. Reed said.

She let out a heavy breath, but her strength was still withering at the thought of seeing Naomi again. "Thank God."

"The other kidnappers have identified him as Jesse, uh—"

"Sullivan," Amy finished for him. "He has a criminal record from a few years back. Minor offences, but still on the records."

Jason squeezed Karen's hand even tighter. She inched closer to him. "Criminal record for what?"

"Theft, I think. Jewelry theft?" She scrunched her nose and glanced at Dr. Reed, who shrugged.

"I'm not sure."

"That sounds likely," Karen said. "That was a possible theory at first." That was when they reached Naomi's room. The door was cracked open, and when Karen caught sight of her daughter on the bed, she yanked Jason with her into the room.

Nothing could have prepared her for what she saw.

Naomi was asleep. Morning sunlight fell in amber stripes across her body. She was entirely different from what Karen had molded inside her head during the past year. She expected to see the same girl she had grown used to looking at in photos. This girl was completely different—almost a stranger.

"Her hair's short," she whispered. "Why is her hair short? Jason, she looks so different. Her face, she's …."

She was aged. Worn. Karen wasn't prepared for that at all. She thought Naomi might be different, but not like this.

Jason shifted his feet. "Honey, you knew it would be like this. We haven't seen her for a year. We don't even know what she's been through." He took a deep, shaky breath. "I can't imagine what she's been through."

Naomi stirred and Karen's heart jumped. "Naomi?"

Her eyes opened and she looked up. In a way, she looked empty, and it tore at Karen's heart. Was it emptiness or something else? What needed to be fixed? She would do anything to help her, to ease her pain. It was an odd feeling, something completely new.

"Mom?"

Naomi struggled to sit up as Karen leaned forward to help her. Dr. Reed had said she was in excellent health, but she felt fragile, like a bird, as they embraced each other out of what felt like obligation. She had no words to say. What could she say? She hadn't said anything when her mother passed away, and it was the same now. There was too much pain. Instead, she pushed her fingers into the small of Naomi's back. She was afraid that if she squeezed too hard something might break. Perhaps something already had.

XXX
3 Months Later – May

NAOMI LISTENED TO THE SEAGULLS OUTSIDE. SHE remembered the first few months with her kidnappers and how she had ached to hear seagulls again. Now they were annoying.

She covered her ears and buried her face in her pillow. It smelled different from Evelyn's laundry soap. Not as sweet. She cried as thoughts of Evelyn consumed her. No more yoga. No more cooking in the kitchen. No soft voice and fingers through her hair. No more Jesse.

He was who she thought about the most for the past three months. He had left her shivering in front of the police station. He had left her there with nothing more than his words echoing in her head, just as they were now.

Get out of the car, Naomi.

Her bedroom seemed to close in on her. This wasn't what she had missed while she was held captive. She didn't know what she had missed, but it wasn't her room or this house or the ocean. Since she got home, it seemed the only thing she had done was sit downstairs with counselors who tried to tell her how to think and feel. When she wasn't being hounded by them, she retreated to her room to sleep. She didn't want to talk to anybody, especially her parents. So far they were staying out of her way. It felt good to have them away from her. It felt normal—how things had always been.

Sitting up, she slammed a fist against the wall beside her bed. She wanted to make a dent. She remembered how it had felt when she tried to hit Eric and he had stopped her. Now there was nobody to stop her. They were arrested. Gone. She hit the wall again and again until she couldn't feel her fist. Then she sank back to her bed and buried her face in the pillow.

How could Jesse have just left her like that? Every part of her wanted to scream at him, but maybe that's what he wanted so she wouldn't pine away in misery. Didn't he miss her at all? She was hoping for a secret phone call, a letter, *something.* It was her birthday today. She was nineteen. Something special should happen, but she knew it would end up just like every other day—completely dull and wasted. Her parents might give her something, but it wouldn't matter. It wouldn't really be special.

She sat up and snatched her phone from the nightstand. No calls. Who would call her since she hadn't given the number out to anyone? It wasn't the same number as her old phone from before she was kidnapped, but at her request the service provider had managed to restore her old messages and reroute them to her new number. There was one in particular that she had saved in the archives. Her mother's voice. Her weeping at the end. She had it memorized by now.

Naomi … I miss you. I don't know where you are. I don't know anything right now, but for the first time in my life, I miss you and I'm sorry.

Dialing her voicemail, Naomi listened to the message again. It was strange, because for three months she had listened to it, but still couldn't emotionally connect it to her mother. She had thought something miraculous would occur between them when she returned home, but so far nothing had happened. It was like she was dead inside and outside. A shell surrounding nothing.

She stared at the phone in her hand, wishing she knew how to reach Jesse so she could talk to him about how she felt. He was the only one who could understand. Then she remembered that she had left her journal in his car. He must have read it by now—all those passages rambling on and on about how much she loved him. Maybe it had scared him off. Maybe he never wanted to talk to her again.

That night her parents celebrated her birthday with a cake and presents. They were trying so hard to be a normal family. She blew out the candles and smiled, but after a few minutes she leaned back in her chair and put one of the gifts in her lap. She could tell her mother had wrapped it. The corners were bunched and the ribbon wasn't tight. She wondered if her mother had ever wrapped a present before in her life.

"Thank you for all of this," she said with a hollow sound in her throat. "It means a lot." She looked up at them. Her mother was dressed in a white blouse with pearl buttons. Her hair was down, and she wore little shell earrings that glinted in the dining room lights.

"We just want you to know we love you," her father said. He was in a T-shirt and jeans, something Naomi had rarely seen him wear. His jaw was scratchy from two days' growth. That was also something she had rarely seen.

She glanced at the gift in her lap and tried to keep her tears from breaking free. Her parents didn't need to see her like this, a complete wreck. She had grown up independent, and it was impossible now to pretend that she needed them in the way they seemed to want her to need them.

Her father's last words hung in the air. Did he want her to say she loved both of them back? She did. She was a fool to ignore how grateful she was to be with them again, but at the same time she was like the candles on her cake—white smoke still streaming from the charred wicks. She was blown out. Finished. Spent. She had nothing left.

With tears in her eyes, she looked up at them and forced a smile. Everything felt so awkward. She wondered if it would ever change.

"Can I go back to my room?" she asked softly.

Her mother's face scrunched into a worried expression. "You don't have to ask permission, remember? Your counselors talked to you about—"

"I know." She stood and gently placed the gift on the table. She couldn't open it.

Brad came to see her two weeks later. He was waiting on the deck with his back to her when she stepped through the doors.

She studied him before he turned around. His hair was longer, more messy than she remembered, but still as blond beneath the gray sunshine. The day was overcast and cool. She rubbed her arms and cleared her throat.

"Naomi!" He rushed to her, but she didn't open her arms. He hugged her anyway, his strength the same as she remembered—tight and restricting. He pulled away and gave her a bright smile. "Your mom called me. She said you were finally ready to see me, so I got in my car and drove all the way here. I'm at Berkeley now."

"I know. You're studying medicine." She turned away and sat in one of the chairs facing the ocean.

"Yeah, I am."

Smile fading, he took a deep breath and shoved his hands into his pockets. "I couldn't wait to see you. I called as soon as you were back, but your parents told me you weren't ready to talk to anybody. I think I understand why. I mean, with everything you've been through." He stepped forward. "Aren't you a little bit happy to see me?"

She kept her eyes on the ocean and folded her arms. It was cold today. Brad stepped closer, waiting for an answer. She tore her attention from the horizon to look at him. Was she happy to see him? She had no clue.

"I don't know how to feel about anything these days," she finally answered and looked back to the horizon, a curved line only slightly darker than the gray sky.

She was being terribly rude, but a part of her didn't care. He had long since left her heart. Nothing but a shadow. She hardly thought about him anymore. Even now, with him standing right in front her, she was hollow and wilted.

"Oh." He turned away. His shoulders dropped as he pulled his hands from his pockets and folded his arms across his chest. "I don't know why, but I guess I thought things would be the same. Crazy, huh?"

Her heart did an unexpected flip. His shoulders were strong and broad. She remembered his arms closing around her, cradling her on her bed as he whispered in her ear that he would love her forever, take care of her, keep her safe—all the things Jesse had told her as he pulled her to his chest with the same careful promises breathed so softly against her skin. At least back then she had felt things like anger and passion. At least it was *something.*

He cleared his throat. "I've heard a lot about what happened to you, but I don't know if any of it is true. Nobody's told me anything. I've watched the news reports, but what I've heard sounds so crazy." He bit his lip and tears filled his eyes. "Oh, baby, I was hoping you would let me help you get through this. I was hoping—"

"I don't love you," she blurted, leaning forward in her chair. "I'm not sure I ever did."

She had to look away. How could she do this to him? He was still so obviously consumed with her. She didn't know what she was feeling. Anger? Sadness? Whatever it was, it wasn't love—nothing like what she felt for Jesse. He had made her happier than she had ever been in her life.

Until he let her go.

Now she was alone and sure she would never be happy again. She didn't even know what the hell "happy" meant.

Brad wasn't crying yet, but he was close. She had never seen him cry before.

"I still love you," he whispered. She noticed his fingers twitching into fists. Not angry fists, she hoped. Frustrated.

"I'm sorry—it's been a long time, Brad. I thought you would have moved on by now. I thought you would have …." She couldn't finish the sentence, but the word clung to her mouth like a bitter taste. She thought he would have changed, but he hadn't. He was exactly the same.

He leaned down to take her hands in his. She didn't stop him, and let him to pull her to her feet. His touch was pleasant against her skin. She had forgotten how he could make her feel when he wrapped his arms around her and kissed her—like he was doing now—ever, ever so sweetly, his mouth like hot sugar on her lips. She melted against him, lost for a moment in an unsettled sort of stupor. Feeling. Emotion.

She had forgotten.

Then she remembered his fist coming at her, his hand in hers as they walked toward a bonfire in the dark, his arm tight around her as he took a swig of beer and looked angrily at Damien.

She tried to pull away, but he only kissed her harder. She broke into a sweat. Jesse had never once hit her. He had kidnapped her, but she had never felt trapped by him. Even when he held her, she was free.

Not like now with Brad's arms tightening around her waist, his kiss more passionate until he pulled away, smiled, and whispered, "See, I told you. Nothing's changed. We're supposed to be together, because you wouldn't have kissed me like that if you didn't want me. You'll always want me."

With a furious growl, she stepped back and hurled a fist into his face as hard as she could.

He stumbled backward.

"What ... what was *that* for!" Gasping, he touched his cheek and stared at her with a slack jaw and widened eyes. Thunder rolled through the air as a breeze picked up across the dunes, blowing sand through the tall grass.

Hot from the adrenaline, her body seemed to echo the thunder—low, guttural, and angry.

"You've always done this to me!" she yelled, trying to control the anger in her voice, but failing. It didn't matter. She could be angry with him. He deserved it! And it felt good.

She let her voice get louder.

"You make me feel helpless. Do you understand? Every time I thought about you, for an entire year, I realized it more and more. I hated it. I hated knowing that I felt more trapped with you than I ever did with them. It took me a freaking year to figure out what a complete jerk you are. All you've ever cared about is controlling me to make yourself happy."

There. She had finally said it.

He dropped his hand from his cheek and straightened his shoulders. "I think I already knew that." He lowered his eyebrows and stepped forward as if to strike back at her and then froze. A tear fell down his cheek as he turned away.

The thunderclouds rolled closer, releasing a few raindrops onto the deck. Naomi stared at the wet spots as she unclenched her fists and looked up at Brad's back, wondering if she should have hit him. Her knuckles started to throb. It felt spectacular. She had no idea it could feel that good to stand up for herself.

"It rained last time I was out here," he said calmly, but his body was tense. She stepped back as she noted his squared shoulders twitching with anger. His hands were pulled into fists at his sides.

"I was with your mother," he continued. "I told her you were accepted to Harvard. She had no idea."

Naomi kept her eyes on his fists. They began to relax. No, she hadn't told her mother about Harvard. Was that what she wanted to do with her life now? Go to school? Would that make her happy?

Brad turned around, regaining his composure. "There's something you should know before I leave. That guy the FBI's still looking for ... the one who let you go ...."

Her eyes widened. "Jesse?"

"Yeah, that's him. It's really bizarre. I found out last week his dad is my English professor."

Her heart almost stopped. Rain clouds split open and released a heavy, pelting rain. The world, so gray and dark a moment earlier, turned a pale shade of green.

XXXI

KAREN HEADED TO THE KITCHEN FOR A CUP OF COFFEE. She drank a lot of coffee lately, especially after she tried to talk to Naomi and got no response except a frown and drooping shoulders. It happened day after day, and it was dragging her down. Jason was more patient than her. He simply shrugged and said it would take at least a year for Naomi to adjust back to normal.

"What's normal?" Karen muttered to herself as she started the coffee maker. It wasn't normal for her to make her own coffee. It wasn't normal for her to worry about her daughter every five minutes. It wasn't normal that Naomi had come home alive. It was a miracle any of these things had happened.

She looked up at the sound of voices outside. When she peeked out the window she saw Naomi on the deck with Brad. She froze. She hadn't expected Brad to show up so soon. They had stopped talking and were now kissing. Passionately.

That could be good or bad.

Embarrassed to be watching, Karen started to look away right as Naomi stepped back and slammed a fist into Brad's face.

What on earth?

Shocked, Karen rushed into the dining room where a pair of French doors led to the deck. Then she stopped. Should she interfere? She decided to linger in the shadows instead and watched as Brad touched his cheek, fury sweeping across his face. For a moment it looked like he might hit Naomi, and Karen prepared herself to rush forward and yank open the door, but she didn't need to worry.

Naomi was yelling at him now, and something shifted inside Karen. She remembered staring up at the Harvard poster in her room every night before bed. She had held on to that dream for so long that it buried the smell of her mother's cigarettes and the sound of her constant complaining. Had Naomi done the same? Had Brad been her dream? She hated to think of where that might have led, because as Naomi had admitted more to the counselors in the past few weeks, it had become apparent how abusive Brad had been in the past.

Now Naomi needed her.

She rushed forward once again, eager to do her part and order Brad to leave. She stopped, her hands trembling. Naomi didn't need her. She was holding her ground just fine, the way she stood with her shoulders thrust back, the fiery look in her eyes. She reminded Karen of her own strength. Why didn't that surprise her?

She watched Brad walk down the stairs and out to the beach, and then opened the doors. It was starting to rain, but she stepped out anyway. Naomi turned around.

"Mom."

"Hi, honey." She closed the door. "Anything you want to talk about?"

Naomi shook her head and crumpled into the chair, burying her face in her hands. Karen rushed to her side. "What can I do?"

She looked up, tears streaming down her face. "He knows Jesse's dad. I have to go see him. He's in Berkeley."

Jesse. Karen tried not to cringe. "Honey, that's ...." She couldn't find the words. She didn't want Naomi making connections with her kidnappers in any way yet. Seeing Jesse's father would only slow her progress.

Naomi sighed. "That's *what?* You don't think I should?"

"I think you should be cutting those strings."

Naomi stared down at her hand. Her knuckles were red from punching Brad's face. Karen reached out to touch her, but she backed away. "I really want to see him."

Blinking, Karen stood and watched the beach grass bend in the wind, rolling like waves. She felt Naomi's presence, soaked it in like the rain falling down on them. When all was said and done, she had finally learned that when it came to Naomi, nothing else mattered except one thing.

"I'll always be here to help you no matter what you decide," she said, looking down at Naomi with a smile, resolving to live by those words. "That's what I'm here for."

Karen had never driven to Berkeley before, but it seemed simple. It would take a little over two hours, a good amount of time to spend with Naomi. She glanced at her in the passenger seat, her legs crossed Indian-style, her feet bare. She never wore shoes anymore. She was listening to her iPod, one of the only things she did besides sleep and read and stare out at the ocean.

The day was overcast. The sun kept drifting out from the clouds, bright and glaring. Karen slipped on her sunglasses as Naomi pulled out her earphones and gave her a gentle smile.

"Thanks again, Mom. Are you sure you don't want me to drive?"

She shook her head. "It's all right. You just relax." She rubbed her thumb along the steering wheel. "I'm not sure I understand why you want to see this man."

"I'm not sure either." She twisted the earphones in her lap until they resembled a pretzel. "I'm glad you called him for me. I don't think I could have done that. I need to see him face to face."

"Why, honey? He won't be able to tell you where his son is, if that's what you're hoping. He sounded like an intelligent man. I'm sure he knows better than to keep in touch with a wanted criminal."

"Don't call him that."

"But that's what he is. You and your counselors have talked about this. You can't keep hoping things will work out with him."

Naomi's lips clamped shut. Karen could see the hope in her face, in the way her fingers tensed whenever Jesse was mentioned. She was in love with him. At least what she thought was love. The poor girl had no idea, but how could Karen tell that to a nineteen-year-old who thought she had experienced everything already? How could she help her see her life had barely begun? She tried to think back to when she was nineteen, but the only thing that came to mind was her mother's death and her love of art consequently fading to be replaced by classrooms and studying the law.

She squeezed the steering wheel and chewed on her bottom lip. Ever since Naomi was born, she had avoided every possible situation where Naomi could get angry with her for being too concerned and nosy. Her own mother had pried too much, and it had created a breach of trust. Karen didn't want that for Naomi. The problem, of course, was now the opposite. Naomi had grown up thinking she didn't care at all—and in a lot of ways, she hadn't. But now she did. She relaxed her hands.

"Naomi, honey, I know you think you'll see him again, but even if you do, even if he manages to contact you, you'll have to … you know …."

"Turn him in?"

She tightened her grip and said loudly, "Yes. Turning him in would be the right thing to do—the only thing to do. If you don't, I can't even begin to tell you the trouble you'd land yourself in."

"I know, Mom." She turned to the window and untwisted the earphones. She was about to put them in her ears again when Karen cleared her throat, suddenly desperate to reach her. She couldn't stop herself from asking, "Does he love you, Naomi?"

She paused, the earphones halfway to her head. "What?"

"Does he love you?"

Silence. She lowered the earphones and stared out the window. Minutes passed, but Karen wasn't going to say anything else. In fact, she was beginning to doubt her decision to ask such a question when Naomi finally turned to her with teary eyes.

"I don't know." She lowered her eyes to her lap. "Sometimes I ask myself why he let me go. Sometimes the answer is because he loves me."

Karen waited for her to continue, but she only shoved the earphones back into her ears and stared out the window until they pulled onto the street where James Sullivan lived.

It was a quiet road lined with brightly colored apartment buildings and neatly kept trees. Naomi was suddenly attentive, her shoulders squared and tense as she pulled out her earphones and slipped the iPod into her pocket.

"He said it was the yellow building with a green truck out front," Karen said, studying the surroundings as she slowed to five miles an hour. She saw the green truck and pulled up behind it.

"Maybe I don't want to do this," Naomi said weakly, squeezing the sides of her seat.

"You've been talking about it for days." Karen glanced at the clock. "He's waiting for you. We're later than we said we'd be."

Naomi's shoulders fell as she peered up at the apartment building.

"Are you sure you don't want me to come?"

She turned around, white as a sheet. "No, thanks."

"Okay, but if you need me, I'll be right here." Karen wanted to reach out and hug her, but that seemed too dramatic. It wasn't like she was going to lose her again, but what if she came back disappointed? Or even worse, more troubled than she already was? Karen reminded herself that things were the way they were, and no matter what happened Naomi would work through them. If she needed help, she would ask.

"I'll be all right, Mom. Stop worrying." Naomi slipped on the pair of sandals she had kicked off earlier, stepped out of the car, and walked toward the building.

XXXII

Naomi expected James' apartment to be filled with books. What she didn't expect were piles of books. Everywhere. They were stacked in every corner, on every piece of furniture, even on top of the refrigerator.

"Sorry for the mess," he apologized as soon as he invited her inside. "But it's always like this. Make yourself comfortable."

He rushed to the sofa to clear away a stack of magazines as she stood in the entryway, completely stunned, and not just by the apartment. James was a spitting image of Jesse, only older. He had the same deep red hair curled against his forehead, the same pale skin, scattered freckles, and most importantly, behind a pair of wire-framed glasses, the same green eyes.

He straightened and looked at her, those eyes staring into her own, as if Jesse was standing right in front of her. She tried to erase the stupid look from her face.

"Thanks for letting me come," she stuttered, not sure what else to say. She was still tense from the car ride with her mother. All that talk about Jesse and the obvious fact that her mother hated him. She couldn't understand. Nobody could. Except maybe his father.

"No problem." He motioned her to the sofa. She stepped forward, looking around the small living room. The walls were lined with book-stuffed shelves. On one wall was a pair of tall windows, both cracked open with several stacks of books on the windowsill. She made it to the middle of the room, timidly sat on the cleared cushion, and crossed her legs.

"Do you want something to drink?" James asked as a breeze rushed through the cracked windows. It fluttered across several open books, swishing their pages like butterfly wings. Naomi blinked as a flash of November sped through her mind—orange leaves falling from a branch as Jesse held her close and kissed her, *The Awakening* open at her feet, staring up at her like the desperate eyes of her mother.

"Uh, Coke?" she stammered. This room was exactly what she would expect Jesse's own home to look like—if he had one. She wondered if he had grown up here.

"Sure thing. Jesse told me that's what you like." He gave her a nervous glance and turned to walk through a wide entryway into the kitchen.

Her heart raced. Had Jesse spoken with his father since he had let her go? She hoped so. It was one of the reasons she had wanted to come, because somewhere in her heart, beating wildly, was a glimmer of hope that James might be able to tell her where Jesse was, if he was okay, if he missed her. Maybe it was silly to hope for such things, but Jesse always seemed so close to his father.

She looked up to see him standing in the kitchen, his back to her as he opened a can of Coke and poured half of it into a clean glass filled with ice.

He wasn't exactly as she imagined. Maybe, she thought as she looked at him closer, he didn't look just like Jesse. He was taller, his hair darker, almost auburn. His face was longer and more pronounced. He was as nice as she imagined—gallant and calm, like his son.

He poured some soda for himself, lifted both glasses, and entered the living room with an awkward smile. After handing her a glass he sat down in a tattered armchair across the room. It was probably the chair he always read in, because it was surrounded by books— more than any other piece of furniture in the room.

He set his Coke on top of a volume of Anne Bradstreet's poetry and clasped his hands together as he peered at her through his glasses. Now that all the formalities were out the way, she noticed him tapping a finger on his knee as he shifted his weight in the chair.

"I have to say, first of all," he said slowly, "that I'm incredibly sorry for my son's—for Jesse's—actions. You know, everything he did to you." He stared down at his lap. "He says he never hurt you in any way besides holding you captive, but it's hard for me to imagine you never felt threatened. Terrified, even." He looked up with an apologetic frown.

Unsure of how to respond, she tried to give him a smile, but it only came across as a shaky twitch. He didn't need to apologize. It seemed so long ago that she had felt threatened, buried deep in the past. It didn't matter now, but it obviously mattered to James. His own son. His own flesh and blood. She sensed his shame from all the way across the room.

"I think I understand how you feel," she said carefully. "But honestly, it's okay. Really."

He smiled, looking slightly relieved as her lips turned upward. "Well," he said quickly, "that said, I've been looking forward to meeting you. Your friend, Brad, is in my class. He's told me a little about you."

She gripped the cold glass in her hands and peered into the fizzy, brown liquid. She hadn't really wanted a Coke. She tried to smile at the mention of Brad, but couldn't manage it. She looked up with a wrinkled brow. "Did you tell him you're Jesse's father? How did he know?"

"Oh, several of my students asked me about it as soon as they saw the news reports. We look a lot alike, and I think I'd mentioned him in class before I knew what happened." He reached for his glass and took a long sip.

"I'm sorry. I hope they don't give you a hard time about it."

"Oh, not at all." He took another sip and leaned forward. "So, is there a specific reason you wanted to see me? I mean, this is all right, don't get me wrong, but you look nervous. Is there something you need to know?"

She nearly dropped her glass. Not so soon. She wasn't prepared to ask him yet. Her mouth shaped words as she stared into her glass and shifted her eyes to a pile of books on the cushion next to her. Bills were lying on top. One of them was for Jesse—specifically, Jesse James Sullivan. She looked back up.

"Is Jesse's middle name really—"

"James?" He laughed. "Yes—ironic, huh? I couldn't keep myself from doing it. His mother left before his birth certificate was filled out, so it was up to me to name him." He peered into his glass. "A lot of things were left up to me. Guess it wasn't the brightest idea to name my only child after a notorious American outlaw. Quite foolish, actually. I made a lot of mistakes raising him."

She noticed the frown spreading across his face and turned her attention back to the bill. It was for a magazine subscription, something to do with architecture. She took a sip of Coke and slid her eyes to the stack of books beneath the bills. She nearly choked.

"Is something the matter?" James asked with concern.

She looked up, realizing that she didn't have to ask him if he had recently seen Jesse. She would have recognized that book anywhere—an emerald green cover imprinted with the title *The Great Gatsby* and F. Scott Fitzgerald. She knew that if she opened the cover the print date would read 1925.

She swallowed, unable to stop herself from looking at the book again, knowing without a doubt Jesse had brought it back, probably not too long ago judging from the fact that it was on top of a pile and not at the bottom. She clamped her mouth shut and tried to think of something to say, but nothing came and she took another sip of Coke. It burned its way down her throat.

Maybe Jesse was here right now.

"Are you okay?" James asked again. "Have I said something wrong? Sometimes I make thoughtless remarks."

She shook her head and glanced down the hallway leading from the kitchen. It was dark and empty. "I think I have to ask you something," she finally managed, her voice scratchy and dry. Why was this so difficult? He must be expecting her to ask.

"Yes?"

She glanced at the book again, cleared her throat, and made herself look him in the eyes. "Do you know where he is?"

He blinked, then set his glass back on the books and leaned back in his chair. "No, I don't." He glanced out the windows and took a deep breath. "I don't want to know or need to know. He's smart enough not to tell me. The feds come by here at least once a week."

Her heart sank as she stared at the book with blurry vision.

"Ah, you've noticed the books I let you borrow."

She looked up again, this time with more courage. "Will I ever see him again?"

He stood and walked to the windows with his hands clasped behind his back. "Why do you think he let you go?"

Another salty breeze swept through the room. "I don't know. He tried to explain it, but I still don't understand."

James shrugged. "Why do you think he's done all of this? You know as well as I do that with some patience and planning he could have had anything he wanted— even you. He didn't have to get your other kidnappers caught, either. He could have warned them somehow, given them the chance to run once you were free, but he didn't, and not because he was angry with them. Jesse doesn't have a mean bone in his body."

She knew that was true, right through to her core.

"It's a shame he's managed to get himself mixed up in all this theft business," he continued. "He's always struggled to find the correct outlet for his brilliance, but he, well, he made some foolish decisions in the past. He also made extremely worthless friends. He's managed to land himself in a mess too big to handle, and I think he's still trying to hide from it all. I'm not sure why he's still hiding, but I think things will peak soon."

She watched his fingers tighten around each other, his voice tense but calm as he continued to speak, still staring out the window.

"So you *have* talked to him? You've seen him since he let me go?"

"Yes, I have."

Her heart leapt. "Did he say anything about me?"

He turned around and smiled. "Of course he did."

Her heart racing, she almost stood up, a million questions on her tongue. None of them would come out.

"He told me a lot about you and your mother." He walked to a shelf near the front door. He stood in front of the books for several minutes, tapping his foot until he pulled a thin paperback from the top.

Her throat constricted. She already knew what it was. She didn't want it. He turned and headed to the sofa where she twisted around to face him.

"It's *The Awakening*, isn't it?" she asked stiffly.

His eyes widened. "Yes, it is. Jesse brought it back. He said it belonged to the people he was living with."

She turned around and stared at her hands gripping the glass. "If you're going to give it to me, don't bother."

The familiar anger she had experienced off and on since the moment Jesse drove off without her rushed through her body. She had been trying to figure out why she was so angry all the time, but it was complicated, like a woven net all tangled up. Jesse had left her, and although a part of her was screaming that he loved her, all the facts pointed away from those hopes.

She looked at the books surrounding her, the anger still dilating within her as she thought of the others and what she had done to them. How could she have let them slip into so much danger? She cared about them no matter what they had done, and now they were faced with years in prison, far away from Italy and Evelyn's dream. Her heart sank at the thought of Evelyn in a cold, gray cell. Alone. Her dream of Italy vanished, her husband and brother torn away from her. It was almost too much for Naomi to swallow.

James walked around the couch and stood in front of her with the book dangling from his hand. "Don't bother giving it to you, huh? Jesse said you might feel that way, but I think I'll give it to you all the same."

She pursed her lips and remained still as he placed the book in her lap. Trembling, she took a sip from her Coke and stared at the title, wondering what it meant to her, and for the millionth time, why her mother had said it was her favorite book.

"The woman kills herself at the end," she muttered out loud. "She abandons everything important, just like my mom did to me."

The words were bitter on her tongue. She took another drink, trying to wash away the taste, but it still remained. Finally, she understood why the book in her lap was so revolting, and surprisingly enough, her anger began to melt away. She wanted to cry, but she wasn't going to. She was stronger than that now. She had to be. She bit her lip to fight back the tears.

"Jesse told me about that too. He said it was one of the reasons you stayed so long with him."

She looked up. "Exactly how much has he told you about me? You know a lot."

He gave her an apologetic smile and shrugged. "He's told quite a bit, yes. You know how he is."

"Yeah, I guess. I'd like to know him even better."

"Maybe you will someday." He walked around the couch and moved the stack of books next to her. He sat down and smiled. "I don't know why you came to see me, but I'm glad you did, Naomi."

She smiled. "Would you mind if I come visit you once in awhile? Not just because I hope I'll see Jesse. I don't want you to think that's the only—"

"Please do." He took her drink and set it aside before helping her stand up from the sofa. He walked her to the door, and she glanced behind her shoulder at the piles of books and the bright assortment of color they added to the room.

"You know," he said as he opened the door, his intensely green eyes focused on hers, "I think it took a lot of courage for Jesse to let you go." He looked down at the book in her hands. "The way I see it, he's risked some of his own happiness for yours. Now you can be with your mother." He gave her an encouraging smile. "We never could have met each other if he hadn't let you go."

She remembered Jesse's words just before he told her he was going to release her. *We would never be free, Naomi.* She hadn't thought much of those words then, but now they were screaming at her as she held her breath and kept staring into James' eyes. He was right. Jesse was right. She was free now, but what was freedom without happiness?

She gave James one last grateful look before saying goodbye and went down the stairs to her mother.

The drive home started quietly. Naomi looked out the window and ran her hand over the book in her lap. She looked at her mother's reflection in the glass, wondering who she really was. She didn't know much about when she was a teenager. All she really knew was that her mother had died of lung cancer right before she went to college. That would mean she was Naomi's age when she had lost her mom. Something about that made Naomi feel terrible.

"Do you want to stop for lunch?" Karen asked.

"I guess so."

"What are you in the mood for?"

She shrugged. "I don't know. I haven't eaten in a restaurant since before …." She let the words hang in the air.

"We'll eat at home. It's okay."

Silence again. She looked down at the book in her lap and opened the cover. The pink ribbon she had kept from her birthday present slipped out. She snatched it before it fell to the floor. It was smooth. It reminded her of Jesse and their first kiss. Her heart sank. Jesse knew this book was important to her. He must have packed it up in his car with the rest of his stuff.

"Did James give you something?"

"Yeah." She closed the cover and hid the title. "It's just a book."

"There's no such thing as 'just a book.'"

There was no way around it. She knew fate had brought her and her mother to this moment. She shifted across her seat and moved her hand away from the title. "It's *The Awakening*," she said. "You wanted me to read it, remember?"

A little gasp left Karen's mouth. She let her foot off the gas and the car lurched. "Why would Jesse's dad give you that?" She glanced quickly at the book then back to the road as she regained her composure.

Naomi watched her reaction. "I read it six times when I was with them. They liked to read, and they owned it. It helped me ... remember you."

Karen's hands tightened on the steering wheel. Her chest rose up and down faster than normal. "It's my favorite book."

"I know."

"Did you like it?"

Shrugging, she touched the cover. "It's well-written, but it was really depressing. I guess I don't understand why you like it so much. I kept reading it to figure that out—to figure you out—but I still don't get it."

Karen smiled. "I guess I like how strong she was. She kicked down every wall put in front of her. Don't you think that's pretty heroic?"

"I never thought of it like that."

"It's one way to look at it."

Naomi turned to her and saw a part of herself in the stiff woman who had refused to raise her. She saw the same skin and eyes, the same set of her shoulders when she was nervous, like right now.

"Are you okay, Mom?"

Karen looked at her out of the corner of her eye and squeezed the wheel so tightly her knuckles turned white. Her chin quivered. "I'm more than okay," she said softly. "You're here with me. I know you don't feel very happy right now, but time will change things. I hope you'll let me help you."

Naomi could see the hope in her face as something opened between them. It was only a small crack, a sliver of trust. "I know," she said softly, looking away. "I'll try to let you, I promise."

Nodding, Karen turned her full focus back to the road. "When you were gone I started the foundation. I haven't told you much about it, but it's to help families of missing children. Do you think you'd want to be a part of it someday? It might help you."

She fiddled with the lock on the door. "I guess so, but I don't think I'm ready for something like that yet."

"One step at a time."

They entered the freeway. Naomi watched cars blur past her window. Her mother's fingers closed around her hand and they both smiled.

XXXIII

It seemed colder than normal as May melted into June, but that meant the morning glories along the beach trails kept blooming. Naomi could see them from her window as she sat up in bed. Her eyes were crusty from another night of crying and her body was damp with sweat as she once again saw herself standing on the curb, barefoot and shivering, staring at the taillights of Jesse's car.

She remembered the autumn leaves on the balcony twirling around her and Jesse like wings. They were so orange in her mind. They glowed like fire. She imagined them blowing through her window, surrounding her on the bed as she rubbed her eyes, and she felt the overwhelming urge to step outside with her camera.

She had bought a new one weeks ago, but hadn't taken it out of its box yet—or any of the other equipment, either. It was piled in a corner of her bedroom.

She rushed to get dressed, unable to shake the need to feel sand between her toes again. She hadn't been out to the beach for over a year. She pulled a white sweatshirt from her dresser drawer and stared down at it in surprise.

You're crazy. I couldn't smell fish at all. Just you.

It wasn't the same sweatshirt, but it reminded her of the old one. She pulled it over her head, her heart pounding at the memory of Damien kissing her wrist. Then she remembered Jesse's hands sliding gently down her body, and finally Brad pulling her up from the chair, kissing her like she had never been away.

She hadn't seen him since. She turned around and looked at her camera equipment still packaged so neatly in precise, unbendable boxes. What did she want? Who did she want? She had no idea.

Holding her breath, she looked over at her bookshelf where she had recently left an unopened letter from Harvard. Was that what she wanted?

She shook her head and growled to herself. She didn't have to think about it right now.

🐚

Her parents were in the kitchen when she went downstairs with her new camera bag slung over her shoulder. She cradled a tripod in her arms, reminding herself that she needed to buy a case for it. Her mother looked up from a cutting board where she was dicing a red pepper.

"Oh, sweetheart, your father and I are making some breakfast. You want some?"

That's right. It was Saturday. They always cooked together on weekends now—ever since they had cut back Mindy's hours. She breathed in the scent of red peppers. They reminded her of Eric. She pressed her tripod closer to her chest and watched her father. With his back to her, he cracked an egg with one hand and pulled his ringing cell phone from his hip with the other. Work. Always work. Even now.

Karen looked into her eyes and smiled, sleep still softening the planes of her face. She smiled back, trying not to think of Eric as she breathed in another whiff of peppers.

"Uh, no breakfast for me. I'm going to go take some pictures." She motioned to the double glass doors.

Karen glanced out at the morning sky, still dim, but growing more blue by the second. "Are you sure you don't want to eat something first?"

"No, I'm fine." She turned to head out the doors, but not before her father spun around, still talking on the phone. He grabbed an orange from a bowl on the counter.

"You need to take something to eat," he whispered, a playful smile spreading across his lips as he tossed the fruit to her. She barely managed to catch it without dropping her tripod and gave him an understanding smile. Did he remember how he used to peel them for her? The rinds falling to the floor as he answered phone calls, typed emails, gave her apologetic smiles.

"Don't walk out too far," he urged.

It wasn't a great morning for pictures. The sky was completely empty, the ocean calm and sluggish. There wasn't a bird in sight. At least there were flowers and some tide pools down the beach.

She was too tired to carry her tripod and left it near a few rocks before continuing on. She forgot her father's warning not to head out too far, caught up in the rush of having a camera in her hand. Everything in her head was fading away. Even Jesse. Almost.

She walked on, stopping every now and then to snap a picture. She looked through her lens down the beach.

And she saw him.

This wasn't real. It couldn't be. A man was walking toward her—red hair beneath the sun, hands shoved into his pockets, green eyes focused on her as they drew closer and closer.

She couldn't get the camera bag off her shoulders fast enough and threw it into the sand with a heavy thud. The orange rolled out of a side pocket as she took off down the beach, her toes sliding through the sand, her camera banging against her chest.

He pulled her into an embrace as soon as she reached him, his breath brushing her skin as he kissed her face and mouth. Pushing aside her camera, he pulled her closer and whispered that he had missed her like crazy and please, please stop crying.

Was she crying? She pulled away and reached a hand up to her face. Yes, her face was wet. Could he blame her?

"Jesse," she gasped, gripping him closer. "How can you be here? Are you really here?" He didn't seem real. It had been four months since she had stepped out of his car. Four long, bittersweet months.

He looked into her eyes, but didn't smile. "Yes, I'm really here."

"How?" She glanced up and down the beach, expecting to see a gang of armed policemen any second. There wasn't anybody. They were completely alone.

"How what?" he asked quietly. His heart was pounding against her chest, and as she looked into his face she noticed beads of sweat along his brow.

She chewed on her bottom lip. "How did you know I would be here? Where have you been?" Her voice rose higher and higher. He hadn't cut his hair in awhile. It was long and curly, hanging over his ears. His eyes were filled with fear.

"I didn't know you'd be here," he answered carefully, a soft smile spreading across his face. "I've been expecting you to take walks out here, but you haven't, so today, the day I'm planning to ... well, I needed to see you again before ...."

"I don't understand."

He lifted a hand and smoothed it down the back of her head, rubbing her hair between his fingers as he spoke with a shaky voice. "I was on my way to your house. I was hoping I could find you."

"You can't go to my house!" She almost pulled away. "The second my parents see you they'll call the police."

"I know."

Her feet sank farther into the sand and she stepped out of his arms as she realized what he was about to do. "No," she whispered. "You can't."

He tilted his head. "I have to. Trust me, there's no other place I'd rather be but here with you, but I've thought about it for four months now, and there's no other way for me to live with myself."

She took another step back, her camera suddenly weighing like a noose around her neck. The words staggered out of her mouth. "You're really going to turn yourself in?"

He nodded. "I thought I could live with myself like this, but it turns out I can't."

Closing her eyes, she felt her body sway in the morning breeze. She imagined him handcuffed, sentenced, lying in a cell year after year, growing older without her, a book constantly in his hands. She opened her eyes in time to see him stepping closer.

"You need me to hold you," he whispered, and gathered her to him. "You're safe now." He pressed her head to his shoulder. "I made sure you would be safe."

"Why have you done all this?" She tried to hold onto him so tightly he would never be able to escape.

"Why did you leave me? Why did you run? Why can't we stay together?" Her mind reeled with sudden panic. "I'll go with you. Whatever we have to do, I'll do it."

"Oh, Naomi." He kissed her head and shifted his feet in the sand. "I love you, but you know as well as I do that it could never work. Not like this."

She melted at the sound of those words—*I love you.* She knew it. She had known it all along. But now it didn't matter. He was going to leave her again. She gritted her teeth. "You can't leave me."

"That's not your decision to make."

She pulled away. "Not my decision? What does that mean? I'm tired of people talking to me about decisions."

Cradling her face in his hands, he lowered his eyebrows and smiled. "You have a lifetime of your own choices ahead of you. I hope you make better ones than I have. Besides, I'll only be twenty-seven in January. By turning myself in, my sentence might be lessened. Who knows? I might only get a few years." He shrugged and let go of her face.

That's when she remembered all the reports she had listened to about Eric and Evelyn and Steve. "Don't you know they're trying to blame everything on you? If you turn yourself in, you could be in prison longer than they are!"

"Not if you testify against them."

A tremor rolled through her body. "But I couldn't do that to them. I know I should. My mom said I might be forced to, but I care about them, Jesse. I don't know why, but I do."

"No you don't." He gave her an angry stare. "They deserve everything coming to them. They hurt you— and me. Even though I know everything has stemmed from my decisions, they made their decisions too. Evelyn included."

"What do you mean? Evelyn never did anything wrong."

"Evelyn made a choice, Naomi. Like you, she submitted to Eric's power and stayed there. She knew what she was doing was wrong. I believe it was eating away at her, but she never fought it. None of us did until you tried to get away. I think seeing how much Eric hurt you when you tried to leave helped me realize how wrong it was to keep you. That was when I knew I had to let you go." He lowered his eyes. "I realized how unhappy I would be if I kept you, even if you wanted me to. I love you, Naomi. I could never hurt you that way. I'm sorry I left you so suddenly in front of the police station, and I'm sorry I didn't try to make it easier for you. I had to do it that way or I never would have been able to follow through with it."

"Really?"

"Yes. I've never been as lonely in my life as I have been these last four months. Trust me, I want to stay with you more than anything in the world, but this is how things have to be. I have to fix what I've done wrong. I know you've forgiven me for the horrible things I've done, but I still feel like I need to keep apologizing."

"For what?"

"For keeping you, for being such a sick creep at first and for letting you fall in love with me, for leaving you the way I did. I've hurt you, but you still love me. That means the world to me."

She was still trying to control the fantastic pace of her heart. She was caught in a whirlwind. She felt like she might blow away any second.

"I'm going to stay here with you for a little while," he said, squeezing her to his chest. "Then I have to leave."

She looked into his eyes and saw pain swirling in them—like the water being tugged back into the ocean, reluctant, inevitable.

"Okay," she whispered, her mouth dry. She nodded behind her shoulder to where she had left her camera bag. "Let's head back there."

They walked hand in hand, their footsteps leaving deep marks in the sand. She thought the warmth felt good on her heels and toes, but Jesse's warmth was even better, closed around her hand, gripping her fingers tighter. She knew he didn't want to let go, but he had made his decision.

"Did you get any good shots?" he asked quietly as she kneeled down by her bag.

She unzipped the main compartment of the bag, pulled the camera from around her neck, and slipped it inside. She would get it back out to take a picture of him later. She had to have a picture, at least. "No. The day is too perfect."

"Too perfect?" he laughed.

She stared at the orange lying nearby. "Sorry, that probably doesn't make sense. I mean there's nothing interesting in the sky. Sure, the color is pretty, but it's boring."

"Ah." He sat next to her. She tensed as he turned to her and wrapped his arms around her waist. It could be the last time he would ever hold her. "You want clouds and rain and turmoil. Some sort of resistance. That's what makes things interesting for you, isn't it? I read through your journal. I hope that's okay."

She blushed and looked down. "Yeah, I thought you might."

"I think I cried through the whole thing. I had no idea the things you were going through. Those dreams about the dragons and the fire, all those memories of your mother you didn't remember until we took you." He smiled. "Then me. You talked a lot about me. The way you said things—it really touched me, Naomi."

She looked up. "You mean everything to me."

"I discovered that. I think for a long time I took it for granted and I'm sorry. Do you want the journal back? It's in my car, but I can go get it."

She was silent for a moment, her mind reeling with thoughts of him reading her words and connecting with her like that. It felt intimate in a way she had never experienced. At one point, she had thought the journal was filled with avoidance, but now she saw the truth. It was filled with the most complete honesty she had ever let herself experience.

"I think it might be best if you turn it into the police," she said. "I think it might help your case."

He nodded.

"Jesse?" she whispered, looking into his face once again. His skin was paler than normal.

"Yes?"

"Where have you been? I asked your father, but he wouldn't tell me."

"I know. I met with him yesterday. He told me about your stopping by."

"Oh."

"No, it's a good thing. I've always wanted you to meet him. Things are better this way. I can see it will hurt you at first, and I'm sorry for that, but in the long run it will be better."

"I know."

He turned to look at the ocean. "I've been staying with friends, people who know how to ...well, they're not the best people to be acquainted with unless you're trying to hide from the FBI."

For a second she shrank away from him. "Are you sure you want to do this?" she asked, turning to look at the ocean too.

He nodded. "Yes, I'm positive. How many times do I have to tell you that?"

"I guess a lot."

"Listen, Naomi. I know you still care about them—Evelyn, and maybe even the others. I guess that's all right, but you'll need to tell the truth when you're called to testify, even the truth about me. You can't lie."

She tensed. "Do you think I'll be forced to testify against them? Against you?"

"Maybe. When I turn myself in, things will change. Everything will progress faster. I'm willing to tell the authorities anything they need to know, and I'll need your help in letting them see the whole story, even if it incriminates me more than I'd like." He looked away. "It probably will, but I'm willing to do whatever it takes to redeem myself and be with you again. If you still want to be with me after all that time." Then, more quickly, "I would understand if you didn't. It might be a long time."

"Oh," she whispered, unsure of what else to say.

"They're not going to prison for murder, Naomi. Their sentence and my sentence won't be for life. If you don't feel they seriously hurt you, then say so. I'm not going to tell you to try to hurt them. You need to do what's best for your heart, your conscience."

She shook her head, almost choking on her confusion. He pressed a finger against her lips and made a shushing sound. "You don't have to decide right now, okay?"

Wrapping her in his arms, he lowered her to the sand and kissed her.

XXXIV

MINDY KEPT THE BOWL OF ORANGES WELL-STOCKED. Naomi ate one nearly every morning, but only because her father woke up earlier than she did and peeled one for her. Nobody knew about Jesse visiting her. She was holding her breath waiting to hear about him on the news. Five long days later—nothing. What was taking him so long?

She rested her chin in her hand and scraped a fingernail across the toast on her plate. Her mind filled with thoughts of sugar and cinnamon, but she couldn't ask her father for such a thing. It reminded her too much of Eric. He turned around from the stove and gave her a smile.

"What's that by your plate?" he asked.

Swallowing, she shifted across the bar stool and looked down at the letter. "It's from Harvard. I opened it this morning."

"Oh?"

He stepped over to the counter, a spatula in one hand, an un-cracked egg in another. He really liked eggs. Even though Mindy was around on weekdays, he had been cooking them every morning for the past week—like Eric had. They were just as good, though not as fluffy and delicately salted. Eric had made them just right.

He was slowly disappearing from her heart. Thinking about him and Evelyn and Steve didn't make her cry anymore, but she ached for all of them more often than she wanted to admit. She knew she would see them again, whether in the courtroom or somewhere else in a time and space very different from now.

She stared at the envelope, knowing there was no way out of this one. Why had she brought it downstairs? "They wrote me again to tell me I'm still accepted and I've got a scholarship. I don't know why."

"You don't know why you've been accepted and have a scholarship, or why they wrote you again?"

"Both."

Clearing his throat, he leaned across the counter and looked her in the eyes. "They wrote you again because of a call from your mother, and they've given you a scholarship because you're smart and have amazing potential, of course." He turned around and grabbed the skillet from the stove. "Here are your eggs." He slid a small pile onto her plate. "Have you decided, then?"

Her heart beat faster. "I have no idea, Dad."

She was half hoping he would beg her to go. That's what her mother would do as soon as she saw the letter.

Leaving her eggs untouched, she slid from the stool. "I'm not hungry. I'm sorry."

His face fell. He followed her gaze out the doors and raised an eyebrow. "Another walk on the beach? That's all you've done for the past five days. Why don't you wait for your mother?"

"No." She stared out at the ocean and held her breath. Maybe he would be out there today. He hadn't turned himself in yet.

"I have to get to the office," her father sighed, looking at his watch. "Try to eat something before your walk, all right? Don't head out too far."

She frowned. "I'm sorry you made me breakfast. I'm sorry I'm not very happy right now."

"It's all right." He removed his apron and stepped around the counter to give her a kiss on the cheek. "No matter what choices you make, Naomi, your mom and I are here for you. We love you."

"I know."

The sky was intensely clear and blue. Closing the dining room doors behind her, she headed down the grass-lined paths, camera around her neck. She had to find some tide pools, something to get her mind off things. Her steps grew quick and determined.

There weren't any tide pools near the house. They were clustered miles up the beach where craggy rocks jutted into the water. A faint voice called out from behind.

"Naomi!"

Spinning around, she saw her mother jogging from the house, dressed in capris and a loose, white shirt. Her hair, once pulled into a slack bun, was falling around her face.

"Naomi, wait!"

She looked frantic, red-faced and breathing heavily as she finally reached Naomi, who stood watching her with raised eyebrows. Stopping, she swept back the hair from her face and let out a heavy sigh. "Thanks for waiting. You were walking so fast, I didn't think you'd hear me." She relaxed her face and straightened her shoulders. "Do you mind if I walk with you?"

Lowering her eyebrows, Naomi glanced at an orange in her mother's hand. She shook her head. "I was just going to take some pictures. Are you sure?"

"I'd love to see what you do."

With a shrug, she turned around. "All right."

They headed up the beach, silent until Karen cleared her throat. "I saw your letter on the counter."

"Oh."

"Are you still accepted?"

The air felt cold. "Um, yeah." She stopped walking. "What should I do, Mom?"

"Whatever you want."

Naomi studied her face. She was beautiful beneath the blue sky. Her hair shimmered and her eyes sparkled. Naomi had never seen them so bright before. There was trust between them now, but it was still fragile.

"Don't you want me to go?"

Brushing back more hair from her forehead, Karen smiled. "I think it's a great opportunity. Not everybody gets accepted to a school like that."

She stared down at the sand and ran her fingers over the body of her camera. Her choice. Her life. It sounded so simple, but there were so many *ifs*. What if she hated the school? What if she was too scared to live on her own? What if ....

"I came out to tell you I saw something on the news this morning."

Her heart nearly stopped. "You did?"

"Jesse turned himself in."

"I-I—"

Karen's eyes widened. "You knew, didn't you?"

"I saw him on Saturday."

A few stutters, then Karen seemed to comprehend something. "So you talked him into it?"

"No! He'd already made up his mind. I told you before—he's a good man."

"Relatively speaking."

"No, Mom. He *is.*"

Silence. They both stared down at the orange in Karen's hands and then turned to start up the beach again, walking quietly for several minutes until Naomi took a deep breath, her heart beating in time with their footsteps.

"Mom, I love him."

More silence, until her mother stopped once again. She looked into Naomi's eyes and took a confident breath. "I know you do, sweetheart. It's okay." She held out the orange. "I don't know why I brought this out here. You've probably already eaten one today."

"No, Dad didn't peel me one this morning." She held her breath. "I'll do it."

She took it into her own hands, and they continued on. Her feet were weightless all of a sudden. Looking ahead, she saw the spot where she and Jesse had talked five days ago. She would see him again, that much was certain. For now, she looked up and focused on the clear sky ahead.

Michelle lives and writes in Utah, surrounded by the
Rocky Mountains. She adores cheese, chocolate, sushi,
and lots of ethnic food, and loves to read and write books
in the time she grabs between her sword-wielding
husband and energetic daughter. She believes a simple
life is the best life.

SEQUEL TO THE BREAKAWAY

Naomi's journey continues in *Pieces*

MICHELLE D. ARGYLE

Pieces

A BREAKAWAY NOVEL

ALSO BY MICHELLE D. ARGYLE

Monarch
Bonded
Catch
Out of Tune

Lightning Source UK Ltd.
Milton Keynes UK
UKOW04f0350120915

258472UK00004B/66/P